COVERT INVASION

THE PHOENIX CHRONICLES
BOOK 3

R.J. PATTERSON

First print edition 2022

Published in the United States of America

Green E-Books

PO Box 140654

Boise, ID 83714

PRAISE FOR R.J. PATTERSON

"You can tell R.J. knows what it's like to live in the newspaper world, but with *Dead Shot*, he's proven that he also can write one heck of a murder mystery."

- Josh Katzowitz,
NFL writer for CBSSports.com
& author of Sid Gillman: Father of the Passing Game

"Small town life in southern Idaho might seem quaint and idyllic to some. But when local newspaper reporter Cal Murphy begins to uncover a series of strange deaths that are linked to a sticky spider web of deception, the lid on the peaceful town is blown wide open. Told with all the energy and bravado of an old pro, first-timer R.J. Patterson hits one out of the park his first time at bat with *Dead Shot*. It's that good."

-Vincent Zandri, bestselling author of THE REMAINS

"In *Dead in the Water*, R.J. Patterson accurately captures the action-packed saga of a what could be a real-life college football scandal. The sordid details will leave readers flipping through the pages as fast as a hurry-up offense."

- Mark Schlabach,
ESPN college sports columnist and
co-author of Called to Coach
Heisman: The Man Behind the Trophy

OTHER TITLES BY R.J. PATTERSON

TITUS BLACK SERIES

Behind Enemy Lines

Game of Shadows

Rogue Commander

Line of Fire

Blowback

Honorable Lies

Power Play

State of Conspiracy

The Patriot

The President's Man

The Haitian Assassin

Codename: Killshot

Chaos Theory

BRADY HAWK SERIES

First Strike

Deep Cover

Point of Impact

Full Blast

Target Zero

Fury

State of Play

THE PHOENIX CHRONICLES

COVERT INVASION

For Keenan Luckey,
a good friend, father, and
husband who left us way too early

CHAPTER
ONE

KAKSHAAL TOO MOUNTAIN RANGE | KYRGYZSTAN

BRADY HAWK SET the final explosive in place before hustling across the snow-covered prison yard to take cover. Crouching low behind a dumpster, Hawk initiated the firing sequence. One by one, explosions rocked the compound, setting off a flurry of activity and a violent clash between guards and prisoners. And that was all Hawk needed to complete the next part of his mission.

Hawk carefully approached a gaping hole in the back wall, where prisoners were streaming out into the night air. A spotlight from a guard had swung toward the opening, and a guard was firing shots at all the escapees. However, he stopped suddenly and turned his attention to the dozen or so men racing up the stairs toward him. Hawk waited until the mass exodus had subsided for a moment before entering the building.

As men streamed by Hawk, he looked past them, scanning the cell doors that hadn't been sprung open. He glanced at the picture in his hand, refreshing his memory about the face of the man he was there to extract. On one side was the last known image of Oleg Bocharov when he was in good standing with the

Russian elite. On the other side was a computer rendering of what he might look like after being tortured and deprived in one of the few ruthless prisons that survived from the old Soviet era. That stark contrast made Hawk shudder as he continued his search.

"How's it going?" Alex, his wife and Magnum Group colleague, asked over the coms.

"It'd be going great if I could just find Bocharov," Hawk said.

"Well, you need to hurry it up," she said. "The Kyrgyzstan military installment five miles away has some new activity, and I can only assume that their help has been requested."

"Bocharov was supposed to be in this cell block," Hawk said. "And if he's here, I don't see him."

All of Hawk's intel about the Kyrgyzstan prison had been flawless—until now. And while he wished Alex could help, there was only so much she could do from thousands of miles away watching on a satellite feed. He was on his own, and the already challenging task became more daunting.

Where is he?

Hawk scanned the area once more before he noticed a guard who was storming toward him. The man trained his gun on Hawk, who began to assess what might be the best of his limited options. A gunfight would attract more unnecessary attention. Running could draw the guard outside or he could call for help and make the situation worse. Or he could stand and face the man. Hawk didn't like any of them as he fingered the trigger on the gun in his pocket.

A bitter chill swept inside the freshly ventilated prison. Hawk tugged down on his ushanka's ear flaps as the guard approached.

"*Kto ty?*" he asked.

"Where's Oleg Bocharov?" Hawk asked in Russian, ignoring the man's demands to know who Hawk was.

"*Kto ty?*" the guard repeated.

"*Bocharov idet po koridoru,*" a prisoner shouted as he hustled past.

"So, he's down the hall," Hawk said, eyeing the guard closely. "Take me to him."

The guard didn't flinch. "You're responsible for this, aren't you?"

"Take me to Bocharov," Hawk said, locking eyes with the man.

"No," the guard said. "You're coming with me."

Using his weapon, he motioned for Hawk to turn around, which he did—but only for a moment. Hawk spun back quickly, knocking the gun out of the man's hand. As he dove for the weapon, Hawk kicked the man in the face. He groaned as he rolled over onto his back. When he tried to get up, Hawk put a knee onto the man's chest and punched him repeatedly until he fell unconscious. Then Hawk snatched the keys off the man's belt before tossing the guard's gun to a prisoner racing to freedom.

Hawk jumped to his feet and then maneuvered his way through the latest wave of prisoners headed toward the open hole in the wall.

"Got those prison doors open, I see," Hawk said over his coms.

Alex sighed with satisfaction. "All thanks to you. That's about the simplest hack I've had in a prison system in a long time."

"If only you could locate Bocharov's exact cell for me, it'd save me some more trouble," Hawk said.

"I know I'm amazing, but even I have my limits," she said. "As you might imagine, the record keeping in Kyrgyzstan prisons isn't exactly the most detailed or even available, for that matter. I'm surprised that eighty percent actually survive a year in those places."

Hawk stopped and looked down at the picture in his hand again. He scanned the cells as he continued his slow journey against the tide of prisoners. Most of them were already empty, but the ones that weren't, he tried to compare the faces to those on his picture.

As the prisoners exiting started to thin, Hawk wondered how much time he had left before the only people left in the building would be guards.

"Come on, Hawk," Alex said. "You gotta find Bocharov now or get the hell outta there. I don't want to tell John Daniel that his dad won't be able to read him anymore bedtime stories because he's stuck in a Kyrgyzstan prison."

"That makes two of us," Hawk said.

He squinted as he noticed a man curled up in a fetal position facing a wall. Hawk hustled over to the man and gently rolled him over.

"Found him," Hawk said.

"Good," she said. "Now get the hell outta there."

Hawk tried to help Bocharov to his feet, but the old man wasn't complying, remaining motionless.

"I'm here to help you get out of this place," Hawk said in Russian.

Bocharov looked up at Hawk, their eyes meeting for the first time. "Why me? Why now?"

"I need your help," Hawk said. "And quite frankly, no one deserves to live like this, especially someone as old as you."

Bocharov flashed a hint of a smile. "I prayed last night to God that he would take me. I didn't know he would answer my prayers like this."

"I'm not God," Hawk said, "but I am going to take you if you can get up and come with me."

"I can't walk," the old man said. "I can barely breathe."

Hawk glanced over his shoulder and noticed that there weren't any more prisoners running down the corridor. But he could hear guards shouting in the distance, their voices growing louder.

Hawk scooped up Bocharov's frail frame like a sack of potatoes. As Hawk hustled down the hall toward the opening, he estimated that Bocharov couldn't weigh more than a hundred pounds. With wrinkled skin sagging off his bones, Bocharov appeared too weak to make any type of a getaway, especially in the unforgiving winter conditions. Hawk knew that getting the former Russian army captain to safety would require some ingenuity and a healthy dose of luck.

Bocharov wheezed and looked up at Hawk. "Why are you doing this?"

Hawk glanced down at the man before continuing to scan the yard. "I need your help—and I'm betting you're willing to help me."

Bocharov coughed. He tried to cover his mouth, but the fit came on so quickly and violently that he couldn't.

"Hang in there," Hawk said. "We'll be out of here soon enough."

The prisoner Hawk had given a gun to was firing on prison guards to the east of Hawk's position. Hawk went west, which was a largely unguarded area and nearly devoid of any escapees streaking toward freedom. The move was risky as he'd be an easier target for any guard who decided to pursue the handful of prisoners trudging through the snow. And to the east where all the attention had been focused, there were far more prisoners. Yet they were more focused on getting revenge than getting out.

"How am I looking?" Hawk asked over the coms.

"Great as far as I can tell," Alex said. "Once you reach the woods, it'll be more difficult for me to help you, but I don't see any heat signatures behind you."

Hawk's lungs burned as he ran as far as he could while carrying another man, albeit only a shell of one. After a couple of minutes, Hawk reached the forest, disappearing beneath the thick canopy.

"I'm starting to lose you," Alex said.

"No worries," Hawk said. "I've only got ten minutes until I reach the extraction point."

"Fifteen by my count if you don't pick up the pace," Alex said.

"Roger that."

Hawk's legs and arms joined his lungs, all aching from exertion. The snow depth had gone from a few inches in the more traveled areas to over a foot deep, slowing him down even more. Hawk fought against the urge to stop, attempting to increase his pace despite the conditions. However, he wanted to give up completely and make a dash for the extraction point when he heard motors whining in the distance.

"Is that what I think it is?" Hawk asked.

Alex sighed. "I was hoping that just one time we'd get an assignment to go off without a hitch."

"That ship sailed a long time ago," Hawk said. "I was just hoping we'd get an assignment to go off without a half-dozen hitches. If you want to feel good about things in life, you have to lower your expectations."

"Did you lower your expectations for me?" she asked.

"No," Hawk said with a chuckle. "You exceeded all my expectations—except for the cold feet thing when we're in bed. I'd heard other men complain about that, but I thought those stories were just guys trying to be funny."

She laughed. "That's pretty much universal. But you need to keep moving if I'm ever going to put my cold feet on you again."

"New marriage goals," he said. "I'll never be so happy for you to put your cold feet on me again—or give John Daniel a bath and put him to bed."

The snowmobiles Hawk had heard in the distance were fast approaching. Apparently, Bocharov heard them too.

"You can put me down here," the Russian said.

"I'm not leaving you behind," Hawk said, continuing to slog through the snow.

"If you want me to help you, you will," Bocharov said. "I won't tell you anything if you don't put me down right now."

"I need you alive."

Bocharov shook his head. "I doubt you do."

Hawk paused and looked down at Bocharov, his eyes reflecting the bright moonlight piercing the forest canopy. "You know why I'm here?"

"It's about Operation Alarm Clock, isn't it?"

Hawk nodded. "How did you know?"

"It's why I was in prison," Bocharov said. "And it's the only reason why any American would want to get me out.'

"So, you'll help me?"

"Only if you promise to leave me here," Bocharov said. "And I won't hold it against you. You'll die if you try to take me wherever it is that you want to go, long before I ever tell you what you need to know. And I just didn't want to die in that prison."

Hawk knelt down near a fallen log. He placed Bocharov next to it, providing a small respite from the breeze whipping through the trees. "What do I need to know?"

"There's a locker at the Sirkeci train station in Istanbul, number 437," Bocharov began. "It contains all the details of the operation, including the agents, their aliases, their jobs, everything. It was accurate before I was imprisoned three years ago and will tell you each operative's target."

"And you're sure it's still there?" Hawk asked.

Bocharov coughed, wincing in pain. He took off his watch and handed it to Hawk. "It should still be there. The code to the locker is etched on the back of this watch."

"And the FSB doesn't know about this?"

Bocharov shrugged. "The FSB tortured me for information, demanding to know if I had made copies of all my files. I insisted that I hadn't, but they didn't believe me. They know I hid something somewhere, but they arrested me at the train station in Istanbul, so they probably suspect something is there. You must be careful because they will be watching."

"And if I can't find it there?"

"Your only hope then is to convince General Dimitri Gusev that—"

Bocharov broke into another coughing fit. Hawk cupped his hand behind his ear to listen for the sound of the snowmobile engines. They were getting closer—and fast.

"General Dimitri Gusev," Hawk said. "What about him?"

"He knows everything too, but he won't be willing to help."

"Why not?" Hawk asked.

"There's something you need to know about him."

Hawk heard the sound of a twig breaking nearby. "What do I need to know about Gusev?" he whispered.

Bocharov started coughing again. "I—I—"

His voice grew weak, almost inaudible as he tried to continue. But before he could finish his thought, gunfire shattered the stillness. Bullets pinged off their position, peppering the snow around them. Hawk grabbed Bocharov and tried to roll onto the other side of the log.

Hawk laid prone next to Bocharov as the gunfire continued. "What do I need to know?"

Bocharov didn't say a word. Hawk looked at the man's face, lit only by the moonlight. His eyes were closed and he wasn't moving.

"Bocharov, stay with me," Hawk said.

The old man didn't move.

Hawk gently shook him in an effort to get any type of response from him. But Bocharov didn't stir. Then Hawk reached behind the Russian captain's back to see if he could prop him up at the base of a large nearby tree. However, Hawk felt a sticky substance on Bocharov's back while trying to get him to move. Hawk recognized it immediately—blood.

Bocharov's back was covered in blood. As far as Hawk could figure, the old man had suffered a gunshot wound when they rolled over the log to take cover.

Bocharov was gone.

Hawk cursed under his breath before returning fire. He hit one of the guards, who screamed in pain. The other shooter ran over to help his colleague.

Hawk didn't need an invitation to run. After glancing at his GPS, he entered the coordinates for the extraction point and then started running. He heard a couple more shots fired, but Hawk didn't look back.

"What's happening?" Alex asked. "A few seconds ago, you weren't even moving. Now, watching your heat signature is like watching the Flash speed through Manhattan."

"Bocharov's dead," Hawk said.

"That's it?" she asked. "This was all for naught?"

"Not exactly. I didn't get Bocharov, but we got what we came for. He told me where to find the information."

"I'll let the extraction team know you'll be arriving any minute now."

Hawk pumped his arms as he ran, leaping over fallen trees and trickling brooks, all while heading straight into the stiff wind.

"May you rest in peace, Oleg," Hawk said under his breath. "May you rest in peace."

CHAPTER
TWO

ORANJE BAAI HARBOR, ARUBA

MORGAN MAY SWIVELED the trolling motor back and forth, avoiding a buoy as she navigated toward a boat named *El Cigarro Gordo* anchored some two hundred meters off shore. The cool Caribbean breeze caught the edge of her sunhat and almost whisked it off her head. She tamped it down with one hand while still steering the motor with the other. Secretly, she hoped nobody was watching her less than graceful venture. Over the years, she'd spent plenty of time on the water with her uncle, but he'd always been the one to handle the boating duties. As she fumbled along toward her destination, she wished she'd been more assertive in asking her uncle if he would let her drive the boat more often.

Morgan maneuvered closer to El Cigarro Gordo, squealing as she realized she was going to bump up against it. She killed the engine and lunged for the side of the cabin cruiser. But she was too late, the side of the aluminum boat she'd rented smacked hard against the cruiser, scuffing it. Seconds later, the hit was followed by a high-pitched screeching sound as her boat's metal edge scraped alongside of the cruiser's hull.

She worked quickly to tie off against the larger boat. But she winced as she heard the footsteps thundering across the deck.

"What the hell is going on over here?" bellowed a portly man.

Morgan looked up at him with a sheepish grin. "Just your favorite niece dropping by for a visit."

J.D. Blunt bit down hard on his unlit cigar and shook his head as he offered his hand to help Morgan aboard.

After she gave him a hug, he fished a cell phone out of his pocket. "You know modern technology is pretty amazing. They have these new-fangled things called phones. And you can just dial my number from wherever you are and my phone rings. I answer it. We talk. It's truly unbelievable."

"There's a kink in your theory," Morgan says.

Blunt cocked his head to one side and squinted. "And what's that?"

"You have to answer the damn phone."

A smile crept across Blunt's face. "You got me there."

Morgan nodded. "I actually think you don't answer because you want me to come find you, wherever you are in the world."

"It's how I keep my favorite niece sharp," he said, gesturing toward the cabin. "Come on. Let's go have a few drinks."

"Hold on," she said. "I forgot something on my boat."

She grabbed a soft-sided cooler and returned to the cabin where Blunt had a couple of tumblers already on the table in the galley. He was about to pour her a drink when she held up her hand.

"No, no, no," she said. "I've got something for you."

Blunt wagged his finger. "I doubt it. This is the best stuff in the Caribbean."

"It's bourbon—from Hawk."

He put his bottle down and held out his hand. "Let me see it."

"What do you think?" she asked.

"Well, I'll be. This is my favorite."

Morgan smiled. "Did you expect anything less from him?"

"To be honest, I never expected much of anything from him again. But it's nice to know that he still thinks about me."

"And thinks of you fondly," she said.

Blunt opened the bottle and filled the glasses. "Cheers!"

They both took a sip of the liquor before settling into their seats across from each other at the table.

"So, I think it's safe to assume you didn't come all the way out here just to deliver a bottle of bourbon from Hawk, did you?"

She shook her head. "How intuitive of you."

"Why don't we go up top and fish while we talk about it?"

"Seriously?" she asked. "I went to incredible lengths just to find you and then came almost halfway across the world—and you want to fish?"

Blunt stared blankly at her for a moment before nodding. "Pretty much."

"You're unbelievable."

"Look, I already did my time keeping the country safe. Now, I want to fish. And time is a fleeting commodity for me, so let's go talk while we cast some tight lines into the water."

Morgan sighed and rolled her eyes. "Fine."

Blunt chuckled before he threw back the rest of his bourbon. "You never did like fishing much, did you?"

"I hated it. Still do."

Blunt lumbered up the steps. "But everybody likes catching fish. That's the rub. Sometimes you gotta cast a truck load of lines into the water before you make that glorious catch. Before you pose with that trophy fish, you have to put in the work."

"I don't care about fishing, catching, any of it," Morgan said. "I just want you to give me some advice on how to catch a mole."

Blunt shrugged as he started to thread a line through a hook. "Catching a mole is the same as catching a fish. You have to have the right bait."

He handed Morgan a rod with bait on it. "Thanks," she said, forcing a smile.

She cast her line out into the water and then settled down into a chair.

"So, what's the problem?" he asked.

"We had a mole—or at least, I thought we *had* the mole," she said. "Then I learned that the man we thought was the mole, wasn't."

"You still have a mole in your office?"

Morgan nodded. "Yeah, I'm not sure how to go about flushing him out."

A few seconds later, Morgan noticed the tip of her rod dip toward the water. She jumped up and started reeling in her line. After a brief fight, she landed a fish. It flopped around on the deck for several seconds before Blunt pinned it to the ground and used a cleaver to chop off the head.

"You don't waste any time, do you?" Morgan said.

"I told you already that I don't have much time to waste. Gotta move quick when you're my age."

Morgan waved dismissively. "You act like you've only got a few weeks to live."

Blunt shrugged. "Who knows—maybe that's all I've got left. Gotta seize the day."

He proceeded to chop the fish a handful of times and then place one of the chunks onto Morgan's hook.

"What are you doing?" she asked.

"If you want to land a big one, you need to catch a little one first."

"But that's good eating. At least that's what you told me."

Blunt smiled. "Yes, but there's always better eatin', if you catch my drift."

"Look, I appreciate all your help over the years, but I really want to know what you think I should do. I mean, if you were in my position, what would you do to out the mole?"

"I'd be very careful," Blunt said. "Is the mole your ultimate target?"

"The more he—or she—passes off our most sensitive information to some other entity, the less effective we'll be at stopping terrorists from wreaking havoc on innocent civilians."

"Exactly," Blunt said with a wink. "That's why you need to cut off the head of the snake instead of just trying to starve the snake. One way or another, he'll weasel his way into your nest and select whoever he wants to deliver him the information. If you want to end a mole problem, eliminate the reason you have moles."

Morgan nodded subtly as she stared out at the water, her mind whirring with ideas. Her uncle was a straightforward person, except when he wanted her to grasp a concept or a truth. He wanted her to figure it out—and the lightbulb was flashing in her brain. She knew what she needed to do.

Just then, her rod bent toward the water at almost a hundred-and-eighty-degree angle.

"Look at that," Blunt said. "I guarantee you the fish on your line now is five times bigger than the first one you caught."

Morgan smiled. "I bet you're right."

CHAPTER
THREE

WASHINGTON, D.C.

ROBERT BESSERMAN CRACKED his knuckles as he scrolled through the messages on his phone. Sifting through the avalanche of texts from agents trying to place themselves in his good favor versus those who really needed his help exhausted him. He needed someone to read his texts for him and discern which was worthy of his time.

I should've never given out my cell number.

Besserman had his regrets, but there wasn't anything he could do about it now. Agents had shared it like it was the most valuable intel they'd ever collected. The fact that he'd encouraged new operatives to text him if they had issues only exacerbated the problem. One after the other asked Besserman about different situations. Some he considered work related, the kind requesting advice on how to handle a certain stakeout. The others wanted to know how to handle a difficult supervisor or colleague. And Besserman wanted nothing to do with any of it. He only gave out his number with the idea that it would make him seem accessible without anyone utilizing it. But he was wrong.

He swiped through the messages, deleting most of them from his phone. But a few remained, the ones that intrigued him. Besserman wasn't sure he'd be able to ascertain which ones were legit, but he was willing to try after whittling the number down to less than a dozen.

A few minutes later, a Secret Service agent entered the room and announced President Norris. Besserman always found the ceremonial entrance odd, especially when the two had been friends for so long. But despite Besserman's comments about how silly it was, it never changed. Besserman finally made peace with it and ignored the ridiculousness of utilizing a Secret Service agent in that way.

"Bobby, it's so good to see you," President Norris said as he shook Besserman's hand. "Have a seat."

The two men settled into their chairs and began their conversation in earnest.

"You, too, Mr. President."

Norris rolled his eyes. "Come on, Bobby. Let's dispense with the formal titles. I just want to be normal for a few minutes."

"Okay, Frank. I'll be normal for a few minutes. Who do you think is going to win the Super Bowl this year?"

"Packers? Steelers? I don't know," Norris said. "You know I have bigger fish to fry."

"So, the Dolphins are out?"

"You're not nearly as funny as you think you are, Bobby."

Besserman grinned. "Maybe not, but I know deep down that you're suppressing a chuckle."

"Maybe. Your dad jokes aren't as bad as most, but I'm not going to give you the satisfaction."

Besserman shifted in his seat and leaned forward. "So, what's this all about, Frank? Why'd you call me down here, acting as if this is some grand emergency?"

Norris sighed. "It is an emergency, and this is no joke."

"What happened? Did you get caught doing something you shouldn't have been doing?"

"In a way—but not in the way you might think."

Besserman cocked his head to one side. "What's that supposed to mean?"

"I don't really want to say."

"Come on, Frank. If you want me to treat you like a normal person, just tell me what's up."

"I'd rather not. Plausible deniability and all."

Besserman shifted in his seat. "So, you're doing this to protect me?"

"I think that's a fair assessment."

"That doesn't sit well with me," Besserman said. "If you want me to protect you, I need to know what's going on. So, why am I here?"

Norris took a deep breath and exhaled slowly. "I need you to find out who hacked the White House servers."

"Come on, Frank. I'm not supposed to be running your personal private investigation firm. If you have some real problems that need addressing, you need to let me know every detail. But I must warn you that the job of the CIA isn't to protect the president, per se. I'm supposed to protect the American people from foreign agents and entities, first and foremost."

"I respect that," Norris said. "But there's more to this than I'm willing to reveal."

"And you're protecting me?"

Norris nodded. "The media may come knocking on your door—and I'd rather you not know what this is all about."

"That sounds like an admission of guilt to me."

"Bobby, how long have you known me?"

"Since college."

"Exactly," Norris said. "That's a long time. Now, since then have I done *anything* that would make you question my integrity?"

Besserman shook his head. "But integrity isn't a label you earn once and keep for the rest of your life. It's something you have to earn every day. And if you have a moment of weakness that results in you making an awful decision, I can't just look back on your past track record and deem your most recent transgression as irrelevant. At best, it just makes your integrity shaky. At worst, you've fooled me."

"I haven't fooled anyone," Norris said. "I'm still the same guy that pledged Theta Chi with you at the University of North Carolina back in the day. You should know that."

"I *should* know that, but you're not willing to tell me the whole truth about what I'm supposed to be investigating. Obviously, something happened. If you don't tell me what, I'm not sure I'm willing to help you."

Norris sighed and looked down. "I just want you to have someone at the agency look into who's trying to hack our servers here at the White House, and, more specifically, the server with all my personal files uploaded to it. I don't trust the Secret Service team to be competent enough to solve this mystery. And I really need to know who's behind this."

"What did they download?" Besserman asked. "That'll help our team sort through this."

"There were some old videos uploaded onto the site under the guise that they were my personal videos I was holding on to for safe keeping."

"Why would you do that?"

"I can't answer that right now, nor does it matter at the moment. We're on the wrong end of this deal—and I want to know who's behind this—then we'll be able to figure out the *why*."

"Old videos?"

"Yeah, you know, some things that happened that someone wanted to be made public without any context," Norris said. "The kind of things that can ruin a man's career and his livelihood."

"Why don't you just tell me what they are?" Besserman asked. "You know I'm smart enough to distinguish between some political propaganda and the truth."

"No," Norris said. "If you know that, there's no need to go through everything with you. Just trust me when I say that it's bogus and you should ignore it. Just find out for me who's behind it and we'll be good."

Besserman stroked his chin and squinted as he studied Norris. "And once I find out who did it, then what?"

"I don't know," Norris said. "I'm still working that part out."

"As you well know, we don't live in a police state. Once I find out this information, is it actionable? Can I do anything to the people who hacked the White House servers?"

"Absolutely."

"And then they sue, forcing whatever they found into the public domain?"

"We can suppress it."

Besserman sighed. "That doesn't sound very transparent to me."

"This isn't a competition over who's acting the most above board. This is about doing what's right."

"How do I know what's right if you won't tell me what the video really reflects?"

"Like I said, trust me."

"That's not so easy, nor is it politically expedient."

"I thought our years of relationship would weather any temporary storm," Norris said.

"If you're honest and truthful with me, yes."

"And I am," Norris said. "I've been completely honest with you. I did nothing wrong—and someone is trying to take me down for political gain. I just need you to find out who and expose them."

"Fine," Besserman said. "I'll do my best. But I can't make any promises, especially when you won't tell me who is behind everything—never mind what they're doing."

"Once you catch them, I'm sure you'll be able to figure it out."

Besserman pulled out his notebook and jotted down a few

details from his conversation with Norris. If someone was trying to blackmail the president or expose him as a fraud, Besserman would find them.

But he wasn't sure it'd be the best thing for the country—at least not until he knew more. And Norris wasn't willing to divulge anything else that would ease Besserman's mind.

CHAPTER
FOUR

ISTANBUL, TURKEY

HAWK ADJUSTED THE BURKA over his head and took a deep breath. He peered at himself in the mirror and smiled. He couldn't see his teeth—or anything else, for that matter. The only hint that he was staring back at himself was the glint in his eyes. If he couldn't tell it was himself, no one else would be able to either.

He put his shoulder into the restroom door and pushed his way back into the central space of the Sirkeci train station. Travelers hustled back and forth from one train to another, doing everything they could to make sure they didn't miss their connection. But Hawk wasn't in a hurry. On the far side of the station was a series of lockers, number 437 that contained the secret to unlocking the mystery of Operation Alarm Clock. Once he gathered that intel, he'd forward it back to the Magnum Group headquarters—and hope that they'd be able to apprehend everyone on the list, if not at least figure out who they were. But there was work to be done first before that could happen.

Hawk glanced at his watch and turned on his coms. "Just checking in."

"I hear you loud and clear," Alex said. "One more step and we'll be done with this part of the world."

"I like the sound of that," Hawk said. "Plus, John Daniel needs me to read him a bedtime story very soon."

"Yes, he does," Alex said. "I talked with him last night and all he wanted to know was when daddy was coming home."

Hawk chuckled. "The kid still likes me."

"What boy wouldn't like a dad who plays Superman with him?"

"I don't know," Hawk said. "He might not feel the same way if he knew I was dressing like a Muslim woman right now."

"If only you could make yourself invisible," she said.

"This is as close as I'll get. Nobody will pay me any attention while I'm wearing this thing."

"At least, that's what we're hoping, right?"

Hawk tugged down on the sides of his black floor-length attire. "If not, I'm dressed up for no good reason, kind of like a Vanderbilt football player."

"You know I hate it when you make obscure metaphor jokes, especially when they're related to the world of sports," she said.

"I bet you can figure it out from context, honey."

"So, I'm guessing Vanderbilt is terrible at football. Am I right?"

"Perfect. Not so hard, right?"

"When there's a Bollywood movie with college football as part of the plot, I might make an effort to learn more about the sport."

"Ah, Bollywood," he said. "We haven't watched a good Bollywood film in a while."

"When we get back, okay?" Alex said. "You read John Daniel a book at bedtime and then we'll find the latest Bollywood blockbuster. Deal?"

"Sounds perfect."

Hawk checked himself in the mirror one final time before washing his hands. He wanted to say one more thing but a woman walked into the restroom, cutting short his conversation with Alex. He waited to continue until he reached the main lobby.

"Do we have the all clear to proceed?" he asked.

"I've been monitoring all the security feeds, and I haven't seen anything suspicious over the past hour," she said.

"Good," Hawk said. "The sooner I can get out of this outfit, the better. This thing is hot. I have no idea how Muslim women wear these."

"Right now, I'm just glad they do because an operation like this one might be far more dangerous without being able to disguise yourself like that."

Hawk sighed. "You have a point."

He walked through the lobby, taking smaller steps and moving slower than he usually would. Cloaking himself in a burka was only effective if he moved like a woman wearing a burka. His long commanding strides would surely give him away if anyone with a keen eye was watching.

As he rounded the corner and headed toward a bank of lockers, Alex's voice screeched over the coms. "Hold up," she said. "Just turn around and walk in the other direction."

"What's going on?" he asked.

"I just received an urgent message from our field office here."

"Regarding what?"

"Bocharov's watch."

Hawk braced for the bad news. "What about it?"

"I wanted to have it checked for any tracking," Alex said. "You can't put anything past the FSB."

"And?"

"Sure enough, there was a transmitter inside."

"Damnit," Hawk said. "Bocharov warned me that the FSB suspected he'd hidden his information about the operation. But apparently the FSB didn't have a clue."

"Well, they probably do now."

Hawk lumbered over to an empty bench and sat down. "Should we abandon this operation?"

"Do you want to?"

"They might just be waiting for me to open the locker for them."

"Or they have opened it already."

Hawk stood and paced around the bench. "The FSB could've already removed the information. And I doubt they would care about an agent discovering there's nothing in the locker."

"I agree, but just to play devil's advocate here—what if they were as clueless as we were about the operation?"

"What do you mean?"

"I mean, what if this was a rogue operation?" Alex suggested. "They would be interested if anyone was attempting to either capture the sleeper agents to turn them or to use them in another way."

"And you think the FSB could be lying in wait for any agent who might have information about the sleeper cell?"

"It might be far-fetched, but that's a theory," she said.

"What's your gut telling you?" Hawk asked.

"That the locker has probably already been searched and stripped clean. But either way, I think we have to look."

"Agreed," Hawk said as he started back toward the lockers. "I'm going to have a look. Keep an eye on me."

Hawk glanced up at the security cameras positioned on every corner of the backroom housing all the lockers. However, there wasn't anyone around. Emboldened by the absence of any people, he located the locker number Bocharov had mentioned and then entered the code. When he was finished, the lock clicked and dropped open. Hawk unthreaded the device and yanked open the door.

He cursed under his breath as he shut it back.

"It's empty, isn't it?" Alex asked over the coms.

"Completely," he said.

"Well, not all is lost, right?" Alex asked, trying to remain upbeat. "We can still visit Gusev."

"I'm not as hopeful about that. But you're right—at least we're not back to square one, and this operation has at least narrowed our direction."

As Hawk spun on his heels to leave the lockers and meet up with Alex, two men dressed in suits approached him. Hawk put his head down, acting respectfully to the men. But neither one of them moved.

Hawk turned to his right to go around them, but the men shuffled in front of Hawk, blocking his path. Then he turned to his left and tried to evade them on that side. But his efforts failed when the duo repositioned themselves again to keep him hemmed in.

"Need a little help here," Hawk said with a whisper.

"On it," Alex said.

Within seconds, the fire alarm blared, catching the men off guard. They looked up, which was all the opening Hawk needed. He barreled toward them, throwing his arms out and knocking them aside. With a footrace sure to ensue, Hawk realized he had no chance of winning while cloaked in a burka. Grabbing the hem of his garment, he yanked it up over his head and threw it behind him, hitting both men in the face with it.

"I need a way out of here," Hawk said.

"I'm on it," Alex said. "Watching the whole thing here."

Alex guided him through the train station and back to the street. However, the two men kept pace with Hawk.

"Where to now?" Hawk asked.

"Still working on it," she said.

Hawk pumped his arms as he ran, using windows and side mirrors of vehicles parked along the street to keep track of where the two trailing operatives were.

"Okay," Alex said. "I've got it. You're gonna have to hurry, but I think you can make it in time."

"Where to, Alex?" Hawk said, his legs starting to burn from the all-out sprint.

"Head to the harbor ferry," she said. "It's about a half-mile west of your position. There are signs everywhere."

"And then what?"

"Get on the ferry that's about to depart. That should help you lose them."

"Or trap me," Hawk said.

"If you think you can outrun them forever, go ahead," she said. "But I think you know it'll only be a matter of time before they get picked up in a vehicle and then run you down."

"It'd be nice if you could come get me."

"Sure would be, but you know that'd compromise us both— and that's something we agreed couldn't happen once John Daniel was born."

"I know," Hawk said. "Just keep talking to me and let me know if any other alternate routes open up."

"Roger that."

As Hawk raced along the sidewalk that ran parallel to the Bosphorus, he looked down the coastline at the harbor where several boats were launching.

"Which ferry do I need to take?" Hawk asked over the coms as he glanced over his shoulder. The two men were still furiously chasing after him.

"Take the one headed to Üsküdar," she said. "It's a big one and you should be able to disappear there, at least for a while anyway."

Hawk squinted, straining to see which ferry was the right one. As soon as he spotted it, he made a direct line for it. "You're the best, Alex."

"That's why you let me put my cold feet on you at night, isn't it?"

Hawk tried not to laugh as he continued his rapid pace toward the harbor. "It's your way of reminding me that I'm alive —and I'm only alive because of you."

Hawk sprinted up to the gates, which one man was closing. However, Hawk bowled the man over.

"Sorry," Hawk said, tossing twenty Euros onto the ground near the man.

The ferry pushed off and started to chug away from the dock. Hawk didn't hesitate, hitting the edge of the dock full on and leaping for the railing. He performed the challenging task with ease before hurdling the railing and racing on board.

However, when he glanced at one of the side mirrors of a car on the deck, he saw the two agents scrambling over the railing as they scanned the area for him.

"They made it aboard, too," Hawk said as he knelt behind the trunk of a car.

"Don't worry—I'll help you again," Alex said.

Hawk watched as the men drew closer. "This time, I'm gonna need a lot more than just directions."

CHAPTER
FIVE

LOS ANGELES

MORGAN MAY REMOVED her sunglasses as she entered the Magnum Group headquarters. She flashed a big smile to Arthur, who was staffing the front desk. "Why such the long face? Did the Raiders get bounced from the playoffs again?"

Arthur shook his head and set his jaw. "You know, Miss May, there are days when I think there isn't a greater boss in the entire world than you."

"Aww, thank you, Arthur," she said with a wink.

He didn't flinch. "Today isn't one of those days."

"Now, now, Arthur. You'll get over it."

She smiled and made a note to send him bereavement flowers, continuing her playful harassment. Most of the time, she got to tease him by the time it was late November when the Raiders were already out of playoff contention. But whenever the Raiders did fool around and make the playoffs, she knew the needling would be more fun—for her.

Before she reached her office, she found Dr. Zachary Levinson leaning against the doorjamb leading to her office. He adjusted his bowtie with one hand while offering Morgan a cup with the other.

She cocked her head to one side and smiled, accepting Dr. Z's gift. "What do you want this time?"

"What?" Dr. Z asked, feigning his feelings being hurt. "Not even a good morning or a hello? Just a, what do you want? Why can't you think I'm just being kind to you for once?"

"But you aren't, are you?"

"Oh, of course not," he said, "but that's beside the point."

"No, that is the point," she said, wagging her index finger at him. "You're trying to pretend like there'd ever be another reason for you to bring me a drink. And I'm pointing out that I'd never consider that since it's never happened."

"Well, did I ever tell you about the time I shrank a mouse so small that it could fit inside a woman's shoe with her foot in it and not notice it?"

"First of all, I don't care. Second of all, I don't believe your story at all. So, you're going to have to do better if you think you can distract me from the fact that you really want something."

"Alright, alright—guilty as charged," Dr. Z said, throwing his hands in the air in a gesture of surrender.

"Fine then," she said. "Now that it's all out in the open, I might as well hear it."

Dr. Z clasped his hands together and tilted his head to one side, morphing his face into a picture of despair. "I need ten million in funding for this new project I'm working on to help create an invisibility cloak and—"

"Haven't we already arranged for you to get more than thirty million in funding for that project?" she asked.

"Yes, and we just need a little bit more to finish the project. It'll more than pay for itself."

"You'll need to talk with accounting on that one and find out if it's even possible—newsflash: it isn't—and then pitch me the idea again."

She took a sip of the drink he'd handed her. "Peppermint hot chocolate," she said. "Good thing I didn't decide before I drank this. But you were hoping, right?"

"A man can dream, can't he?"

Morgan smiled and gestured toward the conference room at the end of the hall. "Meet me and the rest of the team down there in about five minutes. We have much to discuss."

"Even my invisibility cloak?"

She shrugged. "It's a possibility."

Morgan grabbed a stack of papers off her desk and returned a quick email before walking into the meeting. Big Earv and Mia were in a heated discussion about which U.S. holiday had the best food, while Dr. Z was fiddling with one of his latest inventions, a pen that captures video as well as audio.

"Well, glad to see that we're all in the right frame of mind this morning," she said.

"Is it that obvious?" Mia asked.

Morgan nodded subtly. "We need to be serious—and do it quickly, especially if we're going to catch the mole."

"Is that what this is about?" Mia asked. "We could just start by threatening people, if you really need to find out more quickly."

"That's the last thing I want to do," Morgan said. "Besides, that's not how you catch the big fish."

"Oh, no, have you been spending time with your uncle again?" Big Earv asked.

Morgan nodded.

Big Earv slapped the table. "Every time, without fail."

"What?" Morgan asked.

"Every time you come back after visiting J.D., you use fishing analogies to describe everything," Big Earv said. "It's like it's a pre-requisite for yourself to prove that you weren't just sunbathing on his yacht."

"Cabin cruiser," Morgan corrected. "And, for the record, I hate sunbathing."

Mia furrowed her brow. "What's a cabin cruiser? I'm not familiar with that term."

"Unlike America, Germany doesn't feel the need to delineate between the super-rich and the just-normal rich," Big Earv said. "The people who own yachts don't want anyone to mistake those with little yachts that they're all in the same kind of wealthy, even though nobody cares."

"I'm confused," Mia said.

"He's not to be taken serious," Morgan said. "I'll explain later, but we need to get down to business—the business of reeling in this mole."

She winked at Big Earv.

"Maybe Dr. Z has something in his tackle box that will help us," Big Earv said with a slight grin.

Morgan pointed at him. "Now you're talking."

"I've got a whale of a new project I want to—" Dr. Z said.

"Nope, Dr. Z," Morgan said. "You're doing it wrong. We don't fish for whales. But we really do need to address how to catch this mole."

"Once we do, how do you intend on handling him?" Big Earv said. "Because I have some ideas for you there."

"Actually, we're not going to do anything to him," she said.

Big Earv cocked his head to one side. "Say what?"

"I want to use him as bait," Morgan said. "You can catch chum or you can use the chum to catch the bigger fish. And our mole is a relatively small fish, doing the dirty work for someone far more powerful."

"Okay, I like this idea," Big Earv said. "Let's not waste an opportunity, right?"

"Exactly," Morgan said as she slapped the table. "We made our mole very comfortable with the fact that we aren't actively searching for a mole. So, I'm hoping that will put him at ease and he'll let his guard down."

"Are you sure it's a man?" Mia asked.

Morgan shrugged. "Considering that eighty percent of our

office is comprised of men—probably so. But if you suspect anyone in the office, let me know."

"So, what's the plan?" Big Earv asked. "If we're going to catch the big fish, we have to have a plan to catch the little fish."

"We chum the waters," Morgan said, "just like we'd do for a bigger fish. We have to draw him—or her—out. And I'm going to need all your help to do this, plus the help of a very special celebrity."

"Celebrity?" Mia asked. "We need a celebrity?"

"In a manner of speaking, yes. I have an idea, but I need someone else to help me implement this in a way that can't be traced back to this office in any meaningful way. And there's only one person I know who can do this, one of the world's richest hermits."

"And who's that?" Big Earv asked.

"Mr. Grant Kingsley," she said.

"*The* Mr. Grant Kingsley?" Mia asked. "He practically invented search engines and Kingsley is the largest search engine optimization service on the planet."

"Yes, *that* Mr. Kingsley," Morgan said.

Mia furrowed his brow. "You really think you're going to convince Mr. Kingsley—a man with outspoken disdain for how the federal government keeps its citizens safe—to help with your little operation?"

"*Our* little operation," Morgan corrected. "And, yes, I do, which is why I need your help to make it happen."

"Me?" Morgan asked. "What can I do? It's like you're trying to enlist the help of a minnow when you're trying to land a shark."

Morgan smiled. "Way to stick with the fishing theme with your analogy. And, you're exactly right. And that's precisely why I need you. It's why I need all of you to make this happen."

CHAPTER
SIX

LANGLEY, VIRGINIA

ROBERT BESSERMAN STARED out the window over the CIA campus, considering how to proceed with President Norris's request. The mystery regarding these personal videos someone uploaded to the White House servers was enough to keep Besserman involved in seeing it through to the end. But due to how dodgy Norris was when discussing the details of the videos, Besserman's suspicion had only grown. They'd been friends for several decades, but Besserman had a line he wouldn't cross—and he felt like Norris was dancing dangerously at its edge. At the end of the day, Besserman valued his integrity and keeping the nation safe more than he did keeping his job.

Besserman watched analysts scurrying back and forth across the courtyard below. They all had a purpose, each one assigned a task to prevent foreign enemies from infiltrating the country and wreaking havoc. And while he oversaw a complex operation under intense pressure dealing with high stakes every day, Besserman felt like he was being dragged into something outside of his purview. Someone stealing old personal videos of the president from White House servers wasn't exactly the kind of crime the CIA handled. But Norris had been burned by the FBI in the past and Besserman was the only one Norris claimed to trust— or maybe it was because Norris trusted Besserman wouldn't blow the whistle on him.

In the past, Besserman would've turned to his most trusted confidante, J.D. Blunt. But Blunt had ditched Washington for a well-deserved retirement. There were plenty of days Besserman wished he was stringing up a fishing line with the warm sun beating on his face while enjoying a cold brew—and today was one of those days.

However, his sense of duty overrode everything else. So, he turned to his most trusted colleague at the agency, Mallory Kauffman, inviting her up to his office to discuss the matter.

Mallory, who had worked her way up the agency's ranks over the years, oversaw the CIA's cyber security division. She regularly collaborated with Besserman, especially on sensitive projects. If there was ever an operation that earned that designation, a special assignment for the president was it.

As she entered Besserman's office, she clutched a notebook against her chest. She pushed her glasses up her nose before settling down into the chair across from her boss.

"Mallory, I appreciate you getting here so quickly," Besserman said.

"Of course," she said. "It sounded urgent—and important. You know I'm always here for whatever you need."

"I know, but I must warn you that what I'm about to ask you to help me with is extremely sensitive and could have a negative impact on your career depending on how things shake out."

She drew back and eyed him closely. After a moment, she placed her notepad and phone on the edge of his desk. "What exactly are we talking about here? State secrets?"

Besserman shook his head. "Not exactly. This is more of a secret that might need to stay that way—or it might need to be shared with the world. To be honest, I don't know the extent of everything until we discover what the video is."

Mallory picked up her pad and scribbled something on it. "But that's not the assignment, is it?"

"Not exactly," Besserman said. "The president wants to know who's behind the breach on the White House servers—and I want to know that as well. But for me, the more pressing issue is what was on those videos. Since he's not being forthright with me, I can only assume that he's trying to hide something. And no matter how long we've been friends and how much goodwill has been built up between us, I refuse to be his lapdog."

"That's understandable," she said. "I also hope you understand that I wouldn't want any of this poking around on the White House servers to come back to the agency. That would surely spell the end of my time here—and yours too."

Besserman drew in a breath through his teeth before exhaling slowly. "Of course. That's why I knew that you could handle this investigation in the most discreet way possible. Think you can find out what Norris wants to keep out of the public eye?"

"I've got a few guys who owe me favors," she said, "guys who'd be in prison right now if I didn't intervene on their behalf."

"Always good to have friends in low places," Besserman said.

Mallory offered a thin smile. "Look around you. We're in Washington. This city is teeming with people in low places. Some of them even sit in high positions."

"I wish that wasn't so true," Besserman said.

She stood up and ripped out a sheet of paper from her pad. "If you've got any other details, write them down and drop them by my office this afternoon. I don't want any official record of our conversation or what we're doing. Gotta make sure nothing that happens could ever be traced back to us."

"You got it," Besserman said.

She turned and headed toward the door.

"And, Mallory, thank you."

"Any time," she said before leaving the room.

Besserman wanted to relax knowing that Mallory would be handling it. But he couldn't. Prying felt like a violation of his trust with Norris—and if he got caught, it'd be disastrous. But so would covering up a crime.

Besserman returned his attention to the courtyard and watched the analysts scurrying about.

Everyone has a purpose.

———

MALLORY GLANCED AT all the details Besserman had written down on the sheet of paper before committing all the information to memory. While the CIA had taught her plenty, what she valued the most from her training was her ability to remember anything anyone told her in the context of an operation. Her reports reflected her stellar ability to recall facts and details about each case. It also helped her avoid getting fingered for any criminal activity. After all, if there was no paper trail, there was no crime.

She fluffed her brunette wig hair and glanced at her phone before entering The Dive, a bar that lived up to its name in every way. After surveying the dining room, she took a seat in a booth against the back wall. The white paint was peeling off in most places, while her table wobbled as she placed her phone on it.

As she was perusing the drink menu, a man wearing a trucker cap pulled down low across his brow slid into the seat across from her.

"Mal," he said, "always a pleasure to see you."

She smiled. "I was beginning to wonder if you were going to show up."

"And miss seeing my favorite spook? No way."

"Favorite spook? Or the only spook you don't want to destroy?"

"Congratulations," he said with a toothy grin, "you're both."

"Lucky me."

Cohen Porter shoved his hands into the pockets of his vest jacket and glanced around the room. "No one else here looks like a spook, so I assume we're safe."

Mallory studied him closely. Porter went by the handle Hash45 online and was one of the most cautious hackers she'd ever met. But he had reason to be careful after getting caught once. That was one time too many for Hash45—and he vowed it would never happen again. Yet it was his arrest that made him feel obligated to her. She could've recommended more charges while working with Homeland Security over Hash45's online transgressions. But she didn't, all for the express purpose of utilizing one of the best hackers she'd ever come across, even if he did make a mistake once. She doubted he'd ever make one again—and hoped if he did, it wouldn't happen while he was freelancing for the CIA.

"You still scared of spooks?" Mallory asked.

Hash45 shrugged. "Scared? Relative to what? I'll always be cautious and vigilant, especially when speaking with one face to face."

"You don't have to worry about this one," Mallory said, pointing to herself.

"Okay, enough beating around the bush. What's the job this time?"

"Do you think these meetings are always about jobs?" Mallory asked. "Couldn't for once this just be a couple of colleagues getting together over a drink to talk shop?"

"That might as well be a pipe dream of yours," Hash45 said. "You know I'm only talking to you because of what you did for me—and how I know you'll protect me in the future."

"Fair enough," she said. "I won't waste any more of your time then."

"Good."

"So, how would you like to hack the White House?"

He closed his eyes and pinched the bridge of his nose. "Please tell me you're not serious?"

"Serious as a heart attack."

"Damn," he said. "Just one time I'd like for you to ask me to hack a bank or a foreign country. But with you, it's always the impossible."

"Oh, so you don't think you could do it? I've got other hackers on my list—apparently some that are better."

"If they were better, you wouldn't have come to me first," he said, winking at her.

"Who said I came to you first?"

"Touché," Hash45 said. "What exactly am I looking for?"

"There are some personal videos of the president that we need to see."

Hash45 tugged on his hat and then rubbed the back of his neck. "This sounds like some serious shit."

"Maybe," she said. "We don't know yet, but supposedly someone uploaded some videos to the White House servers that could damage the president's re-election hopes."

"And that's a bad thing?"

She shrugged. "Not my job to determine if his re-election is a bad thing or not. My job is to catch the people who are doing this for whatever reason."

"I understand."

"You got anything else I need to know?" he asked.

She slid him a piece of paper with printed out notes. It was so generic that if he ever got busted with it, nobody would be able to trace it back anywhere. He studied it for a moment before pulling out his lighter and flicking it. The flame lurched upward onto the paper, causing a brief scene in the bar.

"Hey, man," the bartender said. "Can you try to keep the flames to a minimum?"

"Sorry," Hash45 said as he placed the paper on the desk and then used the palm of his hand to snuff out the flame.

"Don't let it happen again," the bartender said.

Hash45 gave the man a knowing nod before returning his gaze to Mallory. "This is big, isn't it?"

"Like I said, I don't know. That's why I'm hiring you. It could be, but I have no idea at this point. Just find out what's on there and report back."

"10-4," Hash45 said before he stood up and left the bar.

Mallory ordered a drink and waited.

———

TWO HOURS LATER, Mallory was already home and getting ready for bed when her cell phone buzzed with a call.

"Took you long enough," she said as she answered.

"Geez, you spooks are ridiculous," Hash45 said.

"What'd you find?" she asked, ignoring his comment.

"All business tonight, I see."

"Yeah, and I hate suspense. So, tell me what you saw."

"You need to see it for yourself," he said. "I wouldn't believe it myself unless I'd seen it with my own eyes."

"That bad, huh?"

"Like you said, I guess it depends on your point of view. I'm just doing what you asked—but you'll definitely want to see this as soon as possible."

Mallory grabbed her keys and a hat before shuffling out the door.

CHAPTER
SEVEN

ISTANBUL, TURKEY

HAWK FELT his pulse quicken as the two men hustled toward him, their guns drawn and trained on the ground. The moment they found him, they'd detain him by whatever means necessary. And once they reached the next port, Hawk knew he'd be done.

I will read John Daniel a bedtime story again.

Hawk glanced at the vehicle next to him, an empty silver BMW 840i Gran Coupe. The red security light blinked, warning would-be thieves that an alarm would immediately follow any attempt to break in. However, the warning light was more of an invitation to Hawk than a deterrent. He felt for the handle of the trunk for the car in front of him and scrounged around for the tire iron. Once he felt it, he eased it out, clutching it tightly in his right hand.

When Hawk was certain the two men were looking in the other direction, he jumped up and bashed the window of the 840i, setting off a whooping alarm. Hawk backed away from the vehicle, peeking around the side of another car to see if the two men were heading in his direction. As soon as he confirmed that they were, he crouched low and retraced their steps. Undoubtedly, they would continue toward the source of the sound, running past it with the assumption that Hawk would be fleeing the opposite way. And Hawk used those good instincts to his advantage.

As the two men hustled past the car with the blaring alarm, they stopped periodically, kneeling and looking beneath the vehicles in the vicinity. Hawk stood next to the tires to hide his feet and send them deeper into the mass parking lot of vehicles spread out across the ferry.

"Where are you?" Alex asked in a hushed tone over the coms.

"I'm on the starboard side of the ferry near the railing on the middle deck," Hawk said as he waved his hat. "Can you see me?"

"I'm locked on to your position," Alex said.

"Where are you?" Hawk asked. "I don't see you."

"Don't worry about me right now," she said. "I'm still skimming across the water, headed in your direction. Just sit tight."

"I can't exactly sit tight. There are two guys actively searching for me. If I stay here too long, they're going to find me."

"Okay, just do whatever you can to stay out of their way and when I get closer, I'll let you know."

"Roger that."

Hawk scanned the area for the two men but didn't see either of them. He wadded his coat up and tucked it under the tire of the closest car. Then he knelt, acting as if he was tying his shoes. It was how he kept his head down without attracting any unwarranted attention. But it wasn't his best option—and he knew it.

For a couple of tense minutes, Hawk stayed low, wondering when the men searching for him on the ferry would find him. He looked over the starboard side, trying to estimate when the boat might complete its trip across the Bosphorus. Based on the distance they were from land, he guessed it'd be at least another half-hour. That was a long time for a man who had no viable way out and a search party scouring the boat for him.

A few seconds later, he heard a clank on the railing next to him.

"Hear that?" Alex asked.

"That you?"

"The cavalry is here," she said with a chuckle.

Hawk looked at the grappling hook clinging to the side of the boat. "Should I assume that's your invitation for me to get to you?"

"Come on down," Alex said. "You're the next contestant on the Price is Right."

Hawk didn't wait for another invitation. He tugged on the hook and then hurtled himself over the side, grabbing onto the rope as he flew down toward the deck of the boat Alex was piloting.

Alex's boat struggled to keep up with the ferry, which felt like it was pulling the small shrimper to Hawk.

"Cut her loose," Alex said.

Hawk tugged on the rope to create some slack, but it didn't work. The tight line seemed to pull their smaller boat along. Realizing that they were tethered to the ferry, Hawk untied the rope with the grappling hook, enabling them to get free.

"Finally!" Alex shouted as she yanked the wheel to the right, pulling away from the ferry.

However, the elation was short lived when a loud thump hit the deck of their boat.

What the —

Hawk spun around to see one of the men on the deck scrambling to his feet. He struggled to get his gun trained on Hawk, who reacted swiftly with a side kick that knocked the gun out of the man's hand and into the water. Instead of sitting back and evaluating the new turn of events, the man bum-rushed Hawk, hitting him in the chest and driving him to the deck.

Alex glanced over her shoulder and shouted for Hawk to get up. "Come on, honey. Don't let him beat you."

Hawk glanced at her and gave her a forced smile. "That's not helping, dear."

He rolled to his left as the man wielded a wild punch, slamming his hand into the deck. Hawk scrambled to his feet and kicked the man in the face.

"Nice, Hawk," she said. "Keep it up."

"You're not helping," he said with a growl.

"Excuse me, but someone has to pilot this boat. Otherwise, we'd have hit a half-dozen shrimpers by now."

Hawk dove toward the man, knocking him to the deck almost as soon as he got up again. They tussled for a few seconds before Hawk put the man in a headlock and started pounding his face. The man begged for mercy, but Hawk wasn't interested in giving the kind the man wanted. Instead, Hawk wrapped his hands around the man's fully tattooed head before twisting his body and tossing him overboard.

Hawk pumped his fist and shouted as the man sank fast into the water.

"Later," Hawk said, waving at the man, who beat at the water to stay afloat.

The man flashed a few obscene gestures at Hawk as they sped away.

———

HAWK AND ALEX regrouped after returning the boat. At their hotel, they called Morgan to update her and determine their next steps.

"The locker was empty?" Morgan asked.

"Yeah," Alex said. "It's like he knew that the intel wasn't likely to be there."

"Then I guess you need to find a way to get to Gusev—but do it quickly," Morgan said. "There's obviously something going on. And the fact that the FSB knows you're onto them makes this situation even more urgent."

They thanked her before ending the call.

"So, St. Moritz it is," Alex said. "I've been wanting to do some skiing this winter."

Hawk chuckled. "We're on a mission, not a vacation."

"I know," she said. "But I did some poking around already on Gusev's place there. We're going to need to use either snowmobiles or skis to get to him. Of those two options, one's far less noisy, don't ya think?"

"You have a point," Hawk said.

They began packing before Hawk stopped. "What did you think of those men who were after us today?"

"What do you mean?"

"That last guy I threw into the water looked like he was part of Bratva with all those tattoos," Hawk said. "I've never met an FSB agent with facial markings."

"Maybe the FSB hired them."

"Perhaps," Hawk said, "but something felt different about this."

"Are you suggesting that Bratva has moved from organized crime to terrorism?" she asked. "That doesn't fit their MO."

"Yes, but this doesn't fit the MO for the FSB either."

Alex nodded. "Then let's be sure to ask Gen. Gusev this personally when we interrogate him."

CHAPTER
EIGHT

SAN FRANCISCO

MORGAN MAY TUCKED a few loose blonde tendrils behind her ears as she followed the housekeeper to the back porch of Grant Kingsley's spacious estate atop the Pacific Heights neighborhood. The woman, who had a sidearm strapped to her shoulder, pointed toward one of the lounge chairs before retreating to the shadows. Slicing through the lap pool just below the porch was Kingsley. Morgan stood up and leaned over the edge before the woman whistled sharply and pointed back at the chair.

Morgan pleaded with her eyes, but the woman didn't move, her index finger still aimed at the chair.

With a sigh, Morgan returned to her spot and waited for Kingsley to emerge from the water. Several more minutes passed before he turned off the pool's jets and trudged up the steps. His back muscles, scarred from battle wounds, rippled in the day's fleeting sunlight. He casually walked around the edge and ascended the steps without pretending the cool temperature and sharp breeze didn't bother him.

The woman snatched a towel off the table next to a chair on

the other side of the deck and handed it to him. He patted his face dry and then collapsed into a seat near Morgan. On the glass table situated between them, he picked up a glass filled to the brim with a green smoothie and drank all of it without pausing for a breath. When he finished, he smacked his lips before licking off an embarrassing mustache.

Kingsley draped his towel over the vacant chair next to him and turned to Morgan. "Sorry to keep you waiting, Miss May, but I needed to finish my workout before my evening dinner appointment, and there just wasn't a way to carve out more time for you."

"I understand," she said before glancing at his broad, muscular chest. "But what I don't understand is how come you aren't freezing right now."

"Miss May—"

"Please, call me Morgan."

"Okay, Morgan, are you aware that the body sweats even when you're in the water?"

She shook her head. "That's news to me, although I'm more versed in geopolitics and security systems than I am in the human body."

Kingsley looked her up and down. "I'm not sure I believe that."

"Good thing I'm not here to convince you about my biology credentials—or lack thereof."

"Then what are you here for?" he asked with a wink. "Because I'm pretty sure you were enjoying yourself while watching me swim."

"I'm not gonna lie," Morgan said. "I was enjoying it—until Nurse Ratched over there rebuked me for watching you."

Kingsley shot a quick glance over at his housekeeper before cracking a faint smile. "Maria isn't exactly a housekeeper in the traditional sense," he said, turning his attention back to Morgan. "While she can cook and occasionally clean when pressed into service, she's been hired to protect me."

"Protect you?"

"Yeah," he said. "You wouldn't believe how many people want to kill a man just because he has a net worth of five billion dollars."

Morgan shrugged. "In the world I live in, money is low on the list of why people are killed, but I understand. You take plenty of flack—and undeservedly so, in my opinion."

"Thank you," Kingsley said emphatically. "At least someone gets it. I mean, it's not like I started a program to end world hunger within the next decade or have a non-profit that's paid the tuition of more than five thousand underprivileged students in the U.S. in the last three years. No, but I have a private jet and five billion dollars."

"Sometimes life isn't fair, is it?" she asked with a coy grin.

"Now, you're just messing with me, aren't you?"

"Me?" Morgan said, pointing to her chest. "I'd never do anything like that."

Kingsley crossed his arms and eyed her closely. "You're lucky I'm a good sport."

"I wouldn't have said it if I didn't think you were."

A faint smile spread across Kingsley's lips. "All joking aside, I do appreciate the kind words. Now, I assume you didn't fly up here just to get a peek at my backyard training regimen or flatter me about my philanthropy."

"Just an added bonus, I guess."

"If you keep this up, I'm going to ask you to dinner," he said.

"I thought you already had plans."

"I'm sure that a nice dinner with you would be more interesting than a working one discussing the annual Golden Gate Art Gala fundraiser."

She smiled. "While that's a kind offer, I do have prior engagements that I must return to L.A. for. But we can get down to business now so you can make your dinner date."

"Fine, Miss May—"

"Morgan," she said, correcting him again.

"Morgan, what exactly do you want?"

She sat up in her chair and locked eyes with him. "I need your help. It's a matter of national security."

Kingsley ran his fingers through his thick brown hair, still damp from his swim. "Maybe you aren't aware of this, but I regularly meet with Senator Victor Cooley of the Intelligence Committee about cyber threats. If there was anything super pressing, why wouldn't I have heard anything from him first?"

The question was legitimate, one that Morgan had prepared to answer in case it came up.

"There are some things that Senator Cooley isn't privy to," Morgan said. "And this isn't exactly about cyber threats."

He furrowed his brow. "It's not?"

Morgan shook her head.

"What is it about then?"

She took a deep breath and recalled the answer she'd rehearsed on the flight to San Francisco. Her first opportunity to tell Kingsley about the issue was her best one. Any future attempts would be little more than groveling, though she wasn't above that in this instance. If the Magnum Group was going to have any hopes of catching the mole, she needed Kingsley's help.

"Think back to your days as a Ranger," she said. "What would you have done if you had a traitor in your platoon, someone who was constantly sabotaging your missions that endangered the lives of everyone else fighting for freedom?"

"I probably would've strung them up, probably in some painful—yet creative—way," he said.

"Well, my organization, the Magnum Group, fights for Americans from the shadows," she said. "And right now, we've got someone informing our enemies about our plans, jeopardizing the lives of everyone involved as well as that of innocent civilians. And to be quite frank, it's not something I can live with much longer. Right now, we're under some incredible pressure both at home and abroad—and the last thing I want to do is knowingly place my people in harm's way because we have a mole in our midst. So, what do you say? Will you help me?"

Morgan anticipated an unadulterated *yes*.

Kingsley cocked his head to one side. "What kind of help do you need?"

"We need your help in planting some information on the dark web so we can find out who's running the mole."

Kingsley winced and shook his head. "I'm sorry, but I don't think so."

"What do you mean? You're not going to help us?"

He nodded. "That's what I meant. If I start manipulating the Internet and I get caught, my good reputation will be trashed. And in the cyber world, trust is one of the most important commodities you can possess. Without it, I'm as popular as Netscape is today."

Morgan scowled. "Netscape?"

"Exactly. It didn't last ten years. But for a while, it was all the rage. I intend for my company to *remain* the rage."

He stood and stared out over the city.

"Are you sure you won't reconsider?" Morgan asked.

"I appreciate you thinking of me, but I have a dinner engagement to get to," Kingsley said before retreating inside.

Maria marched over to Morgan and gestured for her to get up.

Morgan sighed before standing and leaving Kingsley's mansion empty-handed and dejected.

CHAPTER
NINE

WASHINGTON, D.C.

ROBERT BESSERMAN TUGGED his fedora low across his brow as he entered the Columbia Room cocktail bar. He found Mallory Kauffman seated at a table in the back, sipping on a drink with her laptop in front of her. A waitress ushered him to his seat and handed him a menu.

"You look silly with that hat on," Mallory said before placing the straw between her lips.

"Half this town knows what I look like, while the other half wants me dead simply because I lead the best intelligence agency in the world," Besserman said. "The less attention I draw to myself, the better."

"Wearing that hat in public is going to draw attention—and definitely the wrong kind," she said. "If someone does recognize you while wearing that hat, I can almost promise you it'll be much worse for you. Every new recruit will chuckle about how ridiculous you looked in that hat."

"You won't shame me into taking it off," he said.

Mallory shrugged. "Fine. Just don't say I didn't warn you."

Besserman leaned forward and glanced at her glass. "What are you drinking?"

"It's a mojito," she said before taking another long sip. "It's really good. You want one?"

"I'd rather just have a glass of scotch."

Mallory sighed. "Of course you would. And where's the fun in that? Why don't you live a little sometime?"

He chuckled. "By the time you get to be my age, you've sampled everything—and you know what you like."

"I hope I'm never afraid to try new things."

"I'm not afraid of anything new—I just know what I like. And I can tell you some Spanish-sounding cocktail drink won't wet my whistle like a glass of bourbon will."

Their waitress returned a few seconds later and promptly delivered a scotch neat, just like Besserman was craving. He then glanced around to check for security cameras.

"Are you sure this place is clean?" he asked.

"No windows, no cameras, no worries," she said as she slid her laptop across the table toward him.

Besserman put on his glasses and opened the computer, angling it so no one else could see what was on the display. "What now?"

"Click on the file at the top of the folder in the center of the screen."

He did what she asked and a video window opened up and started playing without any sound.

"Why can't I hear anything?" he asked.

"There isn't anything to hear, according to my source," she said. "It's just a video."

Besserman shook his head in disbelief at the images rolling across the screen. He leaned forward in his seat. "Do you know who that is with Norris?"

Mallory nodded. "I mean, I had to look it up and run it through our facial recognition system."

"I hope you deleted your search."

"Of course."

"Good," Besserman said. "We can't leave any trace behind that we knew about this just in case this blows up and becomes a big scandal."

"Why shouldn't this become a big scandal?" Mallory asked. "Are we just going to bury this?"

He sighed as he closed the window. "Are there any more?"

"That's the most damning," she said. "But you're not answering me. Are we just going to pretend like this never happened and make it go away for Norris? I think we should demand some answers about the nature of this video."

"Absolutely," Besserman said. "However, I'm willing to give the president a chance to explain himself. We've been friends a long time, so I feel like I at least owe him an opportunity to explain what the hell was going on there because it doesn't look good."

Mallory finished her mojito. "Do you know where that was?"

"I'm not a hundred percent certain, but it looks like a bar in Maldives."

"You been there?"

"A couple of times while on official business."

She drew back and scowled. "What the hell kind of official business goes on there?"

"Not the kind you want to be involved with, I can tell you that much."

"That's not really an answer."

Besserman smirked. "You don't become the director of the CIA without being an expert at evading questions you don't want to answer. Perhaps you should try it some time. It might help you advance your career."

"If I'm not mistaken, you're actually the only person who could advance my career outside of the president," she said.

"So, maybe you should listen to me," he said with a faint smile.

"You know I don't like playing the political game, which is why this is about as far as I'm ever going to go."

Besserman took a long pull on his glass of scotch before setting it down on the table. "And you're exactly the kind of person the agency needs in the position you're in. Keep up the good work."

"I thought you just said—"

"Look, I just talked in circles and avoided answering your question a second time, meanwhile getting you focused on an entirely different issue altogether."

Mallory stared at the bottom of her empty glass. "Just when I think you're one of the good guys ..."

Besserman dropped a fifty-dollar bill on the table and winked at her. "Don't worry, Mal. We're on the same team. I just don't always say everything I'm thinking. Now, when you get a chance, would you mind sending a copy of that video to my burner phone? There's someone who needs to see that footage."

"Of course, sir."

He eased out of his booth and exited the Columbia Room. When he returned to his car, he pulled out his cell phone and dialed a number.

"Madam Secretary, this is Robert Besserman. We need to talk."

CHAPTER
TEN

ST. MORITZ, SWITZERLAND

BRADY HAWK TIGHTENED his ski gloves one final time
as he leaned over the side of the helicopter's open door. Above
him, rotor blades beat furiously against the windy conditions
near the peak of Piz Albana, He drew in a deep breath before
exhaling, resulting in a thick cloud of vapor. For a moment, he
wondered if he should've considered other transportation
options.

A heli drop was by far the most dangerous way to reach the
ritzy Swiss enclave located a third of the way down the mountain. However, residents had grown accustomed to the regular
occurrence of thrill-seeking skiers leaping from helicopters in
order to carve up virgin snow. And it would provide Hawk with
the best opportunity to reach General Gusev's chalet without
attracting any unwarranted attention.

"You ready?" Alex asked over the coms.

Hawk took another deep breath. "Is this insane or what?"

"You'll be fine, honey."

"Easy for you to say from the comfort of a luxury condo at
the base of the mountain."

She laughed. "Please come join me—just as soon as you finish the mission."

"Give me an hour and I'll be thawing my toes next to you by a roaring fire. How's that sound?"

"Sounds perfect ... too perfect."

"Will you let me be an optimist for just five minutes, give or take four minutes?"

Alex chuckled again. "Whatever makes you happy."

"See you in an hour," he said before forcing himself through the opening and onto the plush snow.

When he first hit the surface, he sank in a few inches. But his momentum brought him back to the top of the snow, where he glided down the mountain, weaving from left to right and back again. Hawk avoided several jagged rocks jutting above the surface. After a couple of minutes, he found a clean line leading straight for Das Luxusdorf.

For the past twenty years, Das Luxusdorf emerged as one of Europe's most exclusive neighborhoods, serving as a collection of resort homes for some of the region's wealthiest entrepreneurs. And although most of the residents were somewhat famous, there were a handful of those who had amassed a fortune from the shadows. Gen. Dimitri Gusev was one such person.

From all the intel Hawk had read about Gusev, the Russian general relished his privacy, most likely due to his long list of guilty pleasures. His gambling addictions had cost him his position in the military after the top brass recognized how easily he could be compromised. But it was his appetite for illicit drugs—and desire to take them with another partner—that made him dangerous. When Gusev was relieved of his post, intel reports claimed that other Russian generals threw a party, relieved that Gusev wouldn't be able to put them at risk any more. His victories during conflicts on several fronts throughout his career still earned him enough respect that Gusev was given a healthy retirement package including a house in St. Moritz. According to one classified report on Gusev's forced retirement, military leaders selected St. Moritz because it gave him access to everything he craved while keeping him more or less hidden from the rest of the world. But his hideaway was no longer a secret to Hawk.

Once Hawk reached Gusev's property, he placed a transmitter on the wall next to the call button and then notified Alex.

"It's done," he said over the coms.

"Roger that," she said. "Why don't you take a walk?"

Hawk leaned his skis against the side of the stone wall that towered twelve feet above the ground. Trudging through the snow, he marveled at the mansions built just below the peak. The architecture was almost Medieval, making Hawk wonder if beyond each gate there was also a moat to protect each fortress. Not that it would do much good considering it was the middle of a harsh winter. The wind nipped at Hawk's extremities, stinging him as he walked. With his hands jammed into his pockets, he appeared to be on a casual stroll around the neighborhood, but he was making mental notes of the area, studying each pathway for possible escape routes should the need arise—a force of habit that had served him well. With all the roads closed during the winter, the options to reach the exclusive property were reduced to helicopters, a private gondola, skis, or snowmobiles. Yet Hawk had only one viable mode of transportation, which made him a little nervous.

Ten minutes later, Alex notified him that she had access to Gusev's security system.

"You'd think that a home worth fifteen million dollars would at least have some formidable firewalls, but not this one," she said.

"Nobody ever thinks of everything."

"At least, we hope they never do," she said. "Now, I can get you inside the gate, but the front door has a deadbolt lock, so you're going to have to improvise there."

"No problem," Hawk said, "as long as the glass isn't bullet proof."

"I was thinking about something a little less violent, maybe posing as a courier."

"Of course, honey. I was just teasing."

"Something tells me you weren't," Alex said. "And remember, Morgan said no high body counts. The president has authorized us to do this, but he doesn't want an international incident as well."

Hawk strode up the path toward the front door. "Don't worry ... I've got an extra gun loaded with Dr. Z's tranq bullets. No dead bodies."

"I'm not convinced you're going to stick to that plan."

"When have I ever strayed from the plan?" Hawk said, trying hard to suppress a laugh.

"I'm not going to comment on that," she said. "But I'll be watching. Let me know if you need some help. But be careful. I can see from the infrared imaging that there are two heat signatures inside the house."

"Roger that."

Hawk took a deep breath before ringing the doorbell. He took a step back and clasped his hands behind his back. A few moments later, a man who appeared to be in his early 40s opened the door.

"Kann ich Ihnen helfen?" the man said.

Hawk forced a smile. "Ist Herr Gusev verfügbar?"

The man scowled before Hawk explained that he needed Gusev to sign for a letter. The man hesitated for a moment.

"Er ist nitch hier," he said before slamming the door.

I don't believe for one second that he's not there.

Undaunted by the rejection, Hawk rang the doorbell again. This time when the man opened it, Hawk didn't say a word. Instead, he forced his way inside and grabbed a fistful of the man's shirt.

"I want to speak with Gusev right now," Hawk said before pulling back one side of his jacket to reveal his gun.

He released the man whose expression quickly morphed from annoyance to terror. He motioned for Hawk to follow him down the hall. Hawk remained just a few feet behind the man, who walked briskly before darting into the dining room. He tipped over one chair, creating a hurdle for Hawk, who was surprised by the move, let alone the man's moxie. By the time Hawk scrambled through the other doorway and returned to the hallway, the man was gone.

"Alex, I'm gonna need some help," Hawk said.

"On it," she said. "What exactly do you need?"

"The man who answered the door darted into the room in front of me and I can't get in. I'd shoot my way in if the door wasn't made out of steel."

"Hmmm. Must be a panic room."

"It's not normal, that's for sure."

Hawk waited, listening to Alex's fingers pounding on her keyboard. "Give me a minute. I'm still working on this."

He stood in front of the door, his weapon trained on it, anxiously awaiting any kind of movement.

"Okay," Alex said a couple of minutes later. "I've got it."

"What's gonna happen?" Hawk asked.

"I've hacked the internal security system, which was different than the one for the perimeter. I'm going to unlock the door and then it's up to you."

"That's it?"

"Yeah, but you should know that I only see one heat signature in the room now."

Hawk furrowed his brow. "Where could the other man have gone?"

"There must be some other way out of there," Alex said. "Maybe you can force Gusev to show you once I open that door."

"Sounds like a plan."

Seconds later, the thick steel door hummed as it slowly swung open. Hawk moved inside, his weapon aimed in front of him. Across the room, Gusev sat on a small couch, his hands clasped and resting on his protruding stomach. The man looked pale, though not as frail as he'd been led to believe by various intel reports.

"Where's your friend?" Hawk asked in Russian.

Gusev shrugged. "He left."

Before Hawk could continue his interrogation, the doorbell chimed.

"Oh, he left, did he?"

"I don't know where he went."

Hawk grunted. "You think I'm going to fall for this. He's outside right now."

"No, he's not," Alex said over the coms. "There are two police officers outside right now."

After cursing under his breath, Hawk looked at Gusev. "Don't say a word."

"A crime has been reported," Gusev said. "They're not going to just leave."

"You reported a crime?"

"You're in my house and you weren't invited. I don't know what you call that in America, but in Switzerland, that's considered unlawful entry. Plus, you have a gun pointed at me, which is considered a lethal threat, also unlawful here."

"You're going to be quiet until they leave."

"You don't understand—they won't leave on their own," Gusev said. "It's part of the security measures this neighborhood has."

Hawk gestured with his gun for Gusev to get up. "Get rid of them."

"It's not that easy," Gusev said. "I have to verify my identity and answer a series of questions."

"I'm sure you can let them know that you're busy and that it was a mistake."

"For your sake, you better hope they buy it," Gusev said.

"Actually, you better sell it for their sake, as well as your own. Mess around with the bull and you're gonna get the horns. You understand?"

"You Americans all think you're cowboys," Gusev said before walking toward the entryway.

"And you Russians think you're smarter than everyone else. And you're going to find out just how wrong you are."

Gusev stopped as he put his hand on the doorknob to open it and smiled wryly. "You might want to move out of the way so they can't see you, Mr. Genius."

Hawk slipped off to the kitchen, watching the interaction take place through the reflection in the window.

"Greetings, officers," Gusev said in German. "What seems to be the problem?"

"We were notified that there was a security breach at your residence, Mr. Gusev. Is everything all right?"

"Must've been an animal—maybe a dog or a bird," Gusev said. "Everything is fine here."

The lead officer nodded at Gusev. "Sorry to bother you, sir."

They turned and walked away without another glance. Gusev clicked the deadbolt behind them and spun toward the kitchen. Hawk stormed toward him, weapon drawn.

"Please," Gusev said, placing his hands in the air, "I did what you asked. Don't shoot."

"They better not come back. You understand?"

"Of course."

As Gusev turned to go back to the panic room, he took two steps and collapsed to the ground. He convulsed for a moment before clutching his heart. After a few seconds of this, he foamed at the mouth before his body went stiff and then limp.

Hawk knelt next to his body to check for his pulse. There wasn't one.

"Damnit," he said. "I lost him."

"Be careful," Alex said. "I just saw that other heat signature come back online."

Hawk studied the body for a moment before peering closer at Gusev's neck. "I don't believe it."

"What is it?"

Hawk grabbed what appeared at first to be a piece of loose flesh. But as he tugged at it, Hawk realized it was a mask.

"This isn't Gusev," he said.

"How did you get fooled?"

"This guy is wearing a synthetic mask. And it looks like there is a small port of some type on the inside of it."

"Better get outta there," Alex said. "The police are coming back."

Hawk stood and heard pounding on the door.

"We're coming in," one of the officers announced. "We just received a report that someone's been murdered."

That sonofabitch is trying to frame me.

CHAPTER
ELEVEN

SAN FRANCISCO

MORGAN MAY SAT in her car, drumming her fingers on the steering wheel. She'd seen her uncle do the same thing plenty of times while trying to conjure up a solution to an impossible problem. And while she wasn't sure the drumming helped her, it alleviated some tension. Then she picked up Grant Kingsley's file and started reading through it again, hoping something would jump out at her, something she hadn't noticed before.

What's this?

A note caught her eye and she re-read it just to be sure. Seconds later, she dialed her office and asked to speak to Mia.

"How's my favorite hacker doing?" Morgan asked.

Mia laughed nervously. "Why do I get the feeling you're about to ask me to do you a favor?"

"Because you have good intuition."

"I knew it."

Morgan studied the document as she continued. "Did you go over all the details in this workup on Kingsley?"

"I looked at it, if that's what you mean," Mia said. "But I'm sure you know that I wasn't exactly hired to be an analyst."

"Right, I know. But did anything strike you as you read it?"

"Other than his rugged good looks? No. But if you want me to help you by posing as a random woman at a bar and flirting with him for an evening while he buys me drinks, I'm more than willing."

"You'll have to get in line for that," Morgan said. "But on a more serious note, I was wondering if you noticed the timing of the launch of Kingsley."

Morgan heard the rustling of papers before Mia continued. "Yeah, I see the date here."

"Anything strike you as coincidental about that date?"

"No," she said slowly. "Not really. Should it?"

"Do you recall Blackout Friday, the week after Thanksgiving when the entire U.S. government's web services were brought to a halt?"

"Who doesn't remember that? I was still in school, but everyone was talking about it, even in Germany."

"Yes, well, check the dates on the launch of Kingsley."

"It's one year after Blackout Friday," Mia said.

"One year *to the day*," Morgan said.

"That's probably just a coincidence."

"Or maybe it's his big inside joke. I can attest that Kingsley has a massive ego."

"As massive as his chest?"

"Focus, Mia, focus."

"Sorry," she said. "I'm just stuck in the office left to stare at this dossier on the most eligible bachelor in the world. You can forgive me, right?"

"I'm not sure I'd consider anyone headed for prison to be marriage material."

"I think conjugal visits and spending his five billion dollars might sustain me," she said.

"Like I said—focus, Mia, focus."

"Okay," Mia said, "I'm getting a strong sense that you want

me to investigate the possibility that Kingsley was involved in Blackout Friday."

"Now you're back on track," Morgan said.

"And how am I going to prove that? From what I understand the NSA has an entire team still trying to figure that out."

"I'll make a call and get you read in. Then I need you to get back to me within an hour."

"An hour?" Mia's replied, her voice going up several octaves. "Are you mental?"

"Settle down. I don't need the kind of proof that would lead a jury to convict him, just enough for a grand jury to consider a case at all."

"Still a challenge."

"And one I know you're up for," Morgan said.

"Do you honestly think he was behind that attack?"

"Just find me something I can work with within the next hour. If not, our best chance to trap the mole might disappear for a while."

"I'll do my best," Mia said. "Just connect me with whoever you know at the NSA and I'll get started."

Morgan pumped her first. "You're the best, Mia."

"Yeah, yeah."

———

MORGAN WATCHED FROM across the street as Kingsley's garage door opened. He drove a black Hummer, pulling out in front of another car, forcing it to hit the brakes while Kingsley peeled away. Dropping into drive, Morgan followed the tech mogul from a safe distance. He headed to Fisherman's Wharf and used valet parking at Gary Danko, the upscale restaurant that was a favorite among the city's elite.

She parked in the garage across the street and bundled up before getting out.

While she waited for Mia to call her back, Morgan strolled

along the pier, watching the last gaggle of tourists feed the seals before the sun dipped below the horizon. The evening chill set in, and Morgan plunged her hands deeper into her coat pockets. She found a bench outside the restaurant and killed time responding to work emails on her phone.

When Mia's call finally came, Morgan stood and paced along the sideway away from the entrance.

"So, tell me the good news," Morgan said.

Mia exhaled audibly. "Well, it wasn't a bad hunch after all."

"What'd you find?"

"The thing about hackers is that they like to pretend as if they do everything anonymous, but deep down they want recognition," Mia said. "Without it, it's like an unsigned painting by da Vinci or van Gogh. You might recognize the brilliance in the work, but you can't definitively ascribe it to a particular painter without a signature."

"That was the case with Blackout Friday," Morgan said. "The NSA experts combed through the code written to infiltrate government servers and never found a hint of a hidden signature. It was as generic of a code as any agency cryptologist had ever seen."

"That's because cryptologists don't think like hackers," Mia said. "Speaking from experience, we all leave a fingerprint, whether we think we do or not. The way we write code says as much about as the type of code we write."

"So, am I to assume that you found this fingerprint with Kingsley?"

"Not exactly," Mia said.

"Damnit, Mia. You got me all excited about this thing, but now you're going to let me down."

"Wrong again."

Morgan sighed. "Stop toying with me and spit it out."

"Kevin Gonzalez has been part of Kingsley's team since the inception of the company. However, before he was a well-respected computer programmer within the industry, he was a hacker who went by the name James Wells, AKA Crasher. He avoided jail time as a 19-year-old student at NYU by cooperating with the feds on another case. Wells worked once with Lord Dominion, who had stolen more than a half a billion dollars from several Cayman Island banks. Since I knew this, I went back and compared the codes. Turns out, Gonzalez's fingerprint from his heists with Lord Dominion match those on the Blackout Friday case."

"That's not definitive."

"You didn't ask for grand jury proof, remember? That should be enough to scare Kingsley so that you can coerce him into helping you."

"Are you sure there isn't some way he could wriggle out of it?"

"If he's most worried about his reputation, he'll have to weigh which one he deems more damaging—getting caught tweaking some algorithms or hiring a known cyber thief."

"Okay, we'll give it a whirl," Morgan said. "It's not like I have any other play at the moment."

She wandered over to his car and waited until the valet came for it twenty minutes later. "I'll give you a five-hundred-dollar tip if you let me drive this to the client."

"Ma'am, I wish I could, but I'd lose my job if I got caught doing it."

Morgan flashed a badge. It was merely her access badge to Langley, but most civilians couldn't tell with such a quick glance. "I'll talk to your boss if he finds out. Deal?"

The valet held out the keys to Kingsley's Hummer. "Deal."

Morgan made the exchange with the young man and promptly pulled up to the valet stand and rolled down the driver's side window. As Kingsley approached his vehicle, his eyes met Morgan's.

"Get in," she said. "We're not done talking."

Kingsley walked around to the other side of the car and

climbed into the passenger seat. "You are quite the little minx. I love a woman who likes to take charge."

Morgan didn't say a word as she put the vehicle in gear and drove across the street to the parking deck. She pulled into a spot and stopped.

"I'm not playing games," Morgan said. "And I'm done asking. You're going to help me."

Kingsley cocked his head to one side. "Forgive me if I'm wrong, but didn't we already have a discussion about this a few hours ago?"

Morgan nodded. "I don't handle rejection well. Besides, since we last spoke, some new information has come to light."

"Oh? Such as?"

"Your lead programmer is a thief—and we also found his fingerprints all over the Blackout Friday hack," Morgan said. "Curiously enough, you launched exactly one year after the hack that brought the government computer systems to its knees. And the money that was paid for that ransom covered your launch. Not many companies get the kind of funding you did and stay private. And I think there's a reason for that."

"That's a ridiculous claim. Kevin would never do anything like that."

"You're right—but James Wells might," Morgan said. "That's right. Kevin Gonzalez is actually James Wells, who helped Lord Dominion drain all those banks in the Cayman Islands years ago. Just so happens one of my best agents was able to find your guy's digital fingerprints all over the Blackout Friday hack, matching them with the Cayman Island heists. So, what's it gonna be? You still think helping me would damage your *trusted* reputation?"

"I don't believe you," Kingsley said. "You're bluffing."

Morgan picked up her phone and asked Mia to send the files to Kingsley's cell. He perused the documents before putting his phone down with a sigh.

"Fine," Kingsley said. "If you promise to make this go away, I'll help."

Morgan smiled and tossed Kingsley his keys.

"Have a good evening, Mr. Kingsley," she said with a wink. "We'll be in touch."

CHAPTER
TWELVE

WASHINGTON, D.C.

ROBERT BESSERMAN EASED a small paper container with scones onto the desk of Barbara Wheeler, who was peering over her glasses at a document. She put her finger on a line and compared it with data on her computer screen, looking over the top of her glasses as she did so.

"If you're trying to butter me up, Bobby, it'll take more than a few scones," she said without glancing at him.

"Madam Secretary, good morning to you, too," Besserman said as he sat down in the chair across from her desk.

She sighed and then rested her glasses on top of her head. "Bobby, what's this really all about? A last-minute meeting with the Chinese ambassador? And you still haven't told me why we're doing this."

Besserman forced a smile. "Would you kill me if I told you that I wanted to talk with him alone?"

"Alone? Are you crazy?"

"I've been called worse."

"Look, when I invite an ambassador to my office, the expectation is that we'll discuss relations. If you set me up like this, it could hurt my credibility."

Besserman leaned forward in his seat and then tugged on the lapels of his sports coat before smoothing them out. "I think you know that's the last thing I'd want to do. But I don't know how else to do this without potentially exposing the Chinese ambassador or jeopardizing our mission."

"And what exactly is that mission, Bobby?"

"We're trying to keep Americans safe, the same as always. But I can't very well do that in this case without a closed meeting."

Wheeler pushed back from her desk before clasping her hands behind her head. "I trusted that you were asking me to do something in good faith—and that you'd read me in. Right now, I feel used. It's like you don't even respect this office."

"That's not at all what I'm trying to convey," Besserman said. "And when I finally get the chance to explain everything, you bet I will. But right now, I'm navigating not only some political landmines but also a literal looming disaster."

Wheeler bit her lip and looked out the window. "And that's all you're gonna give me?"

"I understand you're reticence to go along with this, but how long have we known each other? Fifteen, twenty years?"

"It's been a while, dating back to my days as an intern on Capitol Hill."

"And have I ever given you a reason to distrust me?"

She shook her head. "Never."

"I'm not about to start either. Just give me ten minutes with the Chinese ambassador and I promise to read you in later."

"If you hang me out to dry, I swear, Bobby, I'll—"

"No need for threats," Besserman said. "You'll be pleased with how this turns out in the end, I promise. And if the opportunity arises, I'll be sure to give you as much credit as I possibly can."

"Now, I like the sound of that," Wheeler said.

"So, are you going along with this or not?"

She sighed. "Let's do it. But you owe me."

"I wouldn't have it any other way."

"Good," she said. "You sit over there. I can promise you that Chai Zhen won't be happy about this."

"He'll get over it," Besserman said. "Especially if you give him something he wants."

"Hey, don't push it," she said, wagging her index finger.

Besserman held his hands up in a gesture of surrender. "Of course not."

She eyed him closely before a knock at the door arrested her attention. Wheeler's assistant poked his head inside the room.

"The Chinese ambassador is here to see you, Madam Secretary," he said.

"Send him in."

Besserman watched as Wheeler charmed Zhen for a few minutes before revealing the purpose of the meeting.

"I wish I could stay, Ambassador Zhen, but there's someone else here who has some business with you."

She nodded at Besserman, who'd remained unnoticed in the corner of the room.

Zhen scowled. "What's the meaning of this? I demand to know right now."

"I'm sure Director Besserman will be able to explain everything far better than I can. Bobby."

She nodded at Besserman, who gestured toward the couch.

"Please, Ambassador Zhen, have a seat."

Zhen sat down and crossed his arms in front of his chest. "I don't like being lied to."

Wheeler slipped out of the room, leaving the two men alone.

"I understand," Besserman said. "But you must not hold this against Secretary Wheeler. I'm the one who ambushed her, in a manner of speaking."

"You ambushed her?"

"I asked her to call a meeting with you, but I didn't tell her that I wanted to speak with you alone. I'm going out on a limb here and I'm hoping you can stay with me. I need your help unraveling a mystery."

"What kind of mystery?" Zhen asked.

"The kind that can put our two countries on a collision course for conflict if we don't resolve it quickly."

Zhen moved to the edge of his seat. "Go on."

"If I show you a video clip, could you possibly tell me what's happening?"

"The problem is, there isn't any sound. I'm hoping you can read lips."

"I won't make any promises," Zhen said. "But I'll do my best."

"That's all I can ask for."

Besserman sent the footage saved on his cell phone to a computer, which had its screen mirrored on a projector against the far wall.

"That's General Chow," Zhen said, pointing at the man talking with Norris.

"Do you know where this is?"

"A bar in Maldives. But that's all I know."

"What is General Chow saying?"

"It's not easy to read his lips. He's drunk and appears to be mumbling. Was there any sound with this video?"

Besserman shook his head. "This is all I got. I wish I had more, but this is all I have to go off of. And you can't tell anything else?"

"Maybe you should ask your own president," Zhen said. "He's the one who's invested millions of dollars in Chinese investment firms over the past five years."

Besserman's eyebrows shot upward. "Our president? President Norris?"

Zhen nodded.

"And that's all you have to say about that?" Besserman asked.

"If you want direct answers, perhaps you should ask the president yourself."

"That's all you're going to give me?"

Zhen nodded. "I've probably said too much."

———

WHEN BESSERMAN RETURNED to his office at Langley, he called Mallory Kauffman. A few minutes later, she sauntered inside and sat down across from him.

"So, what'd you learn?" he asked.

"That was quite eye-opening," she said.

"Hopefully in a good way."

"Only if you were running against him in the election."

Besserman rubbed his face with both hands. "Please tell me it's not as bad as I imagined it."

"I can't say for sure, but I'm not in your mind," Mallory said. "But it's bad—real bad. The kind of bad that not even the best fixer in Washington can make disappear."

Besserman shuddered. "You don't have to sound so ominous."

"Just trying to be real so you know what you're up against," she said. "Personally, I hate surprises."

"Lay it on me," Besserman said.

"Over the year, President Norris has deposited more than a hundred and fifty million dollars in Chinese investment banks. He currently had more than two hundred million to his name from those accounts."

"Two hundred million? That's a twenty-five percent increase on his initial investment."

"Uh-huh," Mallory said.

"So, what does that mean for us?"

"It means you're going to be up a creek without a paddle if the media gets a hold of this information."

"I already knew that," Besserman said. "Anything else?"

"What else needs to be said? Isn't that damning enough?"

Besserman could only nod. He knew that Norris was a dead man walking. At this point, it was only a matter of *how*, not *when*.

CHAPTER
THIRTEEN

ST. MORITZ, SWITZERLAND

HAWK SAW the shadows of police officers through the front door's opaque glass and scanned the house for a way out. As they demanded that someone open the door, Hawk realized that Gusev was more than prepared for a moment such as this. The former Russian general was beyond paranoid—and anticipated such a moment when someone came for him. Now Hawk was on his back foot, scrambling to navigate his way out of an unfamiliar house to avoid legal troubles in Switzerland without his own government to back him up, something that went with the territory of engaging in black ops missions.

As Hawk assessed his best possible move, he noticed the shadows of a few officers leaving the front of the house and heading around the side.

"Get to the basement if you can," Alex said. "We'll figure out a way to get you out."

Hawk hustled downstairs and spied his best exit route—a snowmobile. He found a fuel can and dumped as much as he could into the tank. Overhead, he heard footsteps thumping across the floor, serving as a reminder that his time to escape was short.

Hawk opened the garage door and ignited the snowmobile's engine. He pulled back on the handle as the machine lurched forward into the snow. As Hawk churned through the snow, he glanced to his left where an officer had his weapon drawn. He stopped short of firing at Hawk as two other officers sprinted toward him.

Hawk left Gusev's property and entered the street packed with snow.

"What now?" Hawk asked over the coms.

"The street you're on leads to downtown St. Moritz."

"Why does this feel too easy?" Hawk asked.

"Because it's not that easy."

"Great," Hawk said under his breath.

"If you continue on in about a half-mile, you'll reach the security office. And based on what I'm seeing, they're getting ready for you. Not to mention that there's already chatter on the police scanners that a murderer is on the loose."

"This isn't helping."

"You'll need another way down the mountain," she said. "And the only way to get out of there is off-roading it."

"There are rocks jutting out of every spot on the surface of this mountain," he said. "How am I going to navigate that cleanly on this beast?"

"You can always make a short trip back to Gusev's to collect your skis."

"I need helpful suggestions, honey."

"That was helpful, even if it seems impossible. Otherwise, you're gonna have to navigate down the mountain."

Hawk noticed a narrow pathway between two properties, leading to the side of the mountain. Without hesitating, he whipped his handlebars to the right and left the posh enclave. As he did, he glanced over his shoulder and saw that two security guards were following him on snowmobiles.

"You've got company," Alex said.

"I see them," Hawk said. "Any ideas on how to lose them?"

"Hang on a second."

As Hawk rumbled along the path, he dodged large rocks protruding into the path. When he reached a smoother portion, he looked back to see the guards gaining on him. They'd also been joined by another vehicle, a snowmobile driven by a policeman. Alex's second felt like an hour to Hawk.

"I don't need a perfect escape route," he said. "Just something to get these guys off my tail."

"I'm looking at the map and the only place I see where you might be able to lose them is on Dead Man's Bluff."

"Oh, nice, Alex. Do you *want* to be a widower? There's nothing more I'd rather be doing right now than snuggling on the couch and reading John Daniel a bedtime story. But since that won't ever happen if I'm stuck in a Swiss jail for the rest of my life, I need a legit way back to the city."

As he looked over his shoulder, he noticed one of the men with his weapon trained on him. Hawk jerked his handlebars to the right, luring the three men in pursuit along a route parallel to the mountain. Once they'd all fallen in line, Hawk completed his hundred and eighty-degree turn, pointing his machine straight up the mountain. The trio of followers all continued their chase.

With the machines all struggling to get up the mountain, Hawk wove his way back down the mountain, creating some extra separation between him and the men.

"Found anything yet?" Hawk asked.

"Yes," she said excitedly. "Yes, I have. It's called Warrior Ridge, and it's up ahead on your left."

"I think I see it," Hawk said as he sped toward what looked like a ledge. "Am I headed the right way?"

"Roger that," she said. "When you get to the edge, just go for it. It's about a 15-foot drop, according to my calculations. And I think you should be able to land that rather easily."

"I love your confidence in me, hun," he said.

"It's between a cliff drop and a bullet," she said. "Gotta weigh the odds."

"And you're sure this way gives me the best chance?"

"Of course—unless they follow you over the edge."

Hawk took a deep breath and leaned forward, focusing on the upcoming drop. "Just know that no matter what happens, I love you."

A few seconds later, Hawk's snowmobile reached the edge. He pulled back on the handlebars, keeping the vehicle parallel to the ground for as long as possible. As he soared through the air, he felt like he would never come down. He glanced to his left and then his right—nothing but jagged rocks covered with snow and a few scattered trees—all objects that could prove deadly if he hit them at the speed he was moving. Fortunately, the thought was fleeting, one that completely left his mind when his snowmobile made contact with earth again. When he hit the ground, Hawk dug his heels into the side of the snowmobile so that he would fly over the front of it. He whipped around to the left as the vehicle skidded to a stop.

"Good job," Alex said. "I knew you'd nail the landing."

However, when he looked back at the top of the ridge, one of the guards hurtled over the side on his snowmobile.

"Well, it's not over with yet," he said.

Hawk goosed the accelerator and took off, realizing that his chase was still on. He zig-zagged down the mountain with the guard growing closer with each passing second.

"Any other ideas, Alex?"

"You'll have to get creative on the fly. I can't see anything else that's so obvious."

Hawk peered ahead and noticed several large boulders protruding from the ground—and he had an idea. He slowed down enough for the guard to edge closer to Hawk's rear end. Just as the guard was about to overtake Hawk, he sped up and then whipped his snowmobile to the left. By the time the guard reacted, he had turned sideways but smashed against the rocks, knocking to the ground. Hawk scrambled over to the overturned vehicle and snatched the keys out before pocketing them. He hustled back to his vehicle and took off, leaving the guard stranded.

"You all right?" Alex asked as Hawk roared away.

"I am now," he said. "All I have to do is sneak into town without anyone noticing, which seems rather easy given everything else I did just to get to this point."

"I'd say it's time for you to go buy a lottery ticket."

"And why's that?"

"You just stuck the landing off of Dead Man's Bluff," Alex said.

"Dead Man's Bluff? I thought that was Warrior Ridge."

"I may have creatively renamed it to entice you to jump," she said sheepishly.

"That's not funny, Alex."

"No, but it worked. Besides, I'm going to request that they rename the place after you—Brady's Bluff. It's got a nice ring to it, doesn't it?"

"I know what you're trying to do, Alex. It's still not cool."

"You made it, didn't you?"

"Uh huh, but—"

"But I knew you would. There was never any doubt in my mind."

"That makes one of us," he said. "Now, instead of bragging about how you manipulated your husband to do what you wanted—an age-old wife skill—can you help me find Gusev?"

"I suggest you leave that snowmobile at the edge of the city limits and enter on foot. I've been tracking several heat signatures that left the neighborhood at the top of the mountain. So, I think I know where he's at."

"You *think* you know?"

She ignored his question. "There's a hotel two blocks east off the main street. I'll text you the address. I'm betting on him being there."

"You know what the implications are if you're wrong, don't you?"

"He's there," Alex said. "But you have to capture him and bring him in. It's the only way to prove you didn't kill anyone."

"Don't you worry about that," Hawk said. "I'm going to have a heart-to-heart conversation with the General."

"Good luck and I'll be watching from here."

"Let me know if anything changes," Hawk said.

"Roger that."

He hustled down the street, trying to look as casual as possible. If he lost Gusev, Hawk could be arrested on charges of murder. His face would be plastered over every European police station. He wouldn't be able to travel anywhere without getting flagged. Losing Gusev wasn't an option.

While entering through the front door made the most sense when it came to efficiency, he couldn't be sure that the St. Moritz police hadn't already informed businesses and citizens that a crazed murderer was on the loose. Once anyone identified him as the suspect the city's law enforcement were looking for, Hawk would find it next to impossible to escape. Hawk found an empty box just outside one of the side doors. He threaded the slats on the front in order to keep the top shut. Then he eased down the hallway before stopping a concierge and inquiring about Gusev.

"I have a delivery for General Gusev," Hawk said in his best German.

"General Gusev?" the man asked. "I wasn't aware that he was staying with us today. Let me check with the front desk."

Hawk shrugged. "I'll just get someone else to sign for it."

"It's no trouble," the man said. "Please stay here. I insist."

Hawk forced a smile and waited for the man to share what he'd learned from the front desk.

"I understand," the man said in German while scribbling on a notepad on his desk.

When the man finished, he hung up the phone.

"Did you find what room he's in?" Hawk asked.

The concierge stood and held up his index finger. "Would you mind waiting here for just a moment?"

Hawk nodded as the man walked toward the front desk. He spoke with another woman, who cast furtive glances at Hawk. That was all he needed to see.

Hawk scooped up his box and raced toward the stairwell.

"Arrest that man!" the clerk at the front desk shouted.

Hawk didn't wait around to see what the fuss was about. He was halfway up the first flight of stairs when he heard footsteps galloping down the hall after him.

"Alex," he said. "I need a way out—and I need it now."

CHAPTER
FOURTEEN

SAN FRANCISCO

MORGAN MAY STEPPED DOWN from the passenger side of Grant Kingsley's Hummer and followed him to the set of elevators in the corner of the Kingsley parking garage. While they waited for the doors to open, she glanced at the concrete walls livened up by a caricatured version of Kingsley, who was depicted with a royal robe and a scepter. A gold crown was tilted to the right on his head, and one eye was painted closed as if he was winking.

"Do you ever find that painting disturbing?" Morgan asked.

Kingsley chuckled and shook his head. "Should I?"

"It definitely doesn't do justice to your chiseled jaw line."

"I always figured if you're going to be the face of your company, you ought to be comfortable with your company using your face."

She shrugged. "I always thought your logo made you look more like a court jester than a king."

"Everyone's a critic," he said with a low growl.

"But then again if you make as much money as you did last year, I guess you can afford to look like a fool."

Kingsley eyed her closely. "You still want my help, right?"

"Okay," Morgan said. "I'll shut up now."

The elevator dinged as the doors slid open. Once they were inside, Morgan could hear what sounded like a lecture piped in over the sound system. But as she listened, she realized it wasn't a lecture at all.

"Oh my god," she said. "Is this a sound track of you reciting personal affirmations?"

Kingsley shrugged. "Our corporate psychologist suggested it as a way to keep a positive work environment."

Morgan turned her head to one side, straining to hear the one currently being played.

Stay humble. Work hard in silence. Let success make the most noise.

"If I worked here and had to listen to that every day, I might climb to the roof and jump off," Morgan said.

Stay strong. Dream, believe, achieve.

Morgan pantomimed as if she were going to vomit.

Kingsley smiled thinly. "If that's the worst sin I commit in the world of corporate America, I can live with that."

"True," Morgan said. "It's far less egregious than your other real sins."

"Why do I get the feeling that you don't really like me and you're just using me right now?"

She shrugged. "Who knows? Maybe I really do like you and sarcasm is just my first language. It's hard to say. But while we're here, can you just stay strong? *Dream, believe, achieve.*"

The elevator came to a stop and the doors parted. Kingsley led her to his office where he waved his access card in front of the security panel. Once they were inside, Morgan let out a low whistle as she looked around.

"Fancy place," she said, glancing at the putting green in the far corner of the room. "If I didn't know any better, I'd think you were trying to become a golf pro."

"It'd be far less headaches, that's for sure," Kingsley said as he handed Morgan a putter. "You play?"

"On occasion."

He rolled her a ball and crossed his arms. "Show me what you got."

Morgan held up her putter as she knelt, closing one eye and trying to figure out the best line to the hole.

"It's a carpeted level floor. There's no draw to your putt."

She gripped the club with both hands and hovered over the ball. "If there's one thing I've learned in my line of work, it's that nothing is ever as it seems. You can add that to your daily affirmation loop."

Morgan swung the putter, knocking the ball toward the hole.

"Looks like you're off," Kingsley said as the ball started rolling.

Just as the shot looked as if it was going to miss, the ball circled the lip of the cup and dropped in.

"Impressive," Kingsley said, his eyebrows shooting upward. "Maybe I can get a tee time for us after this?"

"So, I make a putt and you suddenly think I like you again?"

"I've never seen a challenge I didn't like."

Morgan chuckled. "One challenge at a time, okay? First, I need your help setting a trap, remember?"

"Of course," Kingsley said. "I didn't mean to get ahead of myself."

He dragged a chair next to his desk, gesturing for her to sit down. "Now, explain to me exactly what you want me to do."

Morgan sat down. "How difficult is it to track information on the dark web?"

"What kind of tracking are you talking about?"

"The kind where we can see who looked at it."

"Easily doable," Kingsley said. "Is that all?"

"Can you track who opened the files down to the exact terminal if it's in a larger office environment?"

"You mean like if it's on a corporate network, you want to know precisely which employee looked at a file?"

She nodded.

"It's a little trickier on the dark web, but it's not impossible."

"Challenging enough for you?" she asked.

Kingsley started typing on the keyboard. "I guess we'll soon find out. Now, what kind of information do you want me to hide?"

"Brad Porter is a prisoner at Leavenworth. I want it to be known that he's going to be transferred soon—and that he's agreed to work with the feds to expose The Alliance."

He stopped typing and looked at Morgan. "The Alliance? That's a real thing?"

"I wish it weren't, but it's as real as it gets."

"I've read about them on some chat rooms. I'd always thought it was just a conspiracy theory."

Morgan sighed. "Maybe I've gotten ahead of myself here. I'm going to need you to sign an NDA."

"You don't have to worry about a thing," Kingsley said. "My lips are sealed."

"I'm sure they will be. But I need to make sure that I have legal grounds to pursue you if you happen to change your mind."

"Whatever you want—just give me the paperwork and I'll sign it for you."

"That's what I like to hear," Morgan said, handing Kingsley a tablet with a space for him to sign one of the Magnum Group's standard agreements.

He hastily signed everything and turned his attention back to his terminal. "If that's all, I'd really like to finish this up before it gets too late."

"Of course," Morgan said. "Time to bait the trap."

CHAPTER
FIFTEEN

ST. MORITZ, SWITZERLAND

HAWK TOOK two steps at a time as he raced up to the third floor using the stairwell. He managed to get a significant lead on the officers pursuing him, but it would amount to nothing if Alex didn't find a way out for him.

"Alex," Hawk said as he yanked open the door to the third floor, "any time now would be a great time to direct me out of here."

"I'm still looking," Alex said. "From what I can see, the police have every exit blocked, and there aren't any other physical ways out."

"Is there a basement?"

"Yes, but—"

"Then all I have to do is get there without them noticing."

"And how are you going to do that?" she asked. "Even with the best of Dr. Z's gadgets, there are still limitations to what you can do with them."

"I won't need any gadgets for this."

Hawk scanned the hallway and spied a cleaning cart parked outside a room with a door propped open. He ran inside the room and found a woman making the bed. She smiled at him after he offered a timid wave.

"How would you like to make five hundred Euros?" he asked in German.

The woman glared at him. "I'm not that kind of woman."

Hawk shook his head. "No, no. That's not what I mean. I need your help."

After explaining what he wanted her to do, she laughed nervously. "I can do that."

"Thank you," Hawk said as he forked over three hundred Euros. "The rest when we get there."

They worked together to unload some of the cart's supplies on the bottom of it, hiding them in the closet. Then Hawk climbed underneath the cart and clutched his legs tight against his chest. As the woman pushed the cart down the hall, she moved slowly, straining due to Hawk's weight.

Before they reached the elevators, Hawk heard the thunder of footsteps from officers searching for him. One stopped and asked the cleaning lady if she'd seen a man, but she told him she hadn't and that it had been quiet on the floor. The officer thanked her before sprinting away.

Once the cart was loaded into the elevator, they descended toward the basement. However, they stopped early on the main floor.

The woman muttered something under her breath.

"What is it?" Hawk asked.

"I don't know."

She tapped one of the buttons repeatedly in an attempt to close the door again, Hawk presumed. Before it closed, Hawk heard the doors jerk as they slid open again.

"Have you seen anyone suspicious while you were cleaning?" a man asked.

"Not any more suspicious than usual," she said with a chuckle.

The man laughed too. "I know, I know. It's life in St. Moritz. But if you see anything else, please let us know right away."

"Is everything all right, officer?" she asked.

"Just be careful and report anything you see immediately. I don't want to alarm you, but there is a suspected murderer on the loose and we're trying to detain him immediately before anyone else gets hurt."

The door slid shut without her saying another word. In less than a minute, they were in the basement and she told Hawk it was safe to come out.

"Thank you," Hawk said, forking over the money. "Here's an extra five hundred Euros. You may have saved my life."

She looked up at him, her hands shaking. "You're not going to kill me, are you?"

Hawk shook his head. "Whatever they say about me, don't believe it."

"Then why are you running?"

"Sometimes things aren't always as they appear—but sometimes you may not be able to convince others of that fact. Running was my only choice."

The woman knelt next to a shelf and grabbed a handful of supplies. "You better get out of here then. I'm sure someone will be looking for you down here soon enough."

"Is there a way to get out from down here?" Hawk asked.

She glanced at the basket of dirty uniforms. "The dry cleaner sends someone by today to collect all our uniforms to wash them. The delivery man will be here in ten minutes. I can push you up top and get you into his van."

"Brilliant," Hawk said. "I can figure out the rest from there."

"Good luck," she said, pointing toward the large canvas basket that was on wheels.

Hawk climbed inside, almost immediately overwhelmed by the stench. "How long have these uniforms been in here?"

"Some of them have been in there for up to two weeks," she

said. "I know it's not pleasant, but it's better than the alternative."

"Thank you again," Hawk said.

Ten minutes later, she was pushing him up a ramp and into the dry cleaner's van.

As soon as the doors shut and the van started moving, Hawk poked his head through the mountain of clothes and glanced at the front of the vehicle. The man driving bopped his head to the beat of techno punk, completely unaware that he was harboring a fugitive. At the next traffic light, Hawk climbed out of the cart and opened the back doors. He jumped out and closed the doors without the man noticing.

"Alex, I'm out," he said over the coms.

"Impressive—but this mission is going to be a giant flop if we don't leave with Gusev."

"Any leads on that front?" Hawk asked as he ducked down an alleyway.

"As a matter of fact, there is," she said. "I just heard a conversation on the police radio channel that someone is going to check on Gusev at his permanent villa at the Suvretta House resort."

"I thought he wanted his privacy," Hawk said.

"Maybe from the rest of the world, but not here," she said. "It's apparent that he wants to be known—and known as someone important if he's bought a permanent residence at the Suvretta House."

"Sounds like it's swanky."

"It is. And you'd have quite a time getting into it under normal circumstances—and it's far from normal right now with a city-wide manhunt for you."

"I'll think of something," Hawk said.

"I'm texting you the address right now."

Hawk glanced at his phone with the message from Alex. Moments later, he was following a GPS app on his phone to the resort.

With his hands shoved into his pockets, Hawk walked

briskly toward his destination. "You ever realize what we're doing and then think we could be at home right now with John Daniel snuggling on the couch and reading a book about a teddy bear who lost his button in a department store?"

"Everything but that last part," she said.

"What? You don't like snuggling on the couch and reading?"

"That's not it. If I'm going to imagine an idyllic scene, that book would have no part of it. I could close my eyes and recite it if I had to."

"I hate that book too, but we both know that if we were all on the couch together reading a book before bedtime, that's the one we'd be reading."

"I know," Alex said, "which is why I don't imagine any scenario where I'm reading to John Daniel before bedtime."

"What do you imagine?"

"I imagine taking a bath and reading a book while you put John Daniel to bed."

Hawk chuckled. "Fair enough—and probably one hundred percent accurate."

"You know I love that little dude," she said. "But when I imagine being somewhere else, it's not where I'm doing the hard stuff. And reading that book for the one thousandth time is hard."

Hawk smiled and shook his head. If there was one trait he admired about Alex—and sometimes simultaneously loathed—it was her blunt honesty. It's also how he could trust her in the field.

"I'm approaching the resort," he said.

"I see you," she said. "The satellite image is getting some interference right now, but it's working for the moment enough that I can see your position."

"Roger that."

Hawk spotted a police car parked along the side of the street just outside the entrance. And there wasn't an officer in sight.

Hawk hustled up to the car, which was unlocked. He pulled

on a lever, releasing the trunk and starting a search for a uniform. After rummaging around for a few seconds, he spotted one and promptly crawled into the backseat to change. His transformation took less than a minute before he emerged in a tight-fitting uniform.

Hawk approached the guard house, which was tended by a plump man enjoying a crisp apple. He eyed Hawk's shirt and cracked a smile.

"Maybe less doughnuts on your break," the man quipped.

Hawk flexed his right bicep and then glanced at it. "Maybe this uniform isn't fitting because I'm getting stronger."

The man shrugged. "Maybe so. Are you here with Officer Schmidt to check in on General Gusev?"

Hawk nodded.

"He's in Alpine Village," the security guard said. "Number seventy-two. Good luck."

Hawk hustled across the common area in the direction of the village the guard had referenced. Once he neared the house, he peered in through the window and noticed Schmidt and Gusev having a casual conversation.

Hawk swapped out magazines in his handgun before creeping around to the back of the home. The backdoor was open, the warm vapors of a cup of coffee still swirling upward on the patio table which also contained a book lying face down.

Hawk glanced around to make sure no neighbors were watching, but only a former military officer from Russia would even consider venturing outside to read in such bitter cold. After easing inside, Hawk crept down the hallway, his gun trained in front of him.

"Remember, low body count," Alex said.

Hawk didn't respond as his target came into view.

Noticing Hawk first, Gusev raised his hands in the air. "Don't shoot."

Before Schmidt could draw his weapon, Hawk hit him twice in the neck, sending him collapsing to the floor. Gusev tried to hide behind the couch, but Hawk rushed toward the Russian general and put one shot in his neck and the other in his chest. Before Gusev could say a word, he was out.

Hawk collected all four of the tranquilizer darts he'd shot and pocketed them as well as Schmidt's keys. He ignored the officer and collected Gusev, throwing him over his shoulder and carrying him to the squad car outside the Suvretta House resort.

As Hawk approached the gate, the security guard was searching for any edible flesh on his apple core. He glanced up at Hawk lugging Gusev to the car.

"I thought you just needed to talk to him," the guard said.

"He wasn't being compliant," Hawk said with a shrug.

The guard didn't seem interested in pushing the issue before tossing the core into the street.

Working quickly to secure Gusev in the back, Hawk finished before communicating with Alex.

"The target is secure," Hawk said over the coms. "Let the pilot know it's time to gas up—and that we'll have one more passenger."

CHAPTER
SIXTEEN

FONADHOO, MALDIVES

ROBERT BESSERMAN STEADIED HIMSELF as he climbed out of the small aircraft, its pontoons teetering in rhythm with the waves. He eased onto the dock and held his hand out for Mallory Kauffman as she followed him. Once she was on the dock, she tugged down on the brim of her sunhat as the wind gusted up.

"Welcome to Maldives," Besserman said with a grin.

"This beats a good day at the office every single time," she said.

"If only we weren't here on business."

They followed their pilot to a small hut just off the beach, where a man directed them to a car and handed them the keys. Besserman had been to Maldives once before but he was more than familiar with the layout of the islands. Based on its remote location as well as proximity to China, Maldives had long been a hotbed of modern day pirates, exiled ex-pats, and crime bosses. But that wasn't all. The archipelago had also emerged as a preferred resort destination for the wealthy all over the world. And it was where they'd learned Chinese General Xi Chow, the man seen talking with President Norris in the video, had spent the last five years.

While Chow had retired, U.S. intelligence operatives kept a close eye on him. The most recent report on him detailed his rigid daily routine, which included drinking two mai tais every afternoon at three o'clock at a beachside bar on Fonadhoo.

Besserman checked his watch, which read 2:30 p.m., as he climbed into the driver's side of their rental car. The palm trees lining the sandy dirt road swayed as they turned on the island's main thoroughfare.

"Do you have all the documents in order?" Besserman asked.

Mallory pushed her glasses up on her nose and sifted through the file folder in her lap. "Everything is good to go. All you have to do is get Chow talking."

"That shouldn't be too difficult," Besserman said. "We'll have plenty to talk about."

While Chow had retired from the military, he hadn't fully retired, according to intel reports. He'd slowly started purchasing uninhabited islands and seeking out investors to build resorts. Two projects were nearing completion while a third had just broken ground. Besserman was about to pitch a fourth, one quite suitable for a large island Chow owned.

A few minutes before three o'clock, they pulled into the parking lot for Bub's Beachside Bar. Besserman had learned that the original owner, Bub Morton, was an ex-pat who'd left the Navy after putting in twenty-five years. He'd fallen in love with the islands while stopping in Maldives on several tours and moved there with his wife, Charlotte. Bub had died in a scuba diving accident a few years ago, leaving his wife to run the place.

As soon as Charlotte noticed Besserman and Mallory, a big smile spread across the woman's face.

"Welcome," she said in English, pounding the bar top. "You two look thirsty."

Besserman and Mallory took a seat in front of Charlotte, who was far more energetic than Besserman had imagined.

"Can I interest you in some rum or maybe a cocktail?" she asked. "Or I know—how about a cold beer?"

"I'd love a scotch, neat," Besserman said.

"And for the lady?" Charlotte asked.

Mallory shrugged. "Surprise me."

"You got it," the peppy owner said.

Besserman turned around on his stool and took in the scene right outside Bub's front porch. The water lapped at the beach as a cool breeze rustled the leaves on the palm trees. While the view was picturesque, he wondered why there weren't more than a dozen people enjoying the sun and the white sand, especially as winter had fallen hard on the northern hemisphere.

"Where is everyone?" Besserman asked.

"What do you mean?" Charlotte fired back as she placed a scotch in front of Besserman and a mai tai in front of Mallory.

"Is this all the people who enjoy this pristine beach each day?" he asked.

"Pretty much. It gets a little busier during the tourist season, but this is par for the course most days."

"How do you stay in business then?" Besserman asked, glancing around the room, which contained only two other patrons.

"For one thing, I don't have to pay a ton of taxes," she said. "My late husband, God rest his soul, also squirreled away a hefty sum so that we weren't dependent upon this succeeding to survive. This was more or less a labor of love for Bub, something for him to pass the time in retirement."

"Did you say your *late* husband?" Mallory asked.

Charlotte nodded. "He died a couple of years ago doing what he loved best—scuba diving. I had a bad premonition that day about him being in the water and I warned him about it, but he told me I was crazy and went anyway. He never came home."

"Sorry to hear that," Besserman said.

"Yeah, me too," Mallory said.

Besserman enjoyed the scene before a few minutes passed. When he checked his watch again, it was ten minutes past three o'clock. He turned back toward Charlotte.

"How well do you know General Chow?" Besserman asked. "I heard he comes in here quite a bit."

Charlotte's face fell. "What? You haven't heard?"

"Heard what?" Mallory asked.

"General Chow died two weeks ago at his home," Charlotte said.

Besserman banged his fist on the bar top. "Damnit. We came all this way to speak with him. What happened?"

"Nobody knows," Mallory said. "We were told he went peacefully in his sleep from a heart attack, but nobody knows for sure—or even believes that's what happened."

"What do you think happened?" Besserman asked.

Charlotte shook her head. "I really don't know. He was such a sweet man. Can't believe his mother outlived him, too."

"His mother?" Mallory asked.

"Yeah, his mother is ninety-three, according to what the general told me. She'd been out here a few times to visit and was spry as anything."

Once they finished their drinks, Besserman thanked the woman and left her a healthy tip. When they were inside their car, Besserman turned to Mallory.

"This isn't good," Besserman said as he ignited the engine.

"What are we going to do about this now?" she asked.

Besserman sighed. "The only thing I can do—I need to confront the president directly."

CHAPTER
SEVENTEEN

LOS ANGELES

MORGAN MAY LOOKED at the report on her desk as she sipped her cup of coffee. Hawk and Alex's capture of General Gusev was a start to finding out the identities of everyone in the Russian sleeper cell, but it wasn't happening fast enough for President Norris. He'd left several messages, demanding an update as soon as there was news. But Morgan didn't want to waste everyone's time with a report that there wasn't anything to report. Now, the Magnum Group had something with Gusev, though it wouldn't assuage Norris's angst over the matter.

A knock at her open door jolted her back to the present, where her own problems were mounting. Big Earv leaned against the door jamb, running a half-dollar coin through his fingers.

"Come on in," Morgan said, gesturing for him to have a seat. "We've got plenty to talk about."

"Good work on Kingsley," Big Earv said.

"You heard?"

"Mia told me," he said. "She said you really know how to put the screws on someone."

Morgan smiled wryly. "It's a skill I learned from my uncle."

"Anyone that fakes his own death is playing on another level," Big Earv said. "And I went to his first funeral. Not planning on going to his second though."

"That's fair enough. You go to a person's funeral where they know you were there, then I think you're exempt from going to the second one."

"I already cried my tears for J.D. He doesn't get any more."

"I doubt he'll have one for you to miss. He'll probably just drift into the ocean and happily die there."

"Going out on his own terms—that's how the Senator always operated. No need to change now."

"Speaking of operations, we need to put one together and quickly," Morgan said.

"So you know how this is gonna work?"

"The plan is simple. I'll explain it all to you now."

Morgan spent the next twenty minutes sharing her idea, which Big Earv endorsed. Then she dismissed him to prepare for the meeting.

LATER THAT MORNING, Morgan called a meeting of her operation leaders, the three people involved in planning missions for the Magnum Group agents. Nick Slavitt, Elaine Downing, and Peter Avant gathered around the conference room table with other department heads, including Mia, Big Earv, and Dr. Z.

When Elaine inquired about Morgan's absence for the past couple of days, she explained it away as a little personal time before diving into the discussion. As far as the team knew, the mole had been eliminated and they were freer to talk about issues. However, Morgan had become more guarded than ever, concerned that if she misspoke, she might provide a clue to the mole. And the length she was going through to rid her office of the mole was a painstaking one that required her to leverage more clout than she wanted to. Even more disconcerting, everything she was doing was just so she could have the *opportunity* to expose the mole. Nothing was for certain, not even taxes or death the way intelligence officers planned—that much she'd learned while serving in the field.

Morgan stood and paced around the table, running her hands along the backs of some of the chairs. "By now, I'm sure you've all heard that we finally got rid of the mole within our midst, which comes as a great relief to me, and I'm sure to all of you as well. That's what's delayed us from obtaining the single most important piece of information that we need to expose The Alliance and bring it down."

"If it's as organized as we think it is," Elaine said.

Morgan stopped and shook her head. "At this point, I don't think there's any question that it exists—and that it's a very well-oiled machine. And based on the intel we've received from a certain asset, we're going to have all the proof we need to not only pin certain crimes on them but also systematically take them apart piece by piece."

"And how are we going to do that?" Avant asked.

"Good question," Morgan said. "It's actually the basis for our meeting today. We need to discuss logistics and create a plan for how we're going to get a specific prisoner to safety and amass the intel we need from him."

Downing's eyebrows shot upward. "You have a willing witness to roll over on The Alliance?"

Morgan shrugged. "This prisoner is someone we need to get to the man who's willing to talk. But at this point, we're keeping all the details quiet. There are only three people who know the name of this prisoner, and that's how it's going to stay. It's not that I don't trust any of you, but it's just not really relevant to this operation."

"Then what *is* relevant?" Slavitt asked. "Can we start there?"

Morgan picked up the remote control and clicked a few

buttons. A diagram of Leavenworth Prison and the surrounding area flashed up on the screen.

"So, this is what we're here to talk about," she said. "We need to move our asset to a safe place. Once this information comes out about who The Alliance is, he's going to become a huge target, one that unfortunately we won't be able to protect even in prison. As we've all discovered, The Alliance, as shadowy of an organization as they are, has their tentacles in everything. Top government officials, former assassins, bureaucrats, diplomats, and other political appointees all do The Alliance's bidding. Some of the people involved may not even realize what they are doing, fooled by a representative who makes requests and tells their asset that it's for a secret mission for the government, all working against it, wholly unaware. So, we have to eliminate the leadership first and foremost. This can't be a slow burn."

"And you think this asset is going to be able to do that?" Avant asked.

Morgan nodded. "If just a quarter of the information the prisoner has given us is true, we'll be able to dismantle them, complete with a handful of prison sentences that won't carry any parole possibilities."

"What do we need to do then?" Slavitt asked.

"I want each of you to design a plan to extract this prisoner, who's going to help assure that the witness talks," Morgan said. "Think of your role as a competition of sorts. Instead of brainstorming on this one, I want each of you to put forth an actionable plan to transfer this prisoner out of Leavenworth by way of the Sherman Army Airstrip. Once the prisoner is on the plane, it will be directed to a location to be determined at that moment. No one will know the final destination of the prisoner, not even the pilot as he'll be gassed up and ready to fly wherever it is he's instructed to."

"Seems like this would be a simple transport," Elaine said.

"*Seems* that way," Morgan said, "but we're talking about securing testimony from an asset who's been privy to conversations between high-ranking government officials involved in conspiring against their own country. Don't you think they would do everything in their power to keep that quiet? Power is only worth something if you can use it from your position. Going behind bars is going to neuter these traitors."

"That's just how we like it," Slavitt said.

"Exactly," Morgan said. "So, do you think you can help me out here? I want your best plans on my desk by tomorrow morning and the plan we select will be implemented right away. The transfer is set to take place in less than forty-eight hours."

Morgan dismissed the meeting and leaned back in her chair. Big Earv lingered to speak with her.

"Well done," Big Earv said. "The trap has been set."

She wagged her finger at him. "The trap has been set for the bait. There's still bigger fish to catch and fry."

He cocked his head to one side and eyed her closely. "You're starting to remind me of the senator every single day."

Morgan huffed a laugh through her nose. "I think that was his plan all along."

CHAPTER
EIGHTEEN

TANGIER, MOROCCO

HAWK SLID OPEN the security panel and stared at the ocular scanner. After a few seconds, the light flashed green and the door unlocked. He helped General Gusev inside and placed him in a chair in the living room. Still woozy from the tranquilizer darts, he stared around the room and mumbled something in Russian.

Hawk drew in a deep breath through his nose. "Nobody's been here in quite some time. It's so musty."

"We do have some fond memories here," Alex said, "though I'd still like to visit the city one time without being on assignment."

"I'm starting to detect a common theme here."

"If I don't say it, you won't know what I want. If I hadn't said anything, I'm not sure we would've gotten married in Hawaii."

Hawk smiled. "I'm getting better at picking up your hints, even though you're far more direct than most women I've ever known."

"There's something to having a man figure out what a woman wants," she said. "It lets us know that you treasure us.

When you pay attention to all the little details about us, that sends the kind of message all women want to hear."

"Why don't you two get a room," Gusev sneered.

"We will," Hawk said. "But first we have to deal with you."

Gusev glared at Hawk. "You dragged me across the world to torture me, didn't you?"

"Making you listen in on our conversation wasn't torture enough for you?" Hawk asked. "I can arrange for far more torturous methods. The Mediterranean Madman is only a short call away."

"So, we're in Tangier," Gusev said. "I was wondering why it was so warm."

Hawk pulled up a chair directly across from Gusev and stared straight at him. Alex set up her laptop, connecting it to a camera on a small tripod. They hoped to get all the information necessary to uncover the identities of every sleeper cell agent that had infiltrated the U.S. border. But Hawk didn't share Morgan's optimism. A hardened spy from the Soviet era wasn't about to glibly out his fellow countrymen for a glass of vodka and a ham sandwich. In fact, Hawk wasn't sure there was any positive enticement even possible for Gusev. According to the agency's intel report on him, Gusev took pride in his stubbornness, making Hawk spend the entire flight from Kyrgyzstan to Tangier mulling over the best way to break Gusev. And Hawk was certain there was only one way that would get the former Russian general's attention.

"General," Hawk began, "it's come to our attention that you might be able to help the United States with a small matter of national security."

Gusev grunted and rolled his eyes. "I have no idea what you're talking about. And if I did, I wouldn't tell you shit."

"I appreciate the honesty," Hawk said. "That way I can skip my attempts to pander to you so we can get down to business."

Gusev laughed heartily. "Do you really think I'm going to

conduct any kind of business with you? I mean, you *look* like a smart man, but looks can be deceiving."

"Yes, they can," Hawk said. "For example, you can look at a woman and think perhaps she is a model or an actress when instead she's just a psychology major who will graduate in the coming months and is starting grad school next year."

Gusev narrowed his eyes and set his jaw. "You tread carefully, Mr.—"

"Hawk."

"Tread carefully, Mr. Hawk. Using my daughter as a pawn isn't exactly the best move you have on the table. I can be coerced in other ways."

"I know you're a slime ball," Hawk said. "The fact that your own country doesn't want you any more speaks volumes to the kind of person you are. But the truth is you would sell your own mother's soul to the devil if it meant you could retain all that power that you once held."

"You think you know me so well, Mr. Hawk. But it's apparent that you know nothing about me. Your *intelligence* community has failed in that regard."

Hawk crossed his arms and leaned back in his chair. "By all means, General, please enlighten me. What other ways can I coerce you?"

"You can bribe me."

"Bribe you?" Hawk asked. "Just offer you some money and you'll give up all the assets that you spent years sneaking into the United States."

"If the price is right."

"What's the price?"

Gusev stroked his beard. "Five hundred million for each asset's name."

Hawk scowled. "That's—eight billion dollars. My government will never go for that—and you know that."

"What's eight billion dollars among friends?" Gusev asked. "Maybe I can buy an American football game, rename them The

Soviets, win every game including the Super Bowl. After all, I'd just be investing it right back into the American economy. The economy always seems like the most important thing to Americans."

"Don't play games with me, General," Hawk said.

"I'm not playing any games, Mr. Hawk. You're the one who brought me here to ask me questions that you know I will never answer. You could cut off my nose and horribly disfigure me in every way imaginable—but I will never tell you a thing."

Hawk sighed and tapped on the back of the chair in a short cadence. "I already knew that, which is why I'm glad we can finally move on to my more direct approach."

"And what is it that you expect will entice me to comply with your demands?" Gusev asked.

Hawk nodded knowingly at Alex, who spun the laptop around so Gusev could see the screen. Kira Gusev glided across the room, completely unaware that she was being watched.

"What did you do?" Gusev asked, raising up out of his chair and starting to move toward Alex and her computer.

Hawk pulled out his weapon and trained it on Gusev. "Have a seat, General."

The General complied, but was visibly shaken by seeing his daughter captured in that manner.

"Didn't think I would find out, did you?" Hawk asked. "Your arrogance, your stubbornness—both on full display for me to leverage for our needs."

"And what are your needs?"

"Getting the names and contact information for all sixteen sleeper agents."

"Oh, you think there are sixteen?" Gusev asked with a smirk. "There's only fifteen, unless the FSB snuck in some more after I left."

"You're lying," Alex said.

Gusev laughed. "You have no idea how many agents have already infiltrated and acclimated to life in the United States."

"We have detailed files from Oleg Bocharov," Hawk said.

"Now you're the one lying. If you had them, you wouldn't have gone through all the trouble to take me prisoner."

Hawk took a deep breath before exhaling slowly. He handed a manila folder to Gusev. "Go ahead. Take a look."

Gusev's eyes didn't even flicker as he looked at the documents in front of him. "What's this all about?"

"We know about Kira," Hawk said.

Gusev shrugged. "It's not a secret. Your government knows all about my daughter. She is her own woman."

"Yes, but perhaps she's a sleeper agent, too," Hawk said. "We'll need to talk with her, maybe even let the admissions office at USC know about her connections to a group of Russian terrorists."

"This is ridiculous," Gusev said. "Kira is studying public relations at USC, mostly because she wants to party with the Americans. What you're insinuating is laughable. I've been in this business long enough to know I would never want my own daughter involved in it. And I suppose if either of you have children, you'd feel the same way."

"On that last point, we can agree," Hawk said. "However, you're going to tell us everything or else your daughter will have difficult days ahead of her."

"You leave her out of this," Gusev said with a hiss.

"The choice of whether she's left out of our dealings is up to you," Hawk said. "Tell us what we want to know, or your daughter will suffer consequences."

Gusev glanced at his watch. "I must warn you that she calls me every Sunday night around this time. If she doesn't hear from me, she will notify the FSB, who will come looking for me. I don't think you want to start an international incident, do you?"

"You mean, like the one you've already started?" Hawk asked, shaking his head.

"If there are Russian agents in the United States, I'm sure they aren't planning to do anything," Gusev said. "It's just a safeguard, like nuclear weapons. But taking a former Russian general prisoner? Now that will raise the Kremlin's ire. And I can promise you that you don't want the consequences that come along with that."

Hawk was prepared for Gusev's demand, one that the Magnum Group team had discussed beforehand and expected. But Hawk played up the decision, as if it was something he hadn't considered before. He huddled with Alex away from Gusev, and they put on a show for their guest. For a moment, they went back and forth, arguing for and against the idea. Alex played the good cop in the routine before Hawk acted as if he'd go along with her suggestion.

"Okay," Hawk said as he walked back toward Gusev, "we will let you call your daughter. The phone call will be monitored here."

Gusev entered the numbers in a phone application on Alex's laptop. Hawk verified the number as one belonging to Kira. After a few rings, she picked up and the two held a conversation in Russian.

"Hello?"

"Kira."

"Oh, hello, Papa. Where are you calling from? I didn't recognize this number."

"I'm with some new friends and left my phone at home. But I wanted to call you so you wouldn't worry."

"Of course. Is everything all right?"

"Everything is lovely. I spent the morning skiing and now I'm drinking wine. It doesn't get much better than that."

She giggled. "I just got back from the beach where I went surfing this morning. It definitely doesn't get better than that."

"I'm glad you've had a good morning, dear. I love you. But I must go now. We'll talk next week. Ciao."

"Ciao, Papa."

Alex pushed a button on the laptop, ending the call.

"All right," Hawk said. "We let you talk to your daughter. Now, it's time you talk to us."

"I'll tell you everything you want to know in the morning," Gusev said. "That tranquilizer has made my mind hazy, and I need a good night of sleep."

Hawk glanced at Alex, who shrugged. "Fine. Let me take you to your quarters."

A few minutes later, Gusev was settled in his room, which was locked and secured.

Hawk retreated to the living room to discuss the events with Alex.

"So," she said, "how do you think that went?"

"I don't know," Hawk said. "Fine, I guess. But we have a big day tomorrow, and I hope he's not stalling."

"They can't track him," Alex said. "Not here, anyway. We might as well be off the grid as far as any tracking devices are concerned."

"That will help me sleep better tonight," Hawk said. "But I won't relax until we have every last one of those agents in custody."

"You and me both," Alex said.

———

BIG EARV SAT in a white van with the USC seal emblazoned on the side, monitoring Kira Gusev's activities. It was getting late but he was ready for a long night. Back at the Magnum Group office, he'd been listening in on the general's conversation with his daughter—and nothing seemed out of the ordinary. But Morgan didn't want to take any chances. If Gusev had communicated a secret message to Kira, Big Earv was going to make sure the young co-ed didn't skip off into the night, losing Hawk and Alex's leverage with their prisoner.

Big Earv listened as Kira told her roommate that she was

going down the dorm hall to the bathrooms. However, that was over an hour ago and Big Earv's bug hadn't picked up Kira's return. The lights had been out for a half-hour, but no sign of Kira.

He called Morgan to update her on what was happening. She suggested he go check it out.

Big Earv lumbered up the steps to the dorm and found her room. He softly knocked on the door several times but didn't get an answer. Finally, he knocked louder. A few other doors along the hallway opened up with girls peering into the open to see who was making all the racket. Finally, Kira's roommate, her hair already in a matted mess, shuffled to the door.

"What do you want?" she grumbled.

"I'm looking for Kira," Big Earv said.

"At this time of night? We have classes in the morning."

"It's urgent."

"Well, she's not here."

The girl tried to the close the door, but Big Earv stopped it with his hand. "Did she tell you where she was going?"

"Yeah, she said was going to the bathroom like an hour ago, but I've got an eight o'clock class. So, if you don't mind, you can try calling her on her cell or check back tomorrow. Good night."

"You don't have any other idea where she could've gone?"

"She's probably playing one of those stupid online games," she said. "She wastes so much time. Now, if you'll please leave, I need to get some sleep."

She shut the door without waiting for a response from Big Earv and locked it.

Big Earv hustled down the stairwell and raced to the parking deck nearby. He'd tagged Kira's car, but it wasn't where he'd found it earlier. The tracking device he'd place beneath the bumper was all that remained in the parking spot.

He cursed and then called Hawk.

"Big Earv?" Hawk asked. "It's—"

"I know. It's early, but this couldn't wait."

"What's happened?"

"It's Gusev's daughter, Kira. She's gone."

"Gone? What do you mean *gone*?

"A little over an hour ago, she told her roommate she was going to the bathroom and she never came back," Big Earv explained.

"Maybe she went to visit a boyfriend."

"No, I just went to the spot where her car was parked. It was gone—except for the tracker I'd place under the bumper. She found it."

Hawk growled. "Let me give the general a rude awakening and find out where she might've gone."

Big Earv paced around the parking garage, mumbling to himself as he waited for Hawk.

"Find out where she might've gone," Big Earv said.

Hawk gasped.

"What is it?"

He sighed. "General Gusev isn't going to be able to help us anymore."

"No," Big Earv said.

"Yeah, I wish it wasn't so. He hung himself."

Big Earv hung up and hustled back to his van. If he was going to have any hope of catching Kira, he had to hurry.

CHAPTER
NINETEEN

WASHINGTON, D.C.

ROBERT BESSERMAN HANDED his security clearance badge to the White House guard before being asked to sign in. The man scribbled down something on his clipboard before inspecting Besserman's credentials.

"Is the White House expecting you?" the man asked.

"I don't have an appointment, if that's what you mean," Besserman said.

The man nodded slowly and then made another note, holding onto the badge. Then he held up his index finger. "Wait right here for a moment while I make a call."

Besserman was used to the process. White House security had been always been tight, but it had grown even more so in recent years. What used to be a smile and a quick check of a person's security clearance had morphed into a procedure of phone calls with internal security agents.

"Okay, you're clear to proceed," the guard said after a brief phone conversation. He handed the badge back to Besserman, who was waved through.

Once inside, Besserman was escorted by a Secret Service

agent to an empty waiting room and instructed to remain there. After a few more minutes, Victor Lloyd, the director of the Secret Service, entered the room with two other agents.

"Good morning, Victor," Besserman said. "How are things going?"

Lloyd smiled and offered his hand. "Oh, you know. Just the same old, same old. Protecting this administration's officials from all the nut jobs out there."

Besserman put his hands on his hips. "Well, I appreciate the welcoming committee, but this is highly unusual to get a visit from you before going to see the president. Things that slow this morning?"

"Not exactly," Lloyd said, the light-hearted smile vanishing. "I was sent to tell you that you won't be able to speak with President Norris today."

Besserman furrowed his brow. "What's going on? Is there a problem?"

"I don't always know what's going on. I'm just doing my job."

"Don't lie to me, Victor. The president doesn't so much as sneeze without you knowing about it."

"Sorry, Bobby. I wish I could tell you more, but I've just been instructed by the president to deny you access today."

Besserman took a deep breath and stepped back. He looked down at the ground as he stroked his chin and considered what to say.

"I know it's not what you're accustomed to, but I have to deliver this news to others all the time," Lloyd said.

Besserman crossed his arms and eyed Lloyd. "Just level with me about what's going on. I mean, it's hard for me to do what he's asked me to do without getting a few of my questions answered. And to be honest, this only raises more of them."

"Like I said, I'm sorry about this, but I'm not at liberty to give you any special treatment. The president has given me a direct order, and I intend to carry that out."

"Will you give him a message for me?"

Lloyd shook his head. "Not my job. I'm sure someone else on the White House staff can convey whatever message you have for him."

Besserman raised his hands in a gesture of surrender. "If that's what the president wants, fine. But there's something unusual going on here—and I know you know it."

"These guys will walk you out, Bobby. Thanks for stopping by and it's good to see you."

Besserman didn't say anything, instead putting on his coat and exiting the building. The two agents followed him out to the guard house and then stopped to say something to the guard. Besserman kept walking to his car.

He fumed as he went, baffled by Norris's behavior. Besserman tried to think about what he'd done that would make the president take such a drastic step. Cutting off the director of the CIA seemed like either a precursor to his dismissal or controlling the inner circle of information deemed politically dangerous—or both. Besserman had kept his quick trip to Maldives a secret, only letting the plane's pilot and his deputy director know where they were going. Had Mallory let their destination slip? If she had, that would've been a misstep that she never made. She had her position because she'd become not only one of the best analysts at the CIA but also because she had proven her trustworthiness. If she was ruled out as the source of the leak, who else could've done it? Besserman didn't want to consider that maybe Steve Pickens, his deputy director, told Norris. But he couldn't rule it out.

Besserman had plenty of questions that demanded answers. And he intended to get some as soon as possible and find out if there was something else going on or if he was simply dealing with a paranoid president. Either way, Besserman found the development disturbing.

———

FOR THE REST of the morning and early afternoon, Besserman spoke with Mallory and then Pickens in an effort to determine if either one of them let slip about the Maldives trip. After three decades of working in intelligence, his ability to detect lies was nearly flawless. And both of them swore they'd been extra vigilant in keeping that information to themselves—and Besserman found them both to be convincing.

Establishing that they didn't share that information with anyone else, Besserman struggled to square Norris's behavior. Maybe Besserman was about to lose his job, an unpleasant thought especially given the looming crisis with the Russian sleeper agents. Or maybe there was far more to Norris's meeting with General Chow in the Maldives years ago. But figuring out Norris's reasoning would be a tedious task. The most efficient way to determine what the president was thinking would be to ask him directly. And Besserman knew exactly how to do it.

Later that afternoon, Besserman called Will Alderman, one of Norris's top donors who was hosting a fundraiser for the president that evening at Hillman's, an upscale Washington restaurant. When Besserman arrived, Alderman greeted him and at the door.

"It's great to see you, Bobby," Will said as the two men shook hands.

"You, too, Will. I know this was last minute, but I appreciate you getting me in."

"Of course. I just didn't expect you'd want to show up at a political event given your situation and all."

"Just because I work for the CIA doesn't mean I don't vote or care about who's holding the office of the president."

"Yeah, but if the press heard that you were here ..." Alderman said, his words hanging in the air.

"But there isn't going to be anyone from the press here tonight, is there?"

"No, but I suspect there will be some journalists waiting outside, hoping to get a glimpse of what we're doing."

"I'll leave through the back."

"Good. I'd hate to see some journalist create a story out of this and dent the president's re-election chances."

Besserman maintained his poker face throughout the conversation. "We wouldn't want that to happen, would we?"

"Absolutely not. The country is in a great place right now."

Besserman slapped Alderman on the shoulder and smiled. "The fact that you think that lets me know we're doing our job."

Alderman scowled. "Wait a minute. Is there something I'm missing? I—"

"There's nothing to worry about," Besserman said. "Like I said, we're doing our job."

"Okay. Don't scare me like that, Bobby."

"Sorry, didn't mean to do that. Now, where's Norris at? I need to grab a quick word with him."

"Sure," Alderman said, pointing toward the front of the room. "He's up at the table with Emma Washburn."

"What about the First Lady?"

"She couldn't make it, so I guess he's having his chief of staff stand in for her."

Besserman shrugged. "Interesting. And thanks again, Will."

"Any time."

Besserman wove through the sea of tables toward Norris. After Besserman spied a couple of Secret Service agents who seemed to be watching him, he took a seat at his designated table. He endured a delicious meal with a host of pretentious donors, all talking openly about how they hoped Norris would favor their personal business aspirations over the next four years. Knowing how Washington worked, Besserman thought they were all openly deluded or naïve. If you were at a two-thousand-dollar plate fundraiser, that was just the price of admission to see the president. Meeting with Norris would certainly cost a donor hundreds of thousands of dollars, though that'd be without the guarantee of Norris agreeing to grant any requests. Besserman had been disappointed when he learned that not long after arriving in Washington, but he'd long since accepted it as fact—and it didn't matter which party controlled the White House. While the American people quibbled over which party's leader occupied the Oval Office, Besserman recognized long ago that the real people running the country were all behind the scenes. However, the president had some influence. And if Norris was being influenced by China, that was a most troubling development, one that Besserman couldn't just let go.

After dinner and a short speech from Norris, Besserman slipped into the receiving line to meet the president. When Besserman's turn came, he strode toward Norris. Two of the Secret Service agents stepped forward before Norris waved them off.

"What a pleasant surprise to see you here, Bobby," Norris said before pulling Besserman closer. "Didn't you get the message when you came to the White House today? I'm not interested in talking with you until you find out who was behind those leaked tapes."

"We're still working on it, sir. But I do have some other questions that we need to discuss."

"Just do your job, Bobby," Norris sneered. "Or I'll find someone who will."

Besserman wanted to say more but thought better of it. If China—or someone else—was running Norris, Besserman couldn't do much about it if he was ousted as the CIA Director.

As he slipped out the door, he glanced over his shoulder one more time at Norris, who wore a broad smile as he shook hands with the next donor in line.

What are you trying to hide, Mr. President?

CHAPTER
TWENTY

LOS ANGELES

MORGAN MAY LAID the three plans out on her desk and examined each one carefully. Each one was strong on its own merit, needing only fine tuning to implement. And given all the information she doled out to all of the agents in charge of designing an escape plan, they were all easily implementable. Interestingly enough, they were all about the same: using two decoy vans along with an actual one to transport the prisoner. It was exactly what she was hoping they'd do.

Two of the plans were identical, selecting the first van as the one carrying the prisoner. The other plan had the prisoner in the third vehicle.

Big Earv shuffled into her office, slumping into the chair across from her desk. "How's it looking?"

"Better than expected," she said.

"That good, huh?"

"The plans are all so similar, even if there's water cooler talk about which was the best one, they'll hardly be able to distinguish them."

"You dodged a bullet."

"At least when it comes to outing the mole, which was the whole point of this exercise."

Big Earv cracked his knuckles and then rubbed his face with his hands. "So, what now?"

"Meet me in the conference room in fifteen minutes. Gather everyone from our previous meeting and get them in there. We need to get moving."

Morgan watched Big Earv leave before turning her attention back to the documents in front of her. She concluded that the best way to handle the selection was to privately tell each one that their plan was the one selected and make a slight adjustment to it. That idea was the best way to ferret out the mole.

When she walked into the room twenty minutes later, everyone was gathered and ready to hear what she had to say. She dropped her files onto the table with a thud that echoed off the walls.

"I appreciate all your hard work in presenting some incredible plans to keep our witness safe," Morgan began. "In fact, these are all so good and simple that we should be able to implement them almost immediately to get the prisoner out of Leavenworth and into a safe house where we can interrogate them."

Slavitt lead back in his chair. "So, who's the winner?"

"I'm going to speak with each of you individually about that," Morgan said. "And I trust that you will keep the information to yourself. This is information we'd prefer to be kept quiet, even inside the Magnum Group. Any sharing of this information will be viewed as a breach of trust and grounds for dismissal. Is that understood?"

Everyone at the table nodded.

"Good," Morgan said. "In that case, we can proceed with the overall idea of the plan."

She explained what each analyst had essentially presented: utilize three vans, keeping the location of the actual prisoner a secret. All three vans would go to the nearby airfield and promptly take off. That was the best exit strategy, one so obvious that they almost all came up with the same one.

"I'll be meeting with each one of you in my office at the conclusion of this meeting to go over the merits of your plan and tell you which one we selected. I will reiterate this again; any discussion of your plan in this office will not be tolerated and be grounds for immediate dismissal. Everyone understand?"

Each person seated at the table nodded affirmatively.

"Excellent," Morgan said. "Elaine, you'll go first."

A few minutes later, Morgan was in her office going over Elaine's plans. Next was Slavitt, followed by Avant.

Once Morgan was satisfied her wishes had been communicated to all three analysts, she exhaled as Avant exited her office. A couple of minutes passed before Big Earv sauntered into her office.

"How'd it go?" he asked.

"Better than expected," she said. "They were all told that their plans were selected."

Big Earv raised an eyebrow. "Is that so?"

"If they all think they're right, they're going to report it to their superiors. Whichever van is attacked will reveal the truth about who's the leak. It's that simple."

"It's a great plan," Big Earv. "Let's hope it all goes accordingly."

"Yes," Morgan said as she nodded subtly. "Let's hope."

"And in the meantime?"

"Go home and pack—and tell Mia to do the same," Morgan said. "I want both of you on the company jet by six o'clock tonight headed to Leavenworth. Understand?"

"Of course," Big Earv said. "We'll be there."

Morgan exhaled slowly and looked skyward. "Please, please work. I can't take another failure."

If pushed, she could take another failure or two, but she

didn't want to. She wanted to expose the mole. Basking in all the glory would just be a bonus. But there was still time, plenty of time—even if the clock was ticking.

CHAPTER
TWENTY-ONE

LOS ANGELES

THE NEXT MORNING, Hawk and Alex landed at LAX, rested from sleeping during the flight. When they arrived at the Magnum Group offices, the hive of activity had reached a fever pitch. Hawk and Alex navigated the other employees rushing back and forth across the main room. Analysts huddled over projects. Data specialists pored over information. Interpreters listened in on calls. Meanwhile, Morgan May was waiting for her two operatives in her office, sipping her coffee when they walked in.

"Welcome back," Morgan said.

"Glad to be home," Alex said. "If I never go to that part of the world again, I'd die a happy woman."

"Well, that isn't up to you or me, is it?" Morgan said with a wink. "If we could ask those pesky Russians to stop threatening us, I'd make sure you never have to go back."

"But that vodka though," Hawk said with a smile. "That makes it all worth it."

"Liar," Alex said, punching her husband in the arm.

"It's not ideal," Hawk said. "But it's better than drinking something from Blunt's old bourbon stash."

Morgan smiled. "I save that stuff for interrogation sessions. 'Answer me or I'll make you drink this.' I know it's worse than waterboarding, but what else am I supposed to do with his liquor collection. I'm just surprised he didn't take it with him."

"That ought to tell you what he really thinks of bourbon," Hawk said. "If he was willing to leave it, well, I think it's safe to assume that it wasn't really his favorite. Seemed like more of an act to me anyway—his way of getting attention."

"I can assure you, he *loves* bourbon. He'd only drink scotch if you either forced him to or gave it to him as a gift. And even then he'd probably only pour one glass just out of respect before pouring it all down the drain once you left his house."

Hawk threw his hands up in the air and stepped back. "Who am I to argue? If Director May says it, then I believe it. I'm just sharing my opinion."

Morgan picked up a handful of papers and straightened them by stacking them on her desk. "Let's get to it, shall we?"

Alex nodded and took a seat across from Morgan with Hawk following suit.

"What's the scoop?" Hawk asked.

"I was hoping you could tell me," Morgan said.

"In a nutshell," Alex began, "Gusev is dead—and so is Bocharov. That just leaves us with General Gusev's daughter, Kira, who is on the lam right now from what I understand."

Morgan folded her arms and leaned back in her chair. "All correct, but I want to know the latest. Where are you at with learning more about Kira? Where do you think she went? Do you think she's part of the sleeper cell?"

"Those are all big questions, ma'am," Hawk said.

"And important ones too," Morgan chimed in.

"Of course, of course," Hawk said. "But that doesn't mean that I can give you the answers to these on a moment's notice. There are plenty of factors involved in determining the whereabouts of Kira. But my guess is that she isn't very far. Sometimes the threat of something is greater than the actual threat itself."

Morgan arched an eyebrow. "Meaning?"

"We might be wasting plenty of energy chasing Kira when she was never going to be a threat," Hawk said. "Meanwhile, the other agents get more time while we're consumed with her."

"And we don't know for sure that she's an agent," Alex said. "For all we know, this was Gusev's way of getting into our heads and making us outthink ourselves—or not."

"I see your point," Morgan said. "But at this juncture, we have no leads on any of the agents. And Kira Gusev is our only connection to the general. Either way, she needs to be found and questioned."

"Understand," Hawk said. "We'll head straight over to campus and see what we can learn."

———

HAWK AND ALEX strolled through Queen's Courtyard on their way to Kira's dorm. Students were sprawled out on blankets in the grass, reading textbooks and throwing frisbees, the cares of the real world appearing far out of their minds.

"I'm not sure I would've studied much if I went to school here," Alex said.

Hawk chuckled. "That's supposing you believe that college is all about academics."

Alex looked over the top of her sunglasses at Hawk. "What is college all about? Please do tell."

"It used to be about training students for a profession," Hawk said. "Now it just feels like a way to print money, overcharging students for a subpar experience."

"My, so cynical. I hope you don't talk like this around John Daniel when he gets older because I want him to go to college."

"If that's what you want him to do, I'm fine with it," Hawk

said. "I think we both would rather him do anything other than get involved in the family business."

"Amen to that," she said. "I'm thinking maybe an accountant or a scientist, something safe."

Hawk gave her a sideways glance. "That's a pipe dream with the genes he has."

"I know, I know. But a mother can dream, right?"

They entered Kira's dorm and knocked on her door. After a few seconds, the door swung open.

"Can I help you?" a young woman asked.

"We're looking for Kira," Hawk said. "Do you know where she might be?"

The woman rolled her eyes. "What is it with you people? Does she have a gambling problem? Who are you?"

"Have you seen her lately?" Alex asked, ignoring the woman's question.

"No, but that's Kira. She's Russian. She can drink like a fish and disappear for days at a time. I'm not her keeper."

"And you're not concerned that she hasn't shown up in a while?" Alex asked.

"Why should I be? She's an adult. I'm not her parent."

Hawk sighed. "Look, we're not accusing you of doing anything wrong. We just want to know her whereabouts."

Kira's roommate glared at Hawk and Alex. "I don't know where she is. You sent your friend by a couple of nights ago and then another one this morning. It's getting old, and if you don't stop, I'm going to speak with someone on campus about this."

Hawk handed her a business card. "If you hear from her, would you mind giving us a call?"

The woman huffed. "You think I'm gonna do you any favors?"

Hawk handed her a hundred-dollar bill. "There's plenty more where that came from, okay?"

The woman's face softened. "Okay. I can do that."

"Thank you," Alex said.

Hawk and Alex spent the rest of the afternoon speaking with other acquaintances of Kira's as well as her teachers. Nothing else seemed to signal a red flag. The fact that she had attended all her classes since speaking with her father led Hawk and Alex to believe that she was staying at a boyfriend's apartment.

They returned to the Magnum Group offices and reported their findings to Morgan.

"So, that's it?" she asked. "You think she's oblivious to everything her father was doing?"

"It's hard to draw any other conclusion," Alex said. "She's going to class and seems engaged according to everyone we spoke with. What more are we to assume?"

"She's not staying at her dorm," Morgan said.

"Did you always stay at your dorm at the University of Idaho?" Hawk asked.

Morgan shrugged. "Moscow was nice, but I took off every chance I got. You can't say the same thing about going to school at USC."

"Yeah, but she's in town," Hawk said. "It's not like she's trying to skip out or evade us. She's just being a normal college student."

"I know," Morgan said. "I can't put my finger on it, but I've got a bad feeling about her."

"She seems to be fitting in perfectly," Alex said.

"*Too* perfectly," Morgan said. "We're not done investigating her just yet."

CHAPTER
TWENTY-TWO

ROBERT BESSERMAN AFFIXED the piece of train track to the large piece of plywood resting on a pair of sawhorses in his garage. Picking up another piece, he carefully applied glue to the bottom before putting it in place. When he was finished, he stepped back and put his hands on his hips, surveying the model he'd created.

The newest addition to his growing creation gave him reason to smile. For months he'd been meticulously crafting the small model town but needed another challenge—a tunnel. And now that he'd completed it, he felt a sense of accomplishment. He'd always thought model trains were for men who'd never grown up, but he'd changed all that when a colleague suggested he might enjoy tinkering with them. And Besserman's friend was right. The train sets were something Besserman could finish, something he could actually control—a far cry from the reality of his world as the director of the CIA.

He enjoyed a glass of scotch as he flipped the switch and watched the Bachman HO locomotive pull out of the station for its journey around the track. The small light on the front of the engine was all he could see of it as it sped through the tunnel. As the train completed its first lap, Besserman's phone rang. He glanced at the number—one he didn't recognize—and sent the call to voicemail. Satisfied with his work, he retreated into the house to finish some paperwork he'd brought home.

But the moment Besserman sat down, the reality of his situation hit him hard: His job was in jeopardy, and the one man who could fire him seemed to be embroiled in an impending scandal that Besserman was investigating. And if he didn't investigate, Besserman felt like he wouldn't be doing his job properly.

Won't that be ironic? I'll be fired for doing my job.

Besserman still couldn't figure out why Norris wouldn't be forthcoming with him. The optics of Norris meeting with a Chinese general in such a casual way was damning without the accompanying sound on the video. But what was actually being said? That was the question Besserman had to answer, what he *needed* answered if for anything his own sanity. If he never found out the nature of Norris's discussion with the general, Besserman would be left to draw his own conclusions. And he couldn't imagine it was benign when it came to national security matters. Had Norris's campaign been covertly bankrolled by the Chinese government? Had one of his oldest friends been an actual Manchurian candidate? Was Besserman only in the position he was in because the Chinese wanted him there? The questions plaguing Besserman—and the possible explanations—were enough to drive him mad.

Besserman could ponder these things all night long if he wanted to, resulting in another sleepless night. But that's why he brought home his work, a welcome distraction from the part of his job that had captivated—and demanded—his attention.

Besserman's phone rang again with the same number from a few minutes before. He wasn't sure if he wanted to answer, wondering if the robocall machine had caught up with him again to inquire if he'd like to purchase an extended warranty for his car. No voicemail was left either time, leading him to believe that it was a telemarketer. But five minutes later, a call came in again from the same number—and Besserman needed to make it stop so he could concentrate.

"Hello," he said.

"Director Besserman, my name is Glenn Feller. I'm with the D.C. Connection website."

Oh, great. Worse than a robocall. A political blogger.

Besserman sighed. "What can I do for you, Glenn?"

"I have footage of what appears to be President Norris sharing a drink with a Chinese general, who we've identified as being General Chow. Is the agency aware of this video and what does this say about the president?"

"You need to speak with the president's spokesperson about that," Besserman said.

"So, you're not denying that you haven't seen the video?"

Besserman waited a beat before responding. "Listen here, Glenn. I'm gonna give you a little free advice, the best kind you can get. And it's this—be very careful about what you push out on your website without verifying it. I've not heard of your website, but most of the politicians in this town are very aggressive when it comes to pursuing litigation with reckless journalists."

"So, what you're saying is that this video is true and you don't know the context?"

"I never said that, Glen. All I said is that you better watch yourself. Have a good night."

Besserman hung up and promptly called Mallory Kauffman.

"What is it, sir?"

"Are you familiar with a guy named Glen Feller, a blogger at some site called D.C. Connection, I think?"

"Yeah, he's a real pain in the ass. Poli sci major from Georgetown, if I'm not mistaken. Got fired multiple times as a congressional aide, so he's apparently made it his life ambition to print rumors about everyone on Capitol Hill."

"So, he's not a newbie?"

"Quite the opposite. He's been around a while and is very well connected from what I understand. The agency probably gets three or four complaints about him every week wanting us to look into him, which we can't legally do, of course."

"That might have just changed," Besserman said.

"Oh? Did Glen cross the line?"

"He claims to have seen a video with Norris and some Chinese general."

"Interesting. Wonder where he got it from?"

"I was hoping maybe you could tell me," Besserman said, "if you catch my drift."

"On it, sir."

Besserman thanked her and then hung up.

If Norris was upset that I was looking into the video, just wait until he hears a blogger with an axe to grind has a copy, too.

———

GLEN FELLER HAMMERED on his keyboard, the smile on his lips almost permanent as he mulled over the events of the past few minutes. The director of the CIA didn't deny that the video existed, even going as far to threaten him over it.

A woman walked up behind Feller and put her arms around him from behind. "Glen, when are you coming to bed? You know I have an early morning tomorrow."

He looked up at her and patted her hands.

"What?" she asked. "You look manic right now."

"You won't believe the bombshell that I'm going to drop tomorrow. I'll be on all the talk radio programs for the morning drive and then on all the national shows by the evening. It's going to be a busy one."

"You're not going to destroy my husband, are you?"

Feller shook his head. "Of course not. He's doesn't need any help in that area."

She giggled. "All I ask is that you give me plenty of advance notice before you throw the last shovelful of dirt on his political career. I want to be ready with the divorce papers."

"In due time, dear," Feller said. "In due time. But first things first. Tomorrow I set the city ablaze."

CHAPTER
TWENTY-THREE

LEAVENWORTH, KANSAS

MORGAN MAY SHOOK hands with Capt. Hal Dellinger moments after deplaning at the Sherman Army Airfield. He removed his sunglasses, tucking them away in the breast pocket of his leather bomber jacket, much to Morgan's delight. Dellinger was five years her senior, but she didn't mind. Easy on the eyes and ears, Dellinger greeted her with his smooth voice.

"When I heard I was going to be flying a special person of interest on my flight tonight out of here, I thought about you," Dellinger said, his deep blue eyes twinkling.

"We were here one time, Hal. It wasn't that memorable, as I recall. We ate at Arthur Bryant's for some good barbecue and then drove out to a cornfield and shot glass bottles off a fence post."

"Seems like you remember most of the pertinent details."

Morgan cut him a sideways glance and smirked. "That's all I remember."

"Don't be so coy. I know you remember what we had for dinner and where we went afterward, you remember the rest, too."

She shrugged. "It was a good time. But don't get any ideas about this evening. We're ships passing in the night this time."

Dellinger nodded. "True. But once I finish my mission, I can come back here and pick you up, take you—"

"Wherever I want to go?"

"I was going to say where my next mission is," he said with a chuckle. "But it seems to me that you have quite the pull with my superiors, though from what I understand my final destination is still in your hands."

"I'll make it be somewhere fun."

"Perhaps I can come back and you'll have a mission in Paris that you need my services for. I know a quaint little café on the Seine."

"Paris? The Seine?" Morgan said, her eyes widening. "There's more in your repertoire than I thought."

"Barbecue and cornfields in Kansas, beef bourguignon and rivers in Paris," Dellinger said. "I've learned to work with whatever I've got."

"Well, we'll have to talk about it later because tonight you have a prisoner to fly. Neither one of us are going to have time to do much," she said.

Dellinger nodded. "Well, I've got to finish all my pre-checks and see what the mechanics over here are working on. Always a pleasure, Morgan."

"You too, captain."

Morgan headed toward the dark SUV waiting for her on the tarmac. She took one final quick glance over her shoulder at Dellinger, who was watching her. After a quick wink, she climbed inside.

Almost immediately her phone buzzed with a call from Hawk.

"Did you find Kira yet?" she asked.

"Not exactly," Hawk said, "but I did want to update you on a developing situation."

"Go on."

"This happened right before you took off, so we weren't able to tell you about it beforehand, but we're in Albuquerque."

"Albuquerque? What on earth for?"

"We found out this morning that Kira was using a look-a-like to attend class in her place," Hawk said. "She hardly ever spoke anyway, so nobody really questioned whether it was her or not. But we got a call from one of her professors who recognized that Kira was writing with her right hand, instead of her left. He asked her to remove her sunglasses and hat, which she'd be wearing in class for the past few days. When she did, he didn't recognize her as Kira and called us to report what was going on."

"And how does that put you in Albuquerque?"

"We got a hit on the car at a toll booth leaving California," Hawk said. "Alex stitched together possible stops along the way and found that she pulled into Albuquerque this morning. After calling the Albuquerque police and informing them about how dangerous Kira was, an officer there told us her car was identified as being suspicious and a woman had been seen sleeping inside. We asked the officers to wait for us as it was a matter of national security, and they're keeping an eye on the vehicle until we can get there."

"Good work, you two," Morgan said. "Keep me posted."

UPON ARRIVING AT Fort Leavenworth, Morgan stepped out of the vehicle, where she was met by a pair of guards to escort her to the temporary command center. The waning sunlight from the late afternoon dimmed, dipping beneath the trees to the west. Moments later, she walked into a conference room that had been outfitted at her request. Monitors hung on every wall, computer terminals scattered on various desks, each one manned by Army personnel.

"Everyone, listen up," a barrel-chested colonel barked. "This is your new director and you will address her as such. You will not be told her name, but I expect full cooperation and respect just the same. Is that clear?"

"Yes, sir," said the Army personnel in near unison.

Morgan thanked Col. Hank Ketchum for his introduction and guided her to a specially designed work station.

"We've been testing all the tech, Director," Ketchum said. "Dr. Z has been most gracious with his time to make sure that we have all the details ironed out."

"He's good at that," she said. "And if everything runs smoothly tonight, we'll be out of your hair before you know it."

"Please, Director, take all the time you need. We're for you, especially given the sensitive nature of this mission."

"You've been briefed?"

"Actually, no, I haven't. That's how I know just how secret this must be. All I was told is that I wasn't to refer to you by your name or tell anyone what your name is. I've been involved in some top secret missions before—but not like this."

"You don't recognize me then, do you?"

Ketchum shook his head.

"Good," she said. "Don't even try to remember me. It'll be to your detriment in the long run."

He gestured toward her chair. "If you need anything, please let me or one of my staff know. We're here to serve you."

"Thank you, Colonel."

Outside, Big Earv and Mia were sitting in a van near the outskirts of Leavenworth's federal U.S. Penitentiary, home to some of the country's most dangerous criminals. Once a prisoner arrived at Leavenworth, there were very few ways to leave that included being alive. Most of the ways out were in coffins or body bags after dying of old age or at the hands of fellow hitmen. A rare, live exit by a prisoner who supposedly could secure valuable information about The Alliance? That was sure to arrest the group's attention.

"How are we looking out there, guys?" Morgan asked.

Big Earv and Mia were positioned in an SUV near the only road that had any line of sight on the facility. All transfers took place along this area, though most of the time the feds parked a row of cars farther away from the doors, creating a visual barrier. But this time, the barrier was removed, making it easy for any snipers to remain in the shadows.

"We're clear here," Big Earv said. "No sign of anyone."

"Keep me posted if anything changes," Morgan said.

She checked her watched and leaned back in her chair. The exchange was supposed to take place within the hour. And while she was confident in her team's ability to execute, she couldn't help but feel sick, as if something would go wrong.

Morgan skimmed over her plan again, mentally noting all the details. The plans were nearly flawless, both the fake prisoner transport as well as the one designed to catch the mole. All they had to do was get a nibble—and patience wasn't one of her virtues.

As the time approached to begin the operation, she glanced at her watch and took a deep breath.

"Ma'am," one of the guards said, "we're ready to begin."

Morgan stood, her arms crossed, as the feed came up on the largest screen on the far wall.

"Still quiet out there?" Morgan asked over the coms.

"We've got nothing," Big Earv said.

Morgan watched as Brad Porter was escorted into the first of three vans. The guards went through the charade of pretending to secure him into the transport before a door in the bottom of the van opened up, allowing Porter to exit the vehicle without being seen. On the screen, one of the guard's body cams showed Porter being led through an underground tunnel and back to his cell, a part of the plan she added later working in conjunction with Dr. Z.

The view switched to the outside of the prison where the three vans—all driven remotely—headed to the airfield.

"Get ready to move," Morgan said.

The idea was to entice an attack on the caravan, which would kill Porter. Whichever van from the group was targeted would help Morgan single out the mole.

However, the vans rolled off the base without incident and traveled to the airfield. They retreated into the hangar out of sight to continue the ruse.

"What's going on?" Morgan said. "Is The Alliance that arrogant that they think they can get away with all they've done in court?"

"I don't know," Big Earv said. "But maybe they smelled a trap here."

"How could they? I let it be known that we discovered who the mole was."

"Maybe the mole isn't who we think it is," Big Earv suggested.

"We have to consider all possibilities," Mia said. "It could simply be someone with access to the network."

"But all the files are encrypted and can only be opened with a specific key designed for each individual terminal in the office," Morgan said.

"Sorry to pop your bubble—" Mia said.

"Burst your bubble," Big Earv said. "It's *burst*, not pop."

"You know I'm still learning all the nuances of the English language. It's not the same in German."

"Go ahead," Morgan said.

"It's easy to create a workaround for that," Mia said. "All you have to do is spoof the address of each computer, which isn't all that difficult," Mia said. "In short, your network security isn't as tight as you think it is. But nobody's is, to be honest."

Morgan sighed. "We could be wrong about where the leak is coming from. That's not something I've thought possible, but you could be right."

"Or," Big Earv began, "maybe it is coming from the group we think it is, but The Alliance intend to get to Porter another way."

Morgan gasped. "What do you mean?"

"I mean, what if they decide to go after the plane instead?" Big Earv asked.

"We went over this," Morgan said. "The airfield is so guarded and insulated within the base that nobody would have technologically advanced weapons enough to shoot down the plane."

"I don't know," Big Earv said. "I'm just trying to figure out why The Alliance would pass on taking out Porter. Maybe they have some technology we don't know about."

Morgan asked Col. Ketchum to patch her into Capt. Dellinger's radio feed. Less than a minute later, she was connected.

"Captain, I must level with you," Morgan said. "I actually thought you weren't going to fly anywhere tonight."

"What do you mean?" Dellinger asked.

"We anticipated an attack on the convoy that was going to the hangar. The prisoner was never even in the van when it left the base; that's why the ones there are empty."

"But you're still sending me up tonight?"

"Yes," she said. "Even if the group we were trying to trap didn't take the bait with the prisoner, we still need them to think this was a legitimate operation and that this prisoner may still roll on them."

"I understand. So, where am I headed?"

"What about Edwards Air Force Base? Maybe we could meet up an hour after you land and get some drinks because I'm going to be right behind you."

"It's not Paris but it'll do," he said.

Morgan laughed. "See you soon."

She collected all her papers and thanked Col. Ketchum for all his help before ordering Big Earv and Mia to stay at the airfield where they would leave on the Magnum Group's jet.

"You do know we heard all that, right?" Big Earv said.

"Yes," Morgan said, "and if you tell anyone, I know how to find you."

"Your secret is safe with me," Mia said.

"Suck-up," Big Earv said.

"See you at the hangar," Morgan said.

A pair of military policeman escorted Morgan to her vehicle. As they drove off the base, she buried her face in her hands and growled, frustrated over the fact that her intricate plan had failed. But the trip hadn't been a total waste, at least personally. Seeing Dellinger again was fun—and would lead to so much needed relaxation with someone that wouldn't involve much work talk. She needed a break; that much she realized. This operation had consumed her, and she was wearing thin.

As her car pulled up to the Sherman Army Airfield, it stopped briefly at the gate before proceeding inside. She noticed a vehicle idling just inside the gate.

"Big Earv, is that you in the Tahoe?" she asked over the coms.

"Yes, that's us. Why don't you join us and we can all drive to the hangar together?"

"Sounds good," she said.

Once her SUV entered the base, she gathered her things and walked over to Big Earv's vehicle. As she was loading her bag into the back, she heard a sickening noise and looked skyward.

A plane engulfed in flames was barreling straight toward the ground. She couldn't see the aircraft when it collided with the earth, but she heard the explosion and, seconds later, the sound of emergency vehicles responding to the crash.

There's no way anyone survived—and she knew it.

Dellinger!

CHAPTER
TWENTY-FOUR

ALBUQUERQUE, NEW MEXICO

HAWK AND ALEX were hunkered down in a van outside a half block away from Kira Gusev's car, which had been spotted earlier in the day. Albuquerque police hadn't moved, accepting the fact that Hawk and Alex were legitimate agents. Their credentials had a number to call, which sounded like the FBI but routed the calls to a switchboard at the Magnum Group. The woman there confirmed that Hawk and Alex were FBI agents, and that was the extent of the verification process.

"I'm surprised they don't know the FBI director on a first name basis," Alex said as she peered through a pair of binoculars. "This town is teeming with so many different illegal drugs, it might as well be both a testing facility and a factory."

"Or it'd be a great town to get lost in," Hawk said. "A missing college student is low on the priority list in a place like this."

"Too bad Kira's luck ran out."

Hawk listened in on the radio one of the officers gave him. The Albuquerque Police Department took Hawk's warning seriously. They deployed their only SWAT team vehicle and waited until it arrived before developing a plan for how to approach the vehicle.

"You're sure this woman is dangerous?" an officer asked.

"Yes," Hawk said. "Very dangerous. She has to be armed, but I can't say for sure. All I know is that her father is a criminal mastermind halfway around the world," Hawk said.

"So, what did she do?" another officer asked.

"Nothing yet," Hawk said. "But you need to be alert. We need to bring her in for questioning. She's been privy to some high-level international crime. It's important that we talk to her. Understand?"

"Affirmative. The goal is to do everything possible to apprehend the person of interest, especially since there's no reason to use force. Now, let's move in."

Hawk pulled out his binoculars to watch the scene unfold.

A trio of officers approached Kira's vehicle and gave a status report on her.

"She's still here," one of the officers said.

"Is she awake?" Hawk asked.

"She's covered up in a blanket with a baseball cap over her face."

He watched as another officer tapped on her window several times. But based on what Hawk could see, there was no movement inside.

"Are you sure she's in there?" Hawk asked again.

"There's definitely a woman in the driver's seat," the officer said. "I'm not sure why she's not responding. But this is Albuquerque—and based on my experience, she's likely either overdosed or passed out."

"But do you *see* her?" Hawk asked.

"I can see her hair coming out from underneath her baseball cap," the officer said. "She's turned over on her side and covered up in a blanket."

"Can you see her feet?"

The officer cursed. "What's wrong with you, man? There's a person in here. Would you like to come look for yourself?"

"No, no," Hawk said. "Just be careful."

"I always am," the officer said as he grabbed the door handle.

"Wait," another officer shouted. "Don't open the—"

A large fireball leaped skyward, the boom from the explosion rocking Hawk and Alex's car some fifty yards away. Car alarms went off as did police sirens. In less than a minute, a fire truck rolled on the scene from just down the street and doused the flaming vehicle. First responders rushed back and forth, tending to all three officers who had surrounded the car. Hawk wasn't sure any of them were going to make it based on the amount of explosives Kira had to have used.

Hawk slammed his fist on the steering wheel.

"You think she was in there?" Alex asked.

"Not a chance," he said. "Who knows how long she's been gone now? Five hours? Eight hours?"

"It couldn't be more than twelve," Alex said. "We know that much."

"So we draw a radius that extends about a ten-hour drive from here and put everyone on alert? Do you know how difficult that will be?"

"I'm sure we can at least figure out which direction she went in to narrow the search grid."

Hawk shook his head. "But that's not even the most concerning thing to me."

"What are you really worried about then?"

"Kira—she's not just some run-of-the-mill college student. To rig something like this, she has to be a trained assassin."

"I think we already figured that."

"But that's still not what concerns me."

"Then what does?"

"Gusev activated her with that one phone call somehow. She's not just part of the sleeper cell—I think she might be running the whole damn thing."

CHAPTER
TWENTY-FIVE

WASHINGTON, D.C.

ROBERT BESSERMAN TRUDGED up the sidewalk leading to the White House. After his confrontation with Norris at the fundraiser, the only conversation that Besserman imagined was about to take place was his firing. While Norris had a short leash on everyone in his administration, his relationship with Besserman meant that his dismissal would at least be done in person instead of through another spokesperson.

At least he's man enough to do it himself.

But Besserman couldn't conceive of a worse time to release the director of the CIA, given all the crises happening across the country and around the world. The Alliance still loomed as a threat to Norris's presidency, while the Russians had infiltrated the country with a sleeper cell. Then there was the cybersecurity issue with the White House that posed a serious threat, so serious that even the president was concerned because of what it meant to his political aspirations. Anyone who would take Besserman's place would have to get up to speed on all that and much more. And in the world of espionage and intelligence, the amount of time that would take could be all the country's enemies needed to disappear or worse—commit untold acts of terrorism.

As Besserman checked into a conference room, he sat down and remembered some of his fondest memories with Norris. While they were in college together, one night they were making a beer run when a flash flood overwhelmed Norris's car on a bridge. Between the rushing water, the driving rain, and the thunder rumbling overhead, communicating was nearly impossible. They climbed out of the car through the window and tried to make their way to higher ground. But as they did, they both walked by a car with a woman inside and a small child in the back. Neither one of them hesitated to help when they heard the woman screaming for help, working together to free them both in just a couple of minutes. And when a newspaper reporter tracked them down to talk about it, Norris shrugged it off and said he didn't want to talk about it and didn't want his name mentioned in any article. In hindsight, it would've been a powerful story on the campaign trail that captured the kind of person that he was, but Norris wasn't thinking about crafting a version of himself to sell voters. He was just being himself. That incident years ago depicted the kind of man Norris was—and the reason Besserman was so hopeful about his friend taking over the presidency. But the latest turn of events disheartened Besserman. Maybe that man was gone and Norris had become just like every other politician in Washington, focused on aspirations of power rather than the ability to help people. Besserman wanted to find out for himself—and he considered that this might be his last chance to confront the president.

After a few minutes of sitting alone with his thoughts, the door finally swung open. But instead of a Secret Service agent entering first before Norris, Emma Washburn entered the room, working over a stress ball in her right hand. Seeing the president's chief of staff surprised Besserman—and disappointed him.

That coward won't even fire me himself.

Washburn sat down across from him, still squeezing the ball. With her curly brown hair and fit figure, she was easy on the eyes. Her good looks also served as an effective way to soften up her targets before unleashing her fury on them. Her tirades had already become legendary among White House staffers, and Besserman figured he was about to be the recipient of her trademark rants.

"Bobby, so nice to see you today," she said, offering a thin smile. "I appreciate you coming down to the White House on such short notice. I know you're busy."

He shrugged. "I serve at the pleasure of the president."

"Oh, stop it with that line of bullshit," she said. "You serve at the director of the CIA because you were college buddies with the president. It certainly wasn't on merit."

Besserman narrowed his eyes. "Perhaps you've forgotten that I rose to the position of deputy director of the CIA without his help."

"And that's where you would've stayed with the president. Don't you forget it."

Besserman sighed and stared off into the distance. "Did you just call me down here to berate me? Because I do have things to do, like keeping the country safe from enemies lying in wait, for example."

"Why? Because you've done such a good job with that already, allowing a Russian sleeper cell over our borders on your watch? Please."

"That cell was already here," he said, shifting in his seat.

"Oh, so they came in when you were deputy director? Still on your watch."

"What do you want?" Besserman said. "You have plenty of punching bags in the West Wing, from what I understand. No need to import them unless you've got an actual purpose for this meeting."

"Look, Bobby, I don't know how else to tell you this, but your position within this administration is a tenuous one. And that's a very charitable characterization, to be honest. A more accurate description would be that you're one misstep away from losing your post at Langley and being discarded on the trash heap of failed CIA directors. Can I be any clearer about that?"

Besserman rolled up his sleeves before responding. "If there's one thing I've learned after living in this city as long as I have, it's that you can always make a comeback. I've also observed that those who obtain power without being elected are always just a step away from losing their job. And that goes for you, too."

"I'm well aware of how this thing works," she said. "But you need to be aware that you're not doing your job to the level that the president requires. I spent all morning cleaning up your mess from that blogger Glen Feller. Fortunately, I handled it before it became a bigger issue than it needed to be."

Besserman cocked his head to one side. "What are you talking about?"

"I'm talking about you threatening a reporter last night," she said. "The reason you didn't see it or hear about it was that I happen to know the editor of the website and used up every bit of relational capital I had with her to get Feller fired and a full retraction issued. And that was all before you ate breakfast this morning."

"What?"

"Yeah, that blogger who called you said that you threatened to make him disappear."

"And that was the story?"

"Yeah, but I suppose there was more to it than that, but that's all he made public. He might be making some other things public, too. But I want you to make sure that doesn't happen. You need to meet with him and give him something else, a benign scoop he can use so that he knows you're on his side and that you care about freedom of the press."

"I do care about freedom of the press," Besserman said.

"That's why I encouraged him strongly not to print something without having enough evidence."

"Well, apparently that worked—or he just wanted to play the victim game. Either way, he'll land on his feet, propped up by the people who think being warned against doing something illegal or something that might harm our national security interests—and all for clicks on the Internet—is the bigger story."

Besserman cleared his throat. "The bigger story is that the White House servers have been breached *and* a video of Norris chatting it up with a Chinese general has surfaced. If you think I'm making waves, just wait until that story hits the news cycle."

"I won't have to wait," Washburn said. "You're going to make sure it goes away for a very long time."

CHAPTER
TWENTY-SIX

LEAVENWORTH, KANSAS

BIG EARV WORKED over a toothpick in his mouth and glanced at Mia as a man in a suit approached them. He was wearing a pair of aviator sunglasses and a suit, his jacket unbuttoned with the flaps swaying as he walked. When he reached Big Earv and Mia, the man pushed his sunglasses up the bridge of his nose with his index finger before looking directly at them.

He introduced himself as Chase Walker and didn't waste any time on small talk.

"I understand you two were part of the team that was overseeing an operation that utilized the airplane in this crash," Chase said. "Is that correct?"

Big Earv and Mia both nodded. "The loop was tight."

Walker put his hands on his hips and glanced back across the tarmac toward the charred remains of the airplane. "Apparently, it wasn't that tight."

"Yes, it was," Mia said. "There were only three people who were aware of the full plan."

"Then I guess you two are prime suspects, unless, of course, someone only needed to know *part* of the plan to pull this off."

Big Earv removed the toothpick from his mouth and crossed his arms over his chest. "We had a secure perimeter—at least secure enough that nobody could hit that plane with an RPG. It'd be next to impossible since we were so far away."

Walker stroked his stubbled face. "You think an RPG did this?"

"It's the only explanation that makes sense at this point," Big Earv said.

Walker sniggered at the comment. "I've been doing this a long time, long enough to know that there are a thousand ways to take down an aircraft, some of which you probably couldn't even imagine. But the possibilities feel almost endless. So to suggest that the *only* explanation was someone shooting the plane out of the sky is ludicrous."

Big Earv wanted to punch Walker in the face, even if he didn't deserve it, forgetting that he was probably right. Morgan's insistence that The Alliance wouldn't go after the plane because it would be too difficult wasn't necessarily wrong. She'd just severely underestimated The Alliance's ability to infiltrate any seemingly closed loop. But to have that fact pointed out by someone as slick as Walker angered Big Earv.

"Then how did it happen?" Mia asked.

Walker smiled. "That's why we're here, little lady. Our job is usually to figure out where the pilot screwed up, but this time it sounds like we're to figure out where *you* screwed up."

"Any ideas, wise guy?" Big Earv asked. "Or are you just here to mock our mistake?"

"I'd hardly call this a mistake," Walker said. "Two people are dead and we've got a bunch of journalists over there asking questions about the nature of this flight and who was on it. Despite my pretty face, I'm not real fond of cameras."

"Typical," Big Earv said. "You're evading my question."

"I addressed your second one."

"That one was rhetorical. Do I need to explain to you what that means?"

"All right, all right," Walker said as he adjusted his tie. "We probably got off on the wrong foot, especially since I know you're all sensitive about how your decisions cost a couple of people their lives, not to mention losing a nice aircraft like this, but I digress. We do have some working theories. However, I must emphasize that they are *working* theories, plausible ideas that we're looking into at the moment."

"And what are some of those theories?" Mia asked.

"I'd rather not say since they're very pliable at this juncture in the investigation."

Big Earv narrowed his eyes. "I'd rather not be lied to. You don't have any theories, do you?"

"As a matter of fact, we do—several, even."

"Just give us one," Big Earv said with a growl.

Walker buried his head in his hands and sighed. "God, you people are relentless. I'm sure a classroom full of five-year-olds isn't this annoying."

"If you'd just answer the damn question without lying to us, we could all move on."

After cracking his knuckles, Walker nodded subtly as he looked past Big Earv and Mia. "All right, fine. You want some theories? I'll give you some theories."

"We're listening," Big Earv said.

"Based on what we're seeing in what's left of the fuselage, there appears to have been some sort of blast that came from the interior," Walker said.

Big Earv furrowed his brow. "You think someone planted a bomb in the plane?"

"It certainly appears that way, but, like I said, it's a working theory. It could've been a secondary blast that occurred after the initial one, but at this point that seems less likely. The area of origin seems to be from the inside, not the outside."

"Could you tell if there was an accelerant used?" Big Earv asked.

"Not until we get lab reports back, but that wouldn't surprise me."

Big Earv squinted as he studied Walker. "Why not?"

"The blast penetrated the fuselage, but whoever did this used something to speed up the fire as well as its intensity. They didn't want us figuring out that this fire was started from the inside with a blast. It's almost like they thought you'd believe it was an attack from the outside and that we'd waste months looking for who could fire a shot like that—and how it was done."

"But why?" Big Earv asked.

Walker shrugged. "My job isn't to figure out the *why* in this case; I'm simply here to examine the *what* and the *how*. You will have to piece the rest of this mystery together yourselves—and do whatever you can to make sure it doesn't happen again."

Walker spun on his heels and marched back toward the scene of the crash.

"Thank you," Mia shouted after him.

Walker just raised his hand without stopping or even looking back.

"So, now what?" Mia asked.

"We call Morgan with the bad news," Big Earv said.

"She's not gonna like that."

"Of course not," Big Earv said. "If anything, it's going to highlight how dangerous her obsession is with finding the mole. There were other ways to do this, but she seems to think the mole is the only way to find out who's behind all this."

"And you think she's wrong?"

Big Earv shrugged. "I don't know, to be honest. It seems like we have plenty of other concerns that supersede this one. Besides, this wasn't just a tragedy—Morgan lost a good friend, a guy I think she was rather sweet on."

"And unfortunately, Walker only gave us more to think about, raising more questions than answers," she said.

"Exactly, such as who's really behind this? And how connected is The Alliance?"

"In that case, I'd rather not be the one to tell her," she said. "She's going to ask a hundred questions, none of which I'll know the answer to. I don't want to be the messenger for this."

"I'll do it," Big Earv said, "but you're gonna owe me one—big time."

CHAPTER
TWENTY-SEVEN

COLORADO SPRINGS, COLORADO

HAWK SHOWED his security badge to the guard at the gate of the Cheyenne Mountain Complex before he waved him through. They entered through the main doors and went through another checkpoint before meeting their contact, Col. Zane Ellis, who was waiting for them just off the lobby.

"Sorry I had to drag you all the way out here," Ellis said after they introduced themselves and exchanged pleasantries. "This kind of information isn't one I want shared over the phone or over email, encrypted or otherwise."

"We'll defer to your judgment," Alex said. "Your expertise on how to eradicate sleeper cells is legendary."

Ellis gestured down the hall and began walking with them. "I was blessed with some incredible intel and good fortune. This isn't something that's done in a vacuum, even if that's where you feel like you are."

He led them into a small conference room and they sat down around the circular table.

"We need any tips you can give us," Hawk said. "I've been inside terrorist cells in the Middle East, but not any sleeper cells here. And we feel like we're flying blind right now, especially since we haven't been able to identify anyone in the cell yet. We're working on it, but we know time is of the essence."

Ellis leaned back in his chair. "Well, I read what you sent in your message to me, and I must admit that I'm not sure how much I'm going to be able to help you. Your situation is quite different than mine was, starting with the fact that I was embedded with the sleeper cell, even though I didn't realize it at the time."

Alex cocked her head to one side. "You didn't realize it?"

"No, not at first," Ellis said. "I was just on a mission for the agency to infiltrate a terrorist group. Once I earned the group's trust, I was told that I was needed for a secret mission in the U.S., but they didn't tell me what it was. I thought I was going to help be part of a terrorist attack, but I found out they just wanted me to attend an engineering school along with several other group members, who were all in their early twenties. I seriously started to question if I was really with terrorists or just radical idealists."

Hawk stroked his chin. "What changed?"

"Nothing, honestly. We all went to schools in California and stayed in touch, regularly meeting up. But one day, one of the leaders passed out at my apartment after a night of drinking. I got into his phone and started reading all the messages, the latest of which detailed when everyone in the group was to be activated and trained for a special mission. I'd almost been lulled to sleep."

"What did you do after that?" Alex asked.

"I invited everyone to my apartment for a party the next weekend and laced all the drinks with cyanide. Once they were out, I started a fire and got everyone else out of the building. All the terrorists were reported dead—and so was I. To outsiders, it seemed like an unfortunate accident among friends partying one night. No one else was the wiser, and my role in bringing it down remains classified. But apparently someone over at your organization knew about it or else we wouldn't be talking right now."

"So, what do we need to be looking for?" Hawk asked.

"If everyone in the sleeper cell entered the country legally, I think it would be easy to investigate clusters of people who all migrated here from Russia at about the same time. But that's not the case, is it?"

"Unfortunately, it isn't," Hawk said. "We don't know who these people are or anything about them. We don't know if they're living close together or spread out across the country."

"But you do know Gusev's daughter is involved, right?" Ellis asked.

"If not, she has some dangerous skills and needs to be stopped," Alex said. "But it seems pretty obvious that she's got something to do with it."

"If she hasn't been communicating with a group of people locally, she's been doing it electronically, which is risky, but still possible without getting caught."

"Any ideas on how she might be doing that?" Alex asked.

"Leaving emails in a draft folder and never sending them," Ellis said. "Everyone has the password and they read the messages without ever actually sending them."

"That's a good one."

Ellis nodded. "Yeah, and difficult to find if you can't identify the email address. But there's also the possibility that she's communicating over video games, which is another challenging method to track. But either one of those might give you some insight into how many people she's talking to and where they are. I know it's probably not that great of help, but those are some of the ways I learned that these guys talk. Maybe you'll be able to find the break you need to bring them down before it's too late."

"I hope so," Hawk said. "She's already proved to be slippery and more than adept and keeping our team occupied with red herrings."

"Be relentless," Ellis said. "She'll make a mistake. Just keep the pressure on her."

Hawk and Alex thanked the colonel before leaving the facility.

When they got back to the car, Hawk shook his head as he started the engine.

"This isn't good, is it?" Alex asked.

"I'm afraid this hunt is going to be one of the most difficult ones I've ever done," Hawk said. "But we're not going to stop. Too much is at stake."

Alex nodded. "I'll call Morgan and give her the update. She's not going to like this."

CHAPTER
TWENTY-EIGHT

WASHINGTON, D.C.

BESSERMAN FIDDLED with his watch as he scanned the area beneath the Jefferson Memorial for Glenn Feller. Besserman had reached out to the political blogger after hearing what had happened to him. Even though he was wrong to play up Besserman's comment like he was going to physically harm Feller, Besserman was curious to find out if Feller actually knew something.

After fifteen minutes past their scheduled meeting time, Besserman considered leaving. He figured Feller had changed his mind and wasn't going to show up. But as Besserman was walking toward the steps, he heard footfalls on the stairs and waited. A few seconds later, Feller descended.

"You made it," Besserman said, offering his hand.

Feller glanced at it but ignored it. "I almost didn't come."

"I wouldn't have blamed you if you didn't. But the truth is I had nothing to do with the hit job on your career."

"The truth?" Feller scoffed. "That's rich coming from the director of the CIA, where you thrive on lies and deception. Why should I ever believe a word out of your mouth?"

Besserman put his hands up and took a step back, hoping to reduce the tension. "I understand why you feel that way. If the shoe were on the other foot, I know I'd have serious doubts about you, too. But, like you, I would've come sheerly out of curiosity. If I didn't go, I'd wonder why I was invited."

"If you're so much like me, you'd be wondering how long it takes to bleed out after being shot and left for dead."

Besserman shook his head and eased open the flaps of his jacket. "I'm unarmed. I didn't come to hurt you. I have sincere questions."

"Maybe you should've asked those when I called you a few days ago."

"Much has happened since then, including you getting smeared. I just want you to know that I'm sorry that happened— and also that I had nothing to do with it."

"Who did it then?" Feller asked.

"I—I can't really tell you that."

"You *can't*? Or you *won't*?"

"What difference would that distinction make at this point?" Besserman said.

"It'd let me know if you were being controlled or if you were trying to protect someone, though I suspect that person is yourself."

"It's neither one of those situations. I'm just trying to get to the bottom of this whole ordeal, just like you are. I think if we work together, we might be able to uncover what's going on."

Feller bit his lip and subtly shook his head. "That's what you think? That we're just going to forget the part about you destroying my credibility—the most important trait any journalist can have—and thus ruining any chances I have at a career? Thanks to you, I'm done."

Besserman put his hands on his hips as he surveyed the basement area, which was littered with old displays about Jefferson and his presidency. Then he looked down and scuffed at the ground with his foot.

"Kind of ironic that we're here, isn't it?" Besserman asked. "We're in the basement of a shrine to one of the founding fathers who was most adamant about the importance of the freedom of the press. He famously once told John Jay that, 'Our liberty cannot be guarded but by the freedom of the press, nor that be limited without danger of losing it.'"

"For someone who knows a lot about the freedom of the press, you sure don't act like you care about it."

Besserman shook his head. "I think a free press is vital to our democracy, but an irresponsible press can also endanger it."

"Let me get this straight," Feller said. "You think it's important for the press to have freedoms, but that it shouldn't be free to publish a video of our president chatting it up with a Chinese general at a bar in the middle of the Indian Ocean? Do I have that right?"

"What was on that recording that you have?" Besserman asked. "What were they talking about?"

"Does it really matter?"

Besserman shrugged. "Maybe. Were they talking about who was going to win the NBA Finals or were they discussing military secrets? Those things matter in context. Was the meeting planned or did it happen by chance? I'm curious about those things as well and would like some answers, answers I'm not getting."

"Oh, so now you want to talk about context? After you had your lackeys fabricate stories about me to ruin my reputation? You're not getting anything from me."

"I already told you that you're mad at the wrong person," Besserman said. "I had nothing to do with your character assassination. Honestly, I don't have time for that. I never even saw the original story you wrote."

"Figures," Feller said. "You just shrug it off like another drone missile fired into a compound where a half-dozen innocent children are killed. You don't care because you got what you wanted. And in this case, it's my silence. I'll never have a voice again because of what you did."

"I assure you that you have this all wrong."

"You're lying again. But this time I'm going to put you in a predicament you won't be able to get out of."

"What are you talking about?"

Feller fished his phone out of his pocket and began typing on hit.

"What are you doing?"

"Sending out a little message," Feller said.

"Please reconsider whatever it is that you think you're doing."

Feller didn't look up, his thumbs flying across the screen as he tapped on it. A wry smile crept across his lips. "You ruined my life. Now I'm going to ruin yours."

"Glenn, I don't like the sound of this."

"I bet you don't," Feller said before he snapped a picture of Besserman.

"What are you doing?"

Feller didn't respond before he quickly finished and tucked his phone away. Then he pulled a gun out of his pocket.

"Whoa, whoa, Glenn," Besserman said as he held his hands out. "You don't need to do this."

"Oh, yes, I do."

Feller jammed the gun under his chin and pulled the trigger.

CHAPTER TWENTY-NINE

LOS ANGELES

AT THE MAGNUM GROUP OFFICES, Morgan May sat down at her desk and glanced at the files stacked on the corner of it. She had plenty of pressing issues to attend to, but she needed a moment to mourn. She'd always liked Hal Dellinger. That was part of the reason she requested him for the mission at Leavenworth. She wanted to see him again, not once considering that whoever was behind the attack would outwit her, foiling her plan to expose the mole by shooting down the plane. Dellinger didn't deserve that, but she'd dragged him into her dark world and made him an unwitting participant.

It was early but she wandered over to her wet bar and poured herself a shot.

"Here's to you, Hal," she said. "I don't think I'll ever forgive myself. But I'm going to find the bastards who did this, I promise."

She threw the glass back, the liquid burning her throat as it went down.

Big Earv walked into her office, catching her as she set the glass down on her desk. "So sorry again about Capt. Dellinger.

I'd met him before on another mission. He was one of the good guys."

"And he's dead now, thanks to me," Morgan said before slumping into her chair.

"No, he's dead because someone fired an RPG at the plane and hit their mark. It's not your fault."

"He would've never been on that plane if it weren't for me," she said.

"Maybe not, but someone else would've been dead. We do what we do because there are evil people out there with no regard for innocent life. They crave power and wealth, trampling whoever's in their way to get what they want. You were trying to stop them. We all know the dangers facing us whenever we engage in our job—and I'm sure Capt. Dellinger did, too."

"But he didn't deserve this."

Big Earv shook his head. "No, he didn't. And we can't bring him back now. But we can bring the people who did this to justice—our type of justice."

"I'm right there with you," she said. "I'm just a little bit too numb at the moment to start thinking about that."

Big Earv smiled and winked at her before presenting Morgan with a folder. "Fortunately, I'm not. I've been thinking about how we can turn an unfortunate incident into an advantage for us."

Morgan sat up and opened it. "And you think we can?"

"It's all in there," he said. "Just look it over before our meeting this afternoon. It's just an idea, but I think it'll work."

"Okay," she said, closing the folder. "I'll check this out. And thanks again for all your support. It means a lot to me right now."

"Of course, boss. You know I'm on your side come hell or high water."

"I know. Thanks."

Morgan watched Big Earv exit the room, leaving her alone with her thoughts. She leaned back in her chair and took a deep breath before sitting up and diving into Big Earv's proposal. After reading through it, she smiled and set it aside.

"I think this just might work," she said to herself.

She picked up her phone and made a call.

———

IN THE AFTERNOON meeting, she gathered the team together who'd been part of the planning process. Nick Slavitt, Elaine Downing, and Peter Avant all entered the room, joining Mia, Big Earv, and Dr. Z. Morgan sat at the head of the table, her documents neatly stacked in front of her.

"Thank you for joining me today," she said, her tone somber. "I wish that we could all be here celebrating our victory, but that's not how it turned out. We had an unfortunate turn of events that destroyed all your hard work as well as eliminated one of the most important witnesses we had against The Alliance. If we'd been able to keep him alive, there's no telling how many of their operatives we would've been able to track down and eliminate. But as it stands, we're now at a major disadvantage. Not only are we still groping around in the dark for connections to the organization, but we've also lost precious hours on this mission that could've been spent on tracking down members of The Alliance."

"So, where do we go from here?" Elaine asked.

"That's a good question," Morgan said. "The truth is that we have to go back to the drawing board. And it's a shame too after all the hard work every one of you put into making this operation a reality. But we have no choice at this point. There's much work still to be done, and we don't even really have time to mourn the great people who've been lost in the midst of this struggle."

"Hear, hear," Slavitt said.

"Yes, I agree," Avant said. "From all I've heard about Capt.

Dellinger, we lost a good one on this mission. May God rest his soul."

Morgan forced a smile before asking if Big Earv would like to say a prayer.

"I know you're religious and all," she said. "I just thought it might be appropriate."

Big Earv nodded and said a quick prayer. Once he was finished, Morgan dismissed the team, but Big Earv lingered in the room with Morgan.

"So, what did you think?" Big Earv asked.

"I already made the call," she said. "I'll let you know what I find out."

Big Earv grinned. "Glad I could help."

Morgan gathered her things and trudged back to her office. Despite the suggestion as to how to move forward from Big Earv, she was still having a difficult time processing how her decision ultimately led to Capt. Dellinger losing his life. That ate at her all afternoon until she considered going home. However, as she grabbed her purse to leave, her phone rang with a call from Hawk and Alex.

"What is it?" Morgan asked.

"All business today, huh?" Hawk said.

"I'm not in the mood for small talk," she said.

"I get it. I heard about what happened to Capt. Dellinger. I don't blame you for being upset, but don't blame yourself for what happened. It wasn't your fault."

"I swear, if one more person tells me that—"

"Forget I said it. But we do have some new developments here."

"Where are you?" Morgan asked.

"Seattle," Hawk said. "We figured out where Kira went, at least the general direction."

"So, what do you know at this point?"

"We're closing in on where we think she might be, but I'm

not willing to say anything is definitive at this point. When I know something more concrete, I'll let you know ASAP."

"Appreciate it, Hawk. You and Alex, be careful, okay?"

"Always," Hawk said before he hung up.

Morgan shifted in her chair as she stared at the stack of documents needing her attention. All she wanted to do was go home and sleep. She thought maybe if she went to sleep, she could wake up and the whole thing would just be a nightmare. Glancing over her shoulder at the wet bar, she considered having another drink before deciding against it. She slung her briefcase over her shoulder and headed toward the door. But just before she locked up her office, her phone rang.

"This is Director May," she said as she answered.

"Morgan, this is Grant Kingsley."

"Thanks for calling me back," she said. "Did you get my message?"

"Message received—and implemented," he said.

"And?"

"And I have something else to tell you."

"Go ahead."

"I posted the information you wanted me to on the dark web," he said. "I hinted that there was an issue with the transfer and that it was all a ruse and that the prisoner is still very much alive."

"Excellent," she said. "Any hits?"

"Well, that's actually why I was calling. I tracked one of the hits on the article to your office."

"Who was it?"

"Nick Slavitt," Kingsley said. "At least, that's what I think. His terminal address corresponds with all the IP addresses you gave me—and it matches the one that searched for this information."

"So, you're certain it's him?" Morgan asked.

"I mean, I don't have footage with a timestamp showing Slavitt sitting at that desk during the same time someone was searching the dark web for this information. But from what I know about your office, it'd be highly unlikely that it was anyone else."

"Good work," Morgan said. "I'll check the security footage to verify."

"Glad I could help," he said.

"I bet you are. And I'll make sure that nobody ever hears about what I mentioned when I visited you."

"I appreciate that," Kingsley said. "And just know that I'm here to help in the future, if you need it, too. I kind of liked doing something directly to help secure the country."

"I'll keep that in mind," Morgan said before hanging up.

While Kingsley hadn't identified anything definitive, he'd helped narrow down the person involved in the leaks, provided that Nick Slavitt really was seated at that terminal when Kingsley was tracking. Morgan couldn't say that she was totally surprised, but it didn't mean she was any less disappointed. She'd hired Slavitt and appreciated his work ethic. But he was likely a traitor—and that irked her more than anything. When she started building the Magnum Group, she prided herself on being able to sniff out candidates that weren't trustworthy. But she'd obviously hired one.

Nick Slavitt, just you wait.

CHAPTER
THIRTY

SEATTLE, WASHINGTON

HAWK SHIFTED THE SUV into drive and pulled out of the rental car lot. Entering the surface streets, Alex navigated onto I-5 South, the direction Kira Gusev was last seen heading. She'd stolen a white Tesla sedan outside of Salt Lake City but got quite a jump on law enforcement searching for her. However, when she used an express lane on I-405, the license plate triggered an alert.

The overcast skies spit a light rain, forcing Hawk to use his windshield wipers. They squeaked as they swished back and forth, annoying him even more.

"I think I'd be better off if I just had someone in the backseat running their fingernails down a chalkboard," Hawk said after a few minutes. "It'd be less irritating than this."

Alex snickered as she stared at the map. "According to Mia, the last known location of Kira was right about here, twenty miles south of downtown. Now that we're tracking her on satellite, I don't think it'll be much longer."

"Good because I just don't know how much more of this I can take."

"Oh, honey, admit it. You love this noise. In fact, I think I'm going to record this and add it to our sound machine. I can upload as many as a dozen extra sounds. I think this would be perfect."

"So help me, Alex, if this comes on in the middle of the night while I'm trying to sleep, I can't promise that I won't break your beloved sound machine."

"Sound machines are replaceable," she said.

"And husbands are not," he said, wagging his finger. "Just remember that."

"Says who?"

He gave her a sideways glance and found her grinning.

"If you only knew just how easy you are to rile up, you'd enjoy this game as well."

"Not funny, Alex."

"Maybe not to you, but I must confess that I'm thoroughly entertained."

Hawk growled, deciding that instead of prolonging the torturous conversation to exercise his better judgment and remain silent. His new tactic worked. For the next five minutes, Alex didn't make a peep, concluding Hawk to believe that she would stop if he didn't react.

"What are you so quiet about over there?" Hawk asked. "Am I spoiling all your fun?"

Her eyes were glued to a tablet. She slowly she looked up at him. "I'm sorry. Were you saying something?"

Hawk sighed. "I was just asking if—"

"Didn't Gusev tell us his daughter was a public relations major?" Alex asked.

"Wait. What?"

"When we interrogated Gusev, didn't he tell us that Kira was studying public relations at USC?"

"Yeah, I'm pretty sure that's what he said—something about her wanting to party like Americans, something to that effect."

"Okay," she said. "That's what I remember too. But that's not true at all."

"What do you mean?"

"I asked Mia to work up an in-depth profile on Kira and this is what she sent me," Alex said as she held up the tablet.

"I can't read that while I'm driving."

"I'll read it to you," Alex said. "It says here that Kira Gusev is enrolled in USC's engineering program. She even earned a scholarship after winning a competition in the spring."

"So, she's a legit student," Hawk said.

"Not just a legit student, but she's a good one, too. And based on what we've seen of her already, it's pretty clear that she's not just here to party with Americans. She's here to learn how to make things. Intricate things. Dangerous things."

Hawk nodded. "We shouldn't be surprised. Almost everything out of Gusev's mouth was a lie."

"Kira has been two steps ahead of us this whole time. Her only mistake thus far was not paying a toll, which triggered an alert. We can't lose her this time because I think by now it's pretty apparent that she's far more dangerous than we anticipated."

"Have you asked Mia if she's made any more progress on hacking into any of Kira's accounts?"

"Yes, and she's still working on it. I told her that we need that information as soon as possible."

"I'm afraid she's going to disappear again," Hawk said.

"Only if you forget how to drive. I'm tracking her now. I've got a feed from the Washington Highway Department that's following her as well as a satellite feed. It's going to be very difficult for us to lose her now."

"That statement feels like a setup."

She shrugged. "Well, you're driving—you can take it however you like. Just don't lose her."

Hawk gripped the steering wheel and shifted in his seat before pressing down the accelerator pedal a little more. He didn't want to lose Kira and showed it by weaving in and out of traffic. A few times, people honked at him, displaying their full appreciation for his erratic driving with obscene gestures.

"You sure have a way with fellow motorists," Alex said with a laugh.

"It's a mutual understanding," he said. "You get the hell outta the way so I don't run you over. So far, everyone seems to comprehend this unwritten rule."

After a few minutes of edging closer to the target, Alex got a call.

"It's the Washington State Patrol office," Alex said, placing her hand over the receiver on her cell phone.

"I'm sure they can still hear you, honey," Hawk said.

"Yes, we can hear you just loud and clear," squawked the voice on the other end, which Alex placed on speaker. "And we wanted to let you know that the other vehicle we're tracking must know you're behind them."

"How can you tell that?"

"Once you got within three miles, it started going progressively faster. It's maintained at least that much distance, if not more over the past five minutes. It's really quite fascinating."

"Fascinating? I'd call that disturbing," Hawk said. "How would she know how close we are?"

"I'm not sure if I could explain it," the woman said. "But I can see it happening in real time. My eyes aren't lying to me."

"Is there any way to slow her down?" Hawk asked.

The woman chuckled. "It's almost five o'clock in Seattle traffic. She'll be slowing down whether she wants to or not."

Hawk thanked the woman for her help and then stepped on the accelerator. He jerked the steering wheel to the right, putting the car on the shoulder.

"What are you doing?" Alex asked.

"I'm going to short circuit her."

"Short circuit her? She's not a computer."

"Yeah, but she's using one and I'm going to try and mess with her."

The car gyrated as it rolled across the rumble strips.

"Is there another way to do this?" Alex asked, her voice vibrating.

Hawk smiled and shook his head.

"You're enjoying this too much," she said.

After a couple of minutes, traffic slowed to a halt as brake lights lit up the highway, forming a snaking trail along I-5 South. Moments later, Hawk noticed a plume of smoke rising from the median a few hundred meters up ahead.

"What is that?" Alex asked.

"Looks like an accident," he said, craning his neck to see what had happened.

A few seconds later, the car exploded.

Hawk put his vehicle in park and got out. Darting in between cars he rushed along the media toward the fire that now engulfed the area.

He rushed back to his SUV. "Alex, what are the chances that it's just a coincidence that it's another white Tesla sedan that's now ablaze in the median?"

"You've got to be kidding me," Alex said.

"I wish I was."

She got out and rushed with Hawk over to the fire. A few motorists had stopped to help, but stood around trying to figure out a way to get to the driver. However, there wasn't anything they could do.

Fifteen minutes later, a fire truck rolled up and doused the blaze around the fire. Paramedics worked to get the woman out of the car, but she was badly burned. Hawk flashed his badge to one of the firemen to gain access to the cordoned off area. He looked inside and found a burner phone. It only had one number on it.

Hawk dialed the number. The line rang a few times before going to voicemail.

"Agent Hawk, I've been watching you. Leave a message—if you want to live."

Hawk shook his head and ended the call.

"What is it?"

"An ironic voice mail message from Kira, considering the fact that there's no way she survived this," Hawk said.

Alex shook his head. "Let's get outta here. We've still got a sleeper cell to expose."

Hawk nodded. "Let's just hope it hasn't woken up yet."

CHAPTER
THIRTY-ONE

BESSERMAN CLOSED HIS EYES and braced for the aftermath. He'd seen plenty of people shot dead during his time working in the intelligence field but never a suicide. Glenn Feller wasn't an angel and he certainly didn't deserve to be blacklisted by every news outlet in the city. But he'd seemed incapable of reason and intent on taking his own life.

The click was hollow.

Besserman opened his eyes to see Feller standing there with a grin on his face.

"Scared you, didn't I?" he asked.

Besserman scowled. "Did you think this was some kind of moment to get back at me for what you *think* I did? Because I'm trying to tell you but you won't listen to me—we're sort of on the same team here."

"That's not what it sounds like when you threaten me like you did."

"I warned you because I thought you were being reckless, both personally and professionally."

"How?" Feller asked as he rolled his eyes. "By telling the truth?"

"A good journalist prints the truth *in context*. Anybody with a platform can twist facts to suit the story they want to tell. But a real journalist, the kind this country needs right now, presents as much context around what happened."

Feller smiled and shook his head. "You don't know, do you?"

"Know what?"

"You don't know what Norris and that general were talking about in the video, do you?"

Besserman shook his head. "Even my best lip readers can't tell, especially since they weren't facing the camera the whole time. Does your version have audio?"

Feller shook his head. "But does that even matter? Do we really want the president of the United States getting chummy with a Chinese general? What if they made plans? What if Norris is a traitor?"

"I want answers to those questions just as much as you do, but I can't just assume the worst."

"Why? Because Norris is a longtime friend of yours? You just don't want it to be true."

"This isn't about what I want or don't want," Besserman said. "I took this job because I care about this country and protecting innocent civilians as well as government interests. And while they sometimes clash, I'm adamant about clinging to my moral bearings. I would never look the other way just because it was politically expedient to do so. You have to believe me."

"Then you should've never threatened me."

Besserman sighed. "I'm sorry about *warning* you, okay? I never threatened you. I only warned you to be careful about what you make public as well as told you about how aggressive politicians are in this town about initiating litigation. You apparently took it in a different manner than I intended the comment to be made altogether. And I think that's what has fueled some of this misunderstanding."

"You're just calling this a misunderstanding?" Feller scoffed. "A *misunderstanding*? A misunderstanding is when you tell me to turn at the next traffic light and I instead wait to turn at the one after that because I thought you meant the traffic light after next. I didn't misunderstand what you said at all."

"If you think I was threatening you, you actually did. And instead of simply publishing what you knew, you exacerbated my comment until it sounded like I was guaranteeing you'd be pushing up daisies six feet underground l if you dared to publish what you had learned. Clearly, you misunderstood what I said."

Feller shrugged. "Well, what's done is done. And it'll be a refrain that will follow you the rest of your life as you wonder about what could've been of your career if you hadn't been so overbearing."

"I never look back," Besserman said, shaking his head. "It's a terrible way to live."

"That's about to change."

Before either of them could utter another word, Secret Service agents stormed down the steps, weapons drawn.

"What's this?" Besserman asked as he looked at Feller.

The political blogger stared slack-jawed at the men as they approached. "What do you think you're doing?"

The man leading the group ignored Feller's question and instead looked directly at Besserman. "The president needs to see you."

Feller glared at Besserman. "Nice. Just bring the Secret Service along and have them listen in to try and get me to say something incriminating. You're probably wearing a wire, aren't you?"

Besserman shook his head. "I have no idea what this is about."

The Secret Service agent put his hand on Besserman's back. "I already told you what this is about. The president needs to see you immediately."

"This is bullshit," Feller said. "I'm gonna make your situation worse than you ever imagined."

"Sir," the Secret Service agent said, ignoring Feller and eyeing Besserman, "we have a car waiting for you. We need to go."

Feller spun and kicked one of the agents in his knee. As he fell toward the ground, Feller grabbed the man's gun. Two other agents drew their weapons, but Feller didn't blink.

"I warned you, Director," Feller said. "You're going to live the rest of your life looking back at this moment."

This time when Feller shoved the gun under his chin, the sound that followed wasn't a hollow click. He collapsed on the ground.

One of the agents knelt beside Feller's body and pulled his phone out of his pocket. He swiped a few times before wiping it clean and replacing it inside his pocket.

"Now we've got another mess to clean up," the agent said.

"I'll take the director back to the White House," the lead agent said. "The rest of you take care of this. Mr. Feller just made our jobs a whole lot easier."

"What a shame," the other agent said as he looked at Feller. "Hard to believe this guy was having an affair with Senator Randolph's wife."

Besserman furrowed his brow. "Wait. What?"

"Sorry," the man said. "I shouldn't have said anything. Good luck with the president, sir."

The lead agent nudged Besserman toward the stairs, but he took one step before stopping. "I'm sorry, but what is this all about?"

"You'll find out soon enough, sir. But the president doesn't like to be kept waiting, so we need to go."

Besserman sighed as he glanced back one final time at Feller's body.

We could've worked together.

CHAPTER
THIRTY-TWO

LOS ANGELES

MORGAN MAY STARED at her bookshelf in the corner of her office, reading the titles off the spine. She needed a diversion, something to draw inspiration from as she faced an important decision—how to handle the spy in her midst. Charles Dickens' classic, *A Tale of Two Cities*, jumped out at her. The tension she felt mirrored that of the book's opening line. She had finally solved who the spy was in her office, but beyond the walls of the Magnum Group, the world seemed to be falling apart—and she felt powerless to stop it.

She selected the book off the shelf and eased into the chair behind her desk. After reading a few pages, she leaned back and concocted a plan. Her uncle's words rang in her ear: "If you want to land a big one, you need to catch a little one first."

There was no doubt that Nick Slavitt was a little one. The fact that he was passed over for numerous promotions while serving at the CIA should've been a sign that he wasn't exactly the kind of agent cut out for the Magnum Group. But he came highly recommended by one of the generals at the Pentagon, one who was linked to The Alliance before he drowned in a boating accident a few weeks after she hired Slavitt. Though the coincidences piled up, she ignored them, and obviously at her own peril. However, she was determined to turn her questionable judgment into a big victory.

May rehearsed her speech for Slavitt once more in her head before summoning him.

Ten minutes later, Slavitt knocked on her door and entered. His blue tie was loosened around his neck, the sleeves to his white oxford shirt partially rolled up. However, his sandy brown hair was parted from the side, hardly a strand out of place.

"You wanted to see me?" Slavitt asked as he approached her desk.

She nodded and gestured to the chair across from him. "Please, have a seat."

After he sat down, he crossed his legs and clicked his pen repeatedly. "What do you need me to do?"

"Nick, it's not always about doing something," Morgan said. "Sometimes we just need to talk and make sure we're on the same page."

Morgan studied him closely, almost certain that she noted sweat beading on his forehead.

"Of—of course, I just, uh, I don't know," he stammered. "I usually don't get called here unless you have an important assignment for me."

"And this time is no different," she said. "But it's more of a general assignment than a specific mission."

Slavitt leaned forward. "Oh?"

"Look, I know our plan at Leavenworth was a setback and we're still hunting down leads to The Alliance. But I thought some of your ideas have been ingenious ones, so I'd like to offer you a promotion."

"Seriously?"

"I never joke around when I say things like that," Morgan said.

"Yeah, but I—"

She held up her index finger, silencing him. "Don't try to talk me out of it. I've contemplated this for a while now and recognized that we need someone to head up a task forced dedicated to pursuing The Alliance. How does that sound?"

"That sounds fantastic."

"Good. I was hoping you'd say that. And on that note, I want you to start assembling a team of analysts to dig deeper into everyone with suspected ties to the organization. Then I'd like for you to produce a dossier detailing who might be the next logical targets for us to pursue. Can you handle that for me?"

"Absolutely," Slavitt said, sitting upright in his chair as he uncrossed his legs. "When do you need it by?"

"Have it on my desk in a week."

She put her head down and began perusing several documents stacked in corner of her desk. But Slavitt hadn't moved.

Morgan glanced up at him over the top of her glasses. "Are you waiting for something else?"

"No, I think that's it."

She waved dismissively at him with the back of her hand. "Then run along. You have plenty of work ahead of you."

"Thank you, Director May," he said. "I appreciate the opportunity."

Morgan offered a thin smile. "Don't disappoint me."

Slavitt stood before walking swiftly toward the door. Morgan watched him pump his fist outside the glass walls to her office, almost skipping back toward his cubicle.

"Don't get too comfortable," she said. "You're just the little bait."

———

NICK SLAVITT WENT to his office briefly before grabbing his cell phone and wandering out one of the ground floor exits. He meandered through Paramount Studios, the quasi theme park above the home of the Magnum Group facility. While many of the agents at the company complained about the fact that there was a massive movie set above them, he rather enjoyed it. The unique setting gave him the opportunity to walk around and get fresh air without anyone giving him a second glance. A spy in plain sight was the best kind of spy, even if he never actually had an assignment within the park.

He reached into his pocket and activated a device that scrambled his conversation to any prying ears, friendly or otherwise. Then he entered a number into his phone.

"I told you never to call me from this number while you're still on the premises," the man on the other end of the line scolded. "It's not safe."

"Sorry, but I couldn't wait to tell you this," Slavitt said.

"It better be pretty damn important."

"It is," he said. "I just got promoted to heading up the task force to investigate The Alliance."

"That's not good."

"What do you mean?" Slavitt asked. "It's incredible. I'll be able to protect you from anything now and run interference that will keep the feds—and everyone here—guessing for months if not years."

The man said nothing.

"Well, aren't you going to congratulate me?" Slavitt asked after the long period of silence.

"Congratulate you for what? Being an idiot? I'll pass."

"What are you talking about?" Slavitt asked. "Didn't you just hear me?"

"They're playing you like a fiddle, Nick. The next thing you know, they're going to ask you to produce some names."

"You can help me with that, planting evidence and everything. Then we can get rid of some people we don't trust and deal with the remaining predictable few."

The man growled. "You're walking into a trap. If it's still not too late, I'd march right back into her office and decline the offer."

"But if I do that, she might see that as a sign of weakness and fire me altogether."

"True, but that's a small risk to take. She might see you as assertive if you turn it down. And then if she offers it to you again, drive a hard bargain with what you'll need to be successful. However, I don't think you're in her long-term plans."

"What's that supposed to mean?"

"Sleep on it," the man said. "We'll be in touch."

Slavitt loosened his tie some more and looked skyward. There wasn't a cloud in the sky for as far as he could see in any direction. Just moments ago, that's how he felt. But after his brief conversation with one of the higher-ups with The Alliance, Slavitt realized dark clouds were brewing in the distance.

He hoped his gut feeling was wrong. It made him sick to think that it wasn't.

CHAPTER
THIRTY-THREE

SEATTLE, WASHINGTON

HAWK AND ALEX didn't have the benefit of the Magnum Group jet and were forced to head back to the airport to catch a commercial flight back to Los Angeles. With Kira Gusev out of the picture, Hawk considered the possibility that they'd been wrong about her. Hawk posited to Alex that perhaps Kira was just a scared college student, trying to survive any way she could. While Alex agreed the idea was plausible, she wasn't convinced it was accurate.

"She'd never even had a parking ticket," Alex said as she settled into her chair at the gate. "I mean, who lives a life that clean that they don't at least register some mild offense at some point in their life? Kira didn't have a blemish on her record in Russia or during her time at USC. That's almost inconceivable to me."

"It's odd, yes, but that doesn't mean it's contrived," Hawk said.

Alex leaned close to Hawk and spoke in a hushed tone. "Did you forget about the fact that she stole a car as well as wired her own to blow up in the middle of downtown Albuquerque? That doesn't exactly fall into the *scared college student* category in my book."

Hawk nodded. "That's true. I'm just trying to look at this from all possible angles. For example, what if Gusev sent us on a wild goose chase, knowing his daughter would run and could draw our attention away from the cell?"

"That'd actually be an impressive move on his part," Alex said. "He'd have to be thinking several steps ahead and have a very benign trigger phrase with his daughter."

"But we were right there," Hawk said. "He never said anything that seemed remotely suspicious. It was just a father and a daughter having a conversation."

Alex took a swig from her water bottle. "Or she's exactly who we think she is—the leader of this sleeper cell. If the Russians were slipped into the country, they may have been kept from one another intentionally, so she's the only one who could link them all together. She had to get out of there fast before she was taken into custody for questioning. We couldn't keep her for any potential crime, but she'd be under extreme scrutiny and her ability to activate the cell would be severely hampered."

"That would explain why she ran," Hawk said.

"Make no mistake—she knew something was going down. The only thing we don't know was if her father gave her marching orders or not. And if so, what were they?"

"Whatever they were, I doubt he meant for her to go out like she did. She might have had some training, but she didn't appear to have any field experience."

"Unless she was doing this stuff when she was fourteen."

"I wouldn't put anything past Gusev."

Hawk checked his watch. "A half-hour before boarding begins. I'm going to the restroom."

He got up and walked down the busy concourse, a mix of travelers walking leisurely to their gate and rushing frantically to get there. Before he reached the men's room, he looked up at a television airing a news report about the Colorado River drying up.

More doom and gloom.

Just as he was about to take a hard right for the restroom, the report stopped and the anchor began talking excitedly over dramatic bumper music.

"We have a breaking news report," the man said. "There's been an apparent—"

The screen went dark and Hawk spun around to see if other televisions in the vicinity had also gone blank. Every single one of them was down.

What the hell?

He rushed back over to Alex. "Did you see all the televisions went out?"

She nodded. "That can't be good."

Seconds later, Hawk's phone buzzed with a call from Director May.

"What's going on?" Hawk said as he answered.

"What makes you think something's happening?" she asked.

"I'm in the Seattle airport and every TV screen just went blank," Hawk said. "I know there's generally only one reason that happens."

"Two actually," Morgan said. "An airplane crash or a terrorist attack."

"Please tell me it's the first one."

"We all wish that was the case, but I'm afraid not."

Hawk cursed under his breath.

"In the last half-hour, six Greyhound buses have exploded, killing nearly everyone on board," Morgan continued. "So far, there have been at least two hundred and fifty confirmed casualties."

"Were the bombers on board?"

"That's not something we know at this point. Right now, it's a big challenge just to get any information. Homeland is handling it, as they should. But all the major agencies have been looped in to what's going down and they want us to cooperate in the arrest and capture of the group responsible."

"This has to be the work of the Russian cell, don't you think?" Hawk asked. "The timing just seems too coincidental."

"We don't want to jump to conclusions, but that'd be my first analysis of the situation. Usually before an attempted attack, we hear some chatter from agents embedded within the organization or over the different communication platforms. But this just came out of nowhere—and that's almost exactly how sleeper cells operate. Given that this was the only one we knew about and we are actively hunting them, I don't think it's a stretch to think that this cell was activated ahead of schedule to ensure that it caused sufficient destruction and chaos."

"Do you want us back in L.A.?" Hawk asked.

"Well, here's where things get really interesting," Morgan said. "I got a call five minutes ago from the Washington Highway Patrol officer working the scene of the accident. I had alerted the Seattle patrol post that the woman involved in the accident was likely a fugitive and we wanted confirmation of death or life."

"There's no way she could've survived that crash," Hawk said.

"The woman in the driver's seat didn't," Morgan said. "Apparently, she was already dead before the crash."

Hawk knit his brow. "Wait. She was already dead? Do you mean she had a heart attack or something?"

"No, I mean she was shot in the head."

"Well, then—" Hawk stopped, trying to compute the information.

"The officer also found a synthetic mask on the woman, the kind used to throw off facial recognition software."

"So, what are you concluding? Kira Gusev wasn't in the crash?"

"Nope," Morgan said. "It looks like she was controlling the car remotely from all the way across the country."

"Come again?"

"At this point, my best guess is that she murdered the Tesla owner, put a mask over her head to make her look like Kira, and then programmed the car to drive to Seattle, knowing we would see it and go after it. Meanwhile, we just got a hit on Kira Gusev in Washington, D.C."

"So, she's alive," Hawk said, nodding his head subtly. "That's not what I expected."

"It's not what any of us expected, but if she's the one orchestrating these attacks, we need to apprehend her as quickly as possible," Morgan said. "Homeland is coordinating the efforts to locate the sleeper cell agents based off the pattern of attacks, but since they're buses, their point of origin and multiple stops along the way make this a difficult case to crack in such a short period of time."

"And that leaves us to hunt down Kira?"

"You got it. I'm sending you and Alex everything else we've collected about her since you started your search as well as all the information we've gathered on these attacks. There's a flight leaving for Washington that starts boarding in ten minutes three gates down. I've already purchased you tickets and want you to continue your search for her there."

"We're heading that way now," Hawk said, gesturing for Alex to follow him.

"And Hawk?"

"Yeah?"

"Be careful," Morgan said. "Kira has already proven to be a worthy adversary at best and a damn good spy at worst."

"Roger that," Hawk said before he hung up.

"You mind telling me what's going on?" Alex said.

Hawk sighed. "I'll tell you everything—and it's bad."

CHAPTER
THIRTY-FOUR

WASHINGTON, D.C.

BESSERMAN GLARED at the Secret Service agent as he opened the backseat door. He nodded toward the walkway, his hands clasped in front of him. After sitting there for a few seconds, Besserman took a deep breath and climbed out of the vehicle.

"Can I leave right now if I want to?" Besserman asked the man.

"I wouldn't advise that, sir. The president gave us specific instructions to bring you back to the White House. But if you'd like to take your chances, it's a free country."

"This doesn't feel free."

The agent smiled. "If it wasn't, someone would've probably already put a bullet in your head."

"Are you warning me about what's in store for me?"

"Just fulfilling my mission, sir," the agent said, gesturing toward the walkway. "Now, shall we?"

Besserman paused for a moment before moving in the direction he was urged by the agent. He led the CIA director into the White House, skipping the customary body search and metal detector ritual, and downstairs into a waiting room. Once Besserman took a seat, the agent grabbed the door handle.

"Good choice, sir," the agent said before shutting the door.

Over the years, Besserman had discussed plenty of sensitive security issues with Norris. They figured out how to navigate tricky political quagmires and avoid global conflicts. They'd even talked about their families and their futures. But Besserman knew the imminent conversation wasn't going to be anything like that. In all likelihood, he was about to get fired by someone who he'd known since their days in college together. A lifetime of trust had been washed away in one incident—and Besserman still wondered if he was the one at fault. He tried to give Norris the benefit of the doubt and allow the president to clear the air, but he'd been stubborn about it. There had to be a reason, though Besserman wasn't sure why Norris wouldn't just come out and say it. But the president didn't like to be questioned by anyone, a concerning trait by every measure. Holding the highest office in the land only exacerbated Norris's flaw.

Ten minutes passed before Norris finally entered the room behind a part of agents. He gestured for them to go, leaving Norris and Besserman alone.

"If you wanted to talk, you could've just given me a call," Besserman said. "The fact that you had the Secret Service track me down and force me over here is more than disconcerting."

Norris sat down and chuckled as he stroked his chin. "Wanna talk about disconcerting, do you? How about one of my most trusted confidantes turning on me?"

Besserman stared blankly at the president. "I have no idea what you're talking about."

"Oh, you don't?"

"Not a clue. I've been nothing but loyal to you, though my loyalty to this country trumps our friendship."

"So, secretly meeting with a journalist to discuss the contents of stolen footage after flying to Maldives to learn what you could doesn't constitute betrayal to you?"

Besserman shrugged. "Take it however you want, Frank. The fact of the matter is, you wouldn't tell me what I was getting myself into. And I can't very well do my job—one in which keeping secrets is a vital skill—unless you tell me what's going on. We're allies, not enemies. Remember?"

Norris leaned forward and set his jaw. "You went behind my back."

"Maybe I wouldn't have had to do that if you would've told me *to my face* what was on those videos stolen off your hard drive. You're the one who put me in this position. If you want to continue to hide the fact that you've had secret rendezvous with foreign enemy generals, you probably should get someone else for the job."

"Those videos could ruin me politically."

"Then perhaps they should," Besserman said. "The way you want me to protect them leads me to believe that you were doing some shady dealing with the Chinese. A secret here, a prototype there. Maybe you didn't think it was much at the time, but now it makes you look like a traitor—and you should be very concerned what the American people think about that."

Norris sighed. "You've got it all wrong, Bobby. Your conjecture is so far off base, I'm almost gutted that you think I'm capable of that."

"What am I supposed to think when you when you act like you have?"

"Maybe give me the benefit of the doubt? Maybe consider that I haven't changed and that there must be a reason?"

"So, what is your reason for not telling me? Huh? You've got a captive audience and someone who's on your side. Now is as good of a time as any to tell me why you did what you did as well as the truth about your meeting with that Chinese general."

Norris closed his eyes and massaged his temples with his fingers. He groaned before opening his eyes and staring directly at Besserman. "Okay, I'll tell you."

"I'm listening."

"I thought if this ever got out, there'd definitely be a congressional hearing of some sort," Norris said. "And I didn't want you dragged before a bunch of blood-thirsty senators demanding answers where you'd have to lie about what you knew."

"Is this the kind of secret you'd want to lie about?"

Norris shrugged. "No, not really. But politically, the optics are horrible and largely unprovable."

"What do you mean?"

"General Chow is dead. He's the only one who could verify what we discussed. Everyone who knew is gone, except for me. And it sounds pretty damn convenient, at least politically, for me to be the only one alive who knows what we were talking about."

"So, you're saying this conversation was benign?" Besserman asked.

A knock at the door interrupted the men. "Hold that thought," Norris said. "Come in."

A Secret Service agent poked his head inside the room. "Sir, I'm sorry to interrupt you, but there's been a development."

Norris scowled. "A development?"

"Yes," the agent said before glancing at Besserman. "And I think you'll be needed as well, sir."

"What's going on?" Norris asked.

"There's been an attack, sir. You need to move."

CHAPTER
THIRTY-FIVE

LOS ANGELES

NICK SLAVITT EASED his truck into the small clearing near the top of the Inglewood Oil Field. He checked the pin he was sent on his burner phone one final time before putting the car in park. Near the edge of the clearing, a rusty oil derrick pumped slowly. Aside from a few palm trees designed to hide the monstrous hunk of working metal, the area was rather barren. And there wasn't a soul in sight.

Slavitt stepped out of his vehicle and removed his tie. He unbuttoned the top two buttons on his shirt and stretched after the long drive through the city's crippling traffic. Despite Slavitt's long history of secretly serving The Alliance, he'd only met his contact in person once, a man known as Ranger. Most of their communications were handled via mail or burner phones, which were delivered to Slavitt's home each month. But with the news that Slavitt had been elevated to such a high position, he wasn't surprised when Ranger arranged an in-person meeting with him.

Upon realizing that Ranger was late, Slavitt was annoyed before considering why. The Alliance had to be careful, though

Slavitt was a little bit less so once the Magnum Group had announced that they'd figured out who the organization's mole was—and it wasn't him. The "mole" was dead, leaving Slavitt to operate without even a hint of suspicion. That didn't mean he shouldn't still be careful, but he wasn't nearly as stressed as he had been. But Ranger always took extra precautions and likely wanted to make sure that nobody was following Slavitt, even though he knew it wasn't necessary.

Slavitt checked his watch and surveyed the area again before looking down at the dirt. He knelt and picked up a rock before throwing it at a tree. But the rock missed, curving left and clanking off the chain-link fence surrounding the derrick.

"Good thing your intel is better than your aim," said a man with a gruff voice.

Slavitt turned around and saw Ranger, hands in his pockets as he strode toward him. Ranger wore a pair of aviator sunglasses and was working over a piece of gum, the scar along his left jaw moving in tandem with it. With his hands plunged into his black leather jacket, Ranger appeared at ease. As the corners of Ranger's mouth turned upward in a slight smile, any angst Slavitt had about the meeting vanished.

"How do you know I wasn't aiming at the spot I hit?" Slavitt asked. "You're assuming I missed my mark."

Ranger arched his eyebrows. "I have a gift, and it allows me to know what people are doing, even if they don't. And I happen to know you were aiming at that tree."

Slavitt sighed and raised his hands. "Okay, busted. You got me."

Ranger knelt and selected a rock. He held it open in his hand, showing it to Slavitt.

"Think you can do better?" Slavitt asked.

Ranger nodded subtly. "It's all about the kind of rock you pick. You want to make sure that you find a practical rock, the kind that will get the job done and doesn't decide to go its own way."

Ranger rocked back and fired the rock toward a nearby palm tree, hitting it dead center about six feet off the ground.

"If you make a mistake, it's in choosing the wrong rock," Ranger continued. "Too many rough edges and its trajectory becomes unpredictable."

"Predictability is a good thing, especially when you're taking aim at a target," Slavitt said.

"Exactly, and that's why we didn't strike the van you told us Brad Porter would be in. And while gathering the resources necessary on such a short basis to take out a plane near a heavily-guarded military installation, that was the safest bet. Porter could've been moved at the last minute, potentially exposing you and leading any type of investigation back to me."

Slavitt nodded. "Makes sense. That's why you get paid the big bucks. I'm just the messenger."

"But are you?"

Slavitt furrowed his brow and cocked his head. "Am I what?"

"Are you *just* a messenger? Are you sure you're not being dangled as bait?"

"That's unlikely. The Magnum Group just promoted me, meaning that I'm going to have higher security clearance and access to higher level operations. That's going to be a boon for The Alliance."

Ranger took a step closer to Slavitt before poking him in his chest. "I'm not so sure about that. I think you're endangering all of us."

Slavitt swallowed hard as he realized this conversation had taken a quick turn in a direction that made him uneasy. "What are you trying to say?"

"I warned you," Ranger said. "I told you to keep your head down and just do your job, fly under the radar. But is that what you did? No, you had to make a name for yourself."

Slavitt took a step back. "I thought gaining a higher level of clearance would be good for your efforts. I'm still a relative nobody in the organization."

Ranger put his hands on his hips. "Not if you're getting promotions. You've caught someone's eye. And it's only a matter of time before they look into you."

"And if they did, I'd know all about it."

"They probably already are," Ranger said. "Any organization that's serious would have a dedicated operative surveilling the rest of the team. The only way you'd be safe in that scenario was if you were the one who was in charge of sniffing out moles. And I know for a fact that you aren't or else you would've told me about it already."

"I think you're being overly suspicious," Slavitt said. "If they really didn't trust me, they wouldn't have used my plan on the latest prisoner transfer with Porter. There's no way they would've risked losing an asset."

"You're a fool," Ranger said. "Porter is still alive."

"He survived a plane crash?"

"He was never on the plane," Ranger said as he shook his head and took another step toward Slavitt. "You just don't get it, do you? They're on to you and you have no clue."

"Come on, Ranger," Slavitt said, easing away from his handler. "You're just being paranoid."

"Paranoid, am I?" Ranger said as he walked over toward Slavitt's car. "You think I'm paranoid?"

Ranger produced an electronic wand from his coat pocket and waved it around the car. As he reached the front, the wand beeped. Ranger felt inside the left front fender for a few seconds before holding up a small circular black device. He brushed the dirt off his jeans as he stood up.

"Look familiar?" Ranger asked.

Slavitt shook his head. "How do I know that you didn't just plant that thing in there?"

"Now who's the paranoid one?"

"How do you even know that's from the Magnum Group?"

Ranger looked over the top of his sunglasses at Slavitt. "I

hate to break it to you, but I think you know what kind of rock you are—and you aren't predictable enough for us."

"So, you're just going to cut me loose like that?" Slavitt asked.

Ranger shrugged. "More or less."

"I think you're going to regret this," Slavitt said.

Ranger turned and walked away. "Doubt it."

Slavitt stared in disbelief at Ranger walking away. "You know if it was Magnum that put that tracking device there, they'll know I found it if you don't put it back."

"I doubt they'll care anymore after today."

Slavitt spun on his heels and started walking toward his car. A bullet hit him in the back of the head, and he fell face first into the dirt.

———

RANGER TURNED AROUND and gave a thumbs up to the sniper sitting on a nearby hill. He hustled down to join Ranger before the two men went to work. They loaded Slavitt into his car and set it on fire before rolling it down into a ravine.

"That'll send them a message," Ranger said as he watched the flames engulf Slavitt's car. "Besides, we have other ways of getting to the people at Magnum."

"Good work," the assassin said. "Boss will be pleased."

"He better—and thanks for the tracking device."

The assassin smiled. "He bought it?"

"Who knows," Ranger said. "But it doesn't matter now. He's not our problem and they won't be able to connect him to us either."

CHAPTER
THIRTY-SIX

BARBARA WHEELER CLEARED HER desk and wiped it clean with her hand, sweeping a few stray giblets of paper onto the floor. Aside from her name plate signifying her position as the U.S. Secretary of State, the surface was clean. It was a psychological trick she'd learned from her former boss about what a desk that's completely cleared off conveys to all visitors: Nothing to hide and ultra-commanding. She wanted anyone who sat across from her to understand that she was calling the shots and that other people were doing the grunt work of reading documents and analyzing them—even if that couldn't be further from the truth. But in the game of diplomacy, perceptions were a powerful asset.

Had Wheeler not been so fond of J.D. Blunt, she probably would've never taken on a plucky intern while serving as a U.S. senator from Florida. But Blunt had a charming way about him and convinced her to hire his niece, Morgan May. From the moment Morgan joined Wheeler's staff, the two clashed. Wheeler was idealistic; May was aggressive. If she'd told Morgan once, she'd told her a thousand times: "Morgan, real power in diplomacy isn't leveraging everything you have to get your way. Sometimes, it's what you don't leverage that enables you to ultimately achieve all your objectives and then some. If you aren't patient, you will lose the long game, and there's no shortcut to maintaining peace." Morgan grew to appreciate her boss, eventually developing an affinity for her, even if they still held fast to their methods for achieving the same goals. However, Wheeler wasn't shocked that Morgan chose a different career path. But Wheeler was shocked to receive a call from her former intern requesting assistance in an urgent matter.

"You still need good diplomacy," Wheeler had told Morgan before readily agreeing to help.

As the U.S. Secretary looked over her desk, she dialed her assistant's number and asked her to send in Ilya Fedotov, the Russian ambassador to the U.S. She remained sitting upright behind her desk, fingers templed. He offered a weak smile as he approached her.

"Madam Secretary," he said before sitting in one of the chairs across from her.

"Ambassador Fedotov," Wheeler said with a forced smile. "Thank you for meeting me on such short notice."

"Your message sounded urgent, so how could I refuse?"

Wheeler didn't budge from her position. "I'm sure you've seen the news by now."

"Are you referring to all the exploding buses?"

She nodded. "Quite unfortunate, not to mention unexpected. We pride ourselves on being able to stop terrorist attacks on our own soil."

"No country is an impenetrable fortress, at least that's what I've learned after serving in this role for more than thirty years. And sometimes, your borders seem like an open gate."

Wheeler scowled. "I didn't bring you here to critique our political policies."

Fedotov glanced at his watch. "Well, please do make this

quick. I have a meeting with the ambassador of Turkey in a half-hour."

"Of course," Wheeler said. "I'll get to the point. I wouldn't want to inconvenience you."

"*Spasibo*," Fedotov replied.

Wheeler stood, pushing her chair away with the back of her knees. She paced her office as she spoke. "It has come to our attention recently that a handful of Russian spies have slipped into the country."

"Spies?" Fedotov asked. "We wouldn't sneak spies across your open borders."

"Spoken like a true ambassador," Wheeler said with a wink. "Your qualifiers prevent you from lying, but I know your game."

"I don't believe this is a game," Fedotov said. "I'm simply responding to your accusation."

"It was a statement of fact."

"And I suppose you think I can do something about it?"

"It would be in Russia's best interest if they handled this, especially since we have linked a few of your country's spies to the attacks."

Fedotov shook his head. "That wasn't us. If we ever were to attack your country—which we wouldn't—but suppose we did, we would never go after such small targets. And for what purpose? Just to kill a few random civilians to prove you can do it? That's not how we operate."

"Then how do you operate?"

Fedotov wagged his index finger at Wheeler. "Oh, Madam Secretary, you are a sly one. But I won't fall for your mind games. The Russian government has nothing to hide, especially since we didn't do anything related to that attack."

"How can you be sure?"

"Like you said, I heard about it on the news, knew I was getting called over to the U.S. State Department to discuss this very issue with you, and called my superiors. It's not surprising to me that you asked this exact question, which is why I posed it to him."

"And what did he say?"

"He laughed."

Wheeler squinted. "That's it? He laughed?"

"He used a few choice words before launching into a rant about how American democracy will be the demise of the world. You know, things that would make a diplomatic conversation go sideways."

Wheeler eyed the Russian closely. "I'm all too familiar with people who are incapable of constraining their lips, much less their thoughts."

"Thank you," Fedotov said. "Someone who understands me."

Wheeler stopped in front of Fedotov and leaned back against her desk. "What I don't understand is why you are lying to me."

Fedotov clucked his tongue. "Now, now, Madam Secretary, I would never lie to you. As a diplomat, I'm sure you're aware that our credibility is our most important asset."

"Then I need your helping finding out who's behind these attacks," she said.

"You think I know?"

"It's why you're here, Ilya. I didn't invite you to my office to discuss your feelings on the latest episode of *Law & Order*."

"Guilty," Fedotov said with a grin. "They're always guilty."

"And what about you?"

Fedotov held his hands up in the air. "We didn't do a thing. This is the work of a rogue organization, obviously. But feel free to look into it for yourselves."

"Oh, we already have," Wheeler said. "We were searching for some new answers and thought you might be able to help give them to us."

"What do you want to know? I'll tell you what I can if you promise to get me out of here for my meeting with the Turkish ambassador."

"Deal," Wheeler said. "Now, let's start with this: Who is General Dimitri Gusev?"

Fedotov sighed. "I was afraid of this question."

"Why? Is he a friend of yours?"

"Quite the opposite," Fedotov said. "He went rogue years ago. The FSB tolerated him because he was an extremist in favor of making Russia stronger on the global stage. But he started recruiting agents, paying them likely from all the money he stole while working at the FSB. He was an admired and revered general—but he had his dark side."

"An FSB officer with a dark side?" Wheeler asked with a chuckle. "Now, that's rich."

"Russians are not monsters like you want us to be," Fedotov said. "It's easier for you to hate us if we aren't real. But I can assure you that we're very real and have good reason for doing what we do. However, just like in your government, there are always those who take things too far."

"And in your estimation, General Gusev is one of those people?"

Fedotov nodded. "Without a doubt."

"You realize he's dead, correct?"

"Nothing gets by us, but that is why I expected this call. Gusev was too smart to let you beat him. He was always going to find a way to strike back from the grave."

Wheeler took a deep breath and exhaled slowly as she settled back into her chair behind her desk. "Anything else we should know about Gusev and his sleeper cell?"

"I can't confirm that Gusev was operating a sleeper cell, but I can tell you that the reason he was so dark was thanks to an American military commander, one General Peter Purcell, who years ago murdered Gusev's nephew."

"Murdered him? How come I've never heard of this?" Wheeler asked. "I even helped vet him for his position as the Director of Homeland Security."

"Then you didn't do your job properly."

"What else do you know?"

"I'm sorry, Madam Secretary, but I'm running late for my meeting. But I can assure you that any of the attacks that have occurred today have nothing to do with the Russian government in either an official or an unofficial capacity. I'm sure one of your intelligence agencies can get you up to speed."

"Thank you, Ambassador. I appreciate your candor."

Fedotov smiled before he turned and exited the room.

Wheeler turned and stared out the window, seething at the news she'd just learned. If even Ambassador Fedotov was familiar with the events of the murder of Gusev's nephew, she couldn't conceive that a report detailing General Purcell's actions couldn't have at least been recorded second hand at some point.

Someone has to be covering for Purcell.

Wheeler picked up her phone and dialed Morgan May's number.

"I found out some information for you that you're gonna want to sit down for," Wheeler said.

She proceeded to relay the limited details she'd learned from Fedotov.

"That's troubling," Morgan said. "But it's gotten worse since you've been talking with the Russian ambassador."

"What do you mean? More attacks?"

"Yeah. Three of them, this time on trains during the rush hour commute leaving Washington, New York, and Philadelphia."

Wheeler sighed. "Looks like diplomacy won't be the answer this time."

"Without you, we wouldn't know how to proceed, that is, as long as Fedotov was telling you the truth."

"He was," Wheeler said. "I have no doubt that he was."

"Then we've got one helluva problem on our hands."

CHAPTER
THIRTY-SEVEN

LOS ANGELES

MORGAN MAY ORDERED a triple shot latte from the coffee shop around the corner from her condo before heading into the Magnum Group office. She'd hardly slept a wink and thought 5:30 a.m. was just as good of a time as any to get her day started. The East Coast had been awake from several hours and the hunt for the Mass Transit Bombers, the media's monicker for the group, was underway.

Morgan's phone buzzed with a text message, the third one she'd received since she'd picked up her coffee. She was so early that the Paramount guard was still rubbing his eyes and yawning when she pulled up to the gate.

"Morning, Miss May," he said. "I would say you're here bright and early, but you beat the sun up. Big day today?"

She smiled. "Bigger day than most."

"Well, good luck to you," he said before activating the arm that allowed her to enter.

After returning a friendly wave, she headed straight to the parking deck where she slid into her reserved spot. She hustled down the stairs, refusing to wait for the elevator.

When she walked into the office, she found a bleary-eyed Mia Baumann, the hacker extraordinaire who was now plying her trade for the Magnum Group rather than nefarious people contacting her over the dark web. Mia brushed stray brown tendrils out of her eyes and let out a long breath.

"Been here long?" Morgan asked.

"Never went home," Mia said, offering a thin smile. "I knew I wouldn't be able to sleep until we nailed these bastards."

"You find something?"

Mia nodded. "Hacking into Kira's email account was far more challenging than I thought it would be. I figured she wouldn't use her school email account to run the cell, but she might have used it as a backup for any kind of other email account that she had."

"And?"

"It was easy enough to hack the USC school server and get Kira's password. From there, I got into her account and dug through the emails in her trash. I found one for a gmail account serving as the backup in case she forgot her password. I tried to login to the gmail account and clicked on the option for password recovery. Seconds later, I had a way to reset her email account password and create a new login. That's when I hit the mother lode."

"You have the identities of the entire cell?"

Mia handed Morgan a sheet of paper with the name and contact info for each one. "I even have their burner cells so we can track them that way."

"Excellent work," Morgan said. "I'm going to pass this information along to the appropriate agencies and we'll see what happens."

"Glad I could help," Mia said.

"Go get some sleep."

"Not now," Mia said as she walked away. "There's still the pesky Kira Gusev who needs to be caught. We need to know what she's planning, if anything other than a disappearing act."

According to the document Mia had produced, there were a total of twelve agents in the sleeper cell, which was scattered all across the country. The majority of them were concentrated in the East Coast, but there were two in California and one in Oregon. The one in Houston, Miami, and Columbus had yet to strike, creating an urgency to round them up before it was too late.

After Morgan sent the intel to the FBI and Homeland Security, she leaned back in her chair and wondered how long it would take before arrests started to be made. The response she received from the FBI was that all arrests would be kept secret until every member of the cell had been apprehended. That approach made sense, as it would keep other members from knowing that a nationwide sting was in process. The more the terrorists thought life was normal, the less likely they would be to change their routines.

Morgan sat in her office and watched the text messages roll across her phone with good report after good report. One by one, each member of the Russian sleeper cell was apprehended. And by five o'clock on the East Coast, they were all in custody.

Big Earv walked into Morgan's office as a cable news anchor on the TV against the far wall shared the story that the twelfth and final terrorist had been arrested.

"Good work, Director," Big Earv said. "I think you deserve a raise."

"A leader is only as good as her team," Morgan said with a wink. "And if truth be told, most of this was Mia's doing. She was burning the midnight oil to find out who was involved in all this."

"She found something else out that you need to see," he said.

"Oh?"

"Yeah, come with me and let's talk."

———

PRESIDENT NORRIS ADJUSTED the microphone on the lectern as he waited for the signal that the media was ready to broadcast his remarks. He read over the opening lines a few more times, waiting to deliver what he hoped would become a momentous speech, one that rallied Americans together against a common enemy. It had a been long time since Americans had felt truly united, no matter how much he insisted they were under him as he campaigned. The country had been divided for a long time, but for the first time in a long time, the enemy wasn't their neighbor.

Norris's phone buzzed with a text message. He almost didn't check it, but flipped it over to read it.

Don't do this. It's too soon and there's a chance that there are still more out there.

Norris swiped the text aside, ignoring the warning from the director of the CIA. It was their job to be cautious, but it was the job of the president to be bold and reassuring. And Americans needed a calming assurance after the past thirty-six hours as images from bombed out buses and overturned trains had dominated the country's viewing screens.

He pocketed his phone before he cleared his throat.

"Are we ready?" Norris asked.

"Yes, sir. In three, two, one …" the man pointed at Norris, signaling for him to begin his speech.

"Good evening, fellow Americans. I wish I was speaking under different circumstances, but that's not the hand we were dealt. I would've preferred to be telling you good news about the direction of this country. And I must remind you that there's plenty of encouraging signs in every sector of American society —but Homeland Security has been missing from those conversations over the past couple of days. But this evening, I do have some good news that I wanted to share with you, even before it leaked out to the press."

Norris placed both hands on the side of the lectern, his eyes studying the speech that had been entered into the teleprompter.

"Forget it," Norris said. "I'm not reading what's on that screen. I'm just going to speak from the heart tonight."

He paused and took a deep breath before continuing.

"Twelve violent extremists accused of disrupting our buses and railways, including three who had yet to initiate their attacks, have all been apprehended. And I can promise the families of all the victims out there and the American people that justice will be served. While some of the most talented agents and detectives in the world are out there putting the pieces together as we speak, we do know that all twelve who were actively involved in a secret sleeper cell embedded in this country have been captured. The elevated threat level has been lowered, and we will be getting back to normal today. Although I know for some of you, there will never be a returning back to the way it was. There were husbands, wives, sisters, brothers, mothers, daughters, fathers, sons, cousins, neighbors, and friends—they were all lost in these heinous attacks. And people like them were also lost today. We can't allow this to happen again, which is why I'm reinstating a previously shuttered division of Homeland Security. We're going to make sure that all Americans are free to roam the streets of this great country of ours without fear that a bomb might explode on another train or bus."

Norris's phone buzzed again, alerting him to the arrival of another text message. It was Besserman again.

I told you not to say that. Gusev's daughter is still out there and I think she's more dangerous than we give her credit for. You're going to regret this moment.

Norris wouldn't read that note until he finished, but it didn't matter. He'd already assured the American people that everything would be okay. But deep down, he had an uneasy feeling —and there wasn't anything he could do about it now.

———

MORGAN LOOKED UP from her report to find Mia, wide-eyed and frozen, standing in Morgan's office doorway.

"What is it, Mia? You look like you've seen a ghost."

"We might be seeing plenty of ghosts very soon if Kira Gusev isn't stopped," Mia said.

Morgan motioned for Mia to hand over the stack of papers in her hand. "What do you have there?"

"I finally hacked into Kira's computer."

Morgan eyed Mia closely. "And?"

"I found a set of blueprints that Kira was trying to hide. They're of the Pentagon."

"She's going to blow up the Pentagon."

Morgan slammed her cup onto her desk and then stood. She had to let the proper people know so they could give the order to evacuate the building or else they could have a bigger disaster on their hands.

And given all that had happened in recent days, the last thing Morgan wanted was another crisis.

"Grab your laptop and anything else you might need," Morgan said. "We're all going to Washington."

CHAPTER
THIRTY-EIGHT

WASHINGTON, D.C.

HAWK STRODE PAST the large wooden sign advertising space for lease along the sidewalk leading to the old Phoenix Foundation offices. The two-story concrete building wasn't pretty to look at, drab and gray. It wasn't in the heart of the city either, making it certain to be a casualty in an era of bigger and better and closer. But Hawk wasn't complaining at the moment. They needed a place to base their operations—and one that needed to be separate from any other government intelligence agencies.

Morgan told Hawk that she wanted to remain in the shadows as much as possible, even if Robert Besserman was intent on utilizing the Magnum Group. And while the FBI and Homeland Security had taken the lead on the hunt for the Russian sleeper cell and Kira Gusev, the CIA remained very much involved as the two agencies shared intel. Besserman had been given a small leadership role since the CIA had a better grasp on how Russian-trained agents behaved in the field. It wasn't much, but it gave him an opportunity to influence the hunt for Kira—and that meant he could loop the Magnum Group in.

Hawk keyed in the code on the security panel before the door clicked, allowing him to enter the building. He used a rock to prop the door open.

"Find me a good work station," Alex said. "You probably know which one I prefer."

Once inside, Hawk found most of the desks just where he remembered them being, only covered with large white sheets. He grabbed the corners of one and yanked hard. Dust swirled in the air as the office furniture was exposed.

He then went upstairs and settled on J.D. Blunt's old office for Alex. After exposing all the furniture, he wadded up the sheets and tossed them into a closet. Then he hustled back downstairs to help Alex with her gear.

"This is like old times," Alex said.

Hawk scanned the area before slinging Alex's laptop bag over his shoulder. "Except no Blunt. He's what I associate with this place the most. It certainly won't feel the same to me."

"You were hardly ever here anyway," she said. "But I agree. Blunt was what made this organization what it was, what it eventually became and is now today."

"Don't get too sentimental," said a woman behind them.

Hawk spun to see Morgan May lugging a box loaded with laptops and other computer accessories.

"You two ready to get to work?" Morgan asked.

Alex nodded as she put down her box on the desk.

"But not here," Morgan said. "This is my office now. As I recall, your office was a couple of doors down the hall on the right."

"This was my big chance," Alex said as she snapped her fingers.

Morgan winked. "Not today."

Hawk helped Alex with her things back to her old office before answering calls for help from Big Earv, Mia, and Dr. Z. Mia was struggling to keep from dropping a carton, which had several books stacked on top. He grabbed a few things to steady her balance before turning his attention to Dr. Z, who was pulling a small wagon behind him.

"Dr. Z, there is a small lab here," Hawk said as he gave him a hand.

Dr. Z stopped and pushed his glasses up the bridge of his nose. "But it's not *my* lab. I don't work like everyone else."

"I'm well aware," Hawk said. "But maybe you wouldn't have had to bring all of this."

Dr. Z twirled his cane before slamming the tip hard onto the ground. Two blades ejected from the sides as he whipped the cane toward Hawk, stopping at the last second.

"Whoa there," Hawk said. "It was just a suggestion to make your life easier."

Dr. Z stroked his scraggly white beard. "*I* make my life easier by what I design and build, thank you very much. If you think I can't handle a small red wagon, just remember this demonstration of my hand-to-hand combat skills."

"Using a cane with blades is hardly—" Hawk said before stopping himself. "You know, never mind. Thank you for coming, Dr. Z. I can hardly wait to see what you've concocted for us."

Dr. Z smiled. "Have you ever seen a 65-year-old man cut a backflip?"

"I hardly see how that's useful to me," Hawk said.

The moment Hawk got the words out of his mouth, his jaw went slack as he watched Dr. Z vault into the air and perform a backflip.

"What do you think?" Dr. Z asked as he walked back over to Hawk.

"That cane is just a prop, isn't it?" Hawk asked.

Dr. Z chuckled. "You're probably too young to remember this, but there used to be a commercial for a pair of sneakers and the tagline was 'It's gotta be the shoes.' Well, that's the case here."

"Shoes or no shoes, you're in surprisingly good shape to be able to land that," Hawk said.

"I used to be a gymnast a long time ago," Dr. Z said. "So, maybe I'm cheating a little bit. But back in the day, five-foot-four was still too short to play football—and I hated baseball. It was either gymnastics or a horse jockey. And I wasn't fond of riding horses. But I always loved heights."

"Feeling like you were missing out being so close to the ground?" Hawk asked before whispering. "Spoiler alert: It's not that much different up here."

Dr. Z laughed. "Perhaps I did feel that way. I certainly compensated in other ways and explored things I probably never would have otherwise."

"Such as?"

"I flew powered hang gliders for a while. Hands down the best way to see the world."

Hawk nodded. "You're like an onion, Dr. Z—so many layers to you. But for what it's worth, I'm still impressed that you landed that flip, aided by modern technology or not. Now, there's only one question: When do I get a pair of those shoes?"

Dr. Z shook his head. "Still a lot of kinks to work out between now and then, but I might have something else for you in my wagon here once we figure out what your mission is."

"I look forward to seeing it," Hawk said.

Dr. Z stroked his beard. "In due time."

Over the next half-hour, the Magnum team worked diligently to get their system online and connected to the vast resources of the FBI and CIA. Homeland Security had been dispatched to secure the Pentagon, yet found no signs of any explosives planted around or under the building. The empty search drew sharp criticism of Besserman from other intelligence officials, but he refused to relent to the pressure to say where he got his tips, insulating the Magnum Group and keeping their participation in the effort a secret.

Morgan entered Alex's office, exasperation evident on her face. "Anything new yet?"

Hawk shook his head. "Alex found a few hits of her on various CCTV feeds, but they're so old that it's not really giving us much. If I had to bet, she's probably going around the city and appearing in different spots just to frustrate us. Because if it's not clear to you and everyone else by now, we're not exactly dealing with a novice. There's little doubt in my mind that Kira is a trained pro—and more than a viable threat."

"Yes," Morgan said. "And one we can't talk about now either, thanks to President Norris telling the world that we captured every cell member."

"For the sake of potentially thousands of innocent people, let's prove Norris right."

"And how exactly are we going to do that?" Morgan said. "Because I'm totally open to suggestions right now."

"I've got a suggestion," Alex said. "We just got a hit a few seconds ago near the national mall."

"Kira?"

Alex nodded. "But that's not all. There's also a report of a dirigible drifting over the Potomac."

"A dirigible?" Morgan asked. "Let's just shoot it down."

"I would advise against that," Hawk said.

Morgan squinted as she peered over Alex's computer at the computer screen. "How come?"

Hawk sighed. "You have no idea what's inside of it. And we won't be able to without sending a drone up next to it."

"According to this interagency bulletin I just received, the FBI is already scrambling one up to it to peek inside," Alex said. "Look."

She pointed at the screen where a small drone zipped toward the dirigible, which was unmanned and a tenth of the size of most hot air balloons. Once the drone moved closer, the dirigible emitted a smoke, preventing the drone from getting an image of what was inside the bucket.

"We could just shoot it down and let it fall into the Potomac River," Morgan said.

"Stop suggesting that," Hawk said. "It's too dangerous and you know it. There could be a dirty bomb in there, and the last thing we want is for it to detonate over the city. That would be catastrophic."

"I know we're all acting like we have no clue where this thing is headed, but I think we all know it's going straight to the Pentagon," Morgan said. "And if we do don't something quick, it could destroy our central command, making us very susceptible to a foreign attack."

"I'm not sure a foreign attack is the end game here, based on what we know," Hawk said. "We really just need to get that dirigible down safely. But it's moving so slow that we have time to handle this carefully."

"I understand that, but you're not giving me any viable options here," Morgan said, her voice tinged with a growl.

Dr. Z tapped his cane on the door to Alex's office as he entered. "Did I hear you talking about needing an idea to see what's inside that dirigible floating over the city?"

Hawk eyed Dr. Z closely. "You got a pair of shoes that will make me fly?"

"Hardly, Agent Hawk. This is the real world and I still have to work within the confines of physics and the law of gravity. No, I have something more traditional in the way of flight."

"A rocket booster?" Hawk asked, his eyes wild with excitement.

"Traditional—a powered hang glider," Dr. Z said. "And I know just the place to get one."

"Wait a minute," Hawk said. "How exactly am I supposed to stop that thing from a hang glider?"

"Don't worry," Dr. Z said. "I've got the device to do just that. It's not as flashy as my bouncy shoes, but it will get the job done."

"Will we have time to do this?" Morgan asked.

"That dirigible is moving very slow," Alex said. "Depending on how fast Hawk can get off the ground—"

"I'll make sure it happens lickety-split," Dr. Z said. "But we need to hurry."

Morgan, who'd already been on the phone informing Besserman what they planned to do, held up her hand. "Wait a minute."

"We don't have time to wait," Dr. Z said.

Morgan scowled, her hand still in the air. The rest of the team stood and stared at her for a moment, wondering what was happening.

"I understand," she said. "Tell him I think that's a big mistake."

She hung up and looked at Dr. Z. "The hang glider is out," she said. "The president doesn't want this thing getting any more attention right now."

Alex's mouth fell slack-jawed. "Any more attention? How much attention does he think a bomb exploding over the Pentagon is going to get? It'll be non-stop for months, if not years."

Morgan shrugged. "Don't shoot the messenger. I lodged my complaint."

"Innocent people are going to die," Alex said.

"I know," Morgan said. "But my hands are tied, especially since the airspace over Washington is controlled by the federal government. If you go up there, you'll likely get shot down without authorization."

Hawk grabbed his jacket and put on his sunglasses. He looked at Alex, who gave him a knowing nod. "We can convince him it was the right thing to do after the fact. In the meantime, it's time to ride."

CHAPTER
THIRTY-NINE

BAILEY'S CROSSROADS, VIRGINIA

GUNNER MAXWELL STOPPED his inspection of the canvas on one of his hang gliders and looked up as he heard the roar of car engines growing closer. He spotted an SUV speeding toward his hangar. Curious about the vehicle's obvious urgency, he walked toward the opening and didn't flinch as the SUV skidded to a stop a few feet away.

An older man climbed out of the driver's side and didn't waste any time with introductions.

"Gunner Maxwell?" the man asked.

Maxwell smiled. "In the flesh and—"

"Dr. Zachary Levinson. And we are in dire need of your powered hang glider services," Dr. Z said.

"Dire need? Well, just slow down a minute, partner. We don't operate like a McDonald's out here. We have mountains of paperwork to fill out."

"This is an emergency, and the lives of thousands of people could be at stake, maybe even more," Dr. Z said.

"Sound serious," Maxwell said. "You mind telling me a little bit more about this emergency since I haven't heard about anything like this on the news?"

"You won't hear anything like this on the news," said another man who got out of the passenger side. He was sporting a pair of sunglasses and chewing a piece of gum as he sized up Maxwell.

"That makes me even more suspicious," Maxwell said.

"J.D., more or less, told me you'd say that," the younger man said.

"J.D.? As in J.D. Blunt?"

He nodded. "The man, the myth, the legend."

"And the shyster," Maxwell said. "He stiffed me five hundred bucks the last time he came out to visit me."

"Can we overlook that offense?" the doctor said. "We're willing to pay ten times your regular rate if you can help us get in the air ASAP."

Maxwell scowled. "You guys look like feds. And if you were that good of friends with J.D., he would've warned you that I was a hard sell."

"Who's to say he didn't?" the younger man asked. "J.D. never backed down from a challenge."

Maxwell chuckled. "I miss that old bastard—and my five hundred bucks. But I'm closing up shop for the day. Come back in the morning and—"

Hawk offered his hand. "Brady Hawk, and this is Dr. Levinson, and it's a pleasure to meet you. And while it's entirely possible that you misunderstood just how quickly we need to get up in the air, I'm going to put it this way: If we aren't up in the air within ten minutes, thousands of innocent people could die."

Maxwell grunted. "Innocent people? Nobody's really innocent."

"Can we debate your philosophical positions some other time?" Hawk asked. "I really don't want anyone to needlessly die today because they were in the wrong place at the wrong time."

"Fine," Maxwell said as he wiped the grease off his fingers with a rag. "What do you need?"

"We need a powered hang glider," the doctor said.

"And where are you planning on going with it?"

"Why does that matter?" Levinson asked.

"For starters, I need to know how much fuel to put in the gas tank; otherwise, Mother Nature will be powering you all the way to the ground on a very short flight. And I don't want to have to retrieve you from somewhere else."

"We're flying over Washington," Hawk said.

"No can do," Maxwell said. "That's federal airspace and some fighter jet will put you down faster than you can say, 'No new taxes'."

"We'll buy you a fleet of new ones if we lose this one," Hawk said. "Besides, I doubt we're going to have any trouble given the objective of my mission."

Maxwell nodded. "Are you guys spooks?"

"Something like that," Hawk said. "Look, I'm willing to take the risk—and there's no risk for you. And on top of that, you'll be helping thousands of innocent people survive an unwarranted attack."

Maxwell rubbed his chin and thought for a moment. "J.D. did speak very highly of one of his favorite young agents, though you don't look so young."

"I was probably the last time you saw him," Hawk said.

"Okay, okay. I'll help you," Maxwell said. "Just give me a second and I'll get you going."

———

TEN MINUTES LATER, Hawk was preparing to take off as the engine sputtered to life.

Dr. Z handed him a small gray device about the size of a ring box. "Get close to the dirigible and drop this in the basket. This will prohibit any radio transmissions between someone on the ground and the balloon. You've only got one shot, so don't miss."

Hawk saluted Dr. Z before waiting until he backed away beyond the wingspan of the hang glider. Then Hawk eased onto the accelerator, and the aircraft started to rumble across the airfield. When he got airborne, he banked hard to the right and headed straight for Washington.

"How am I looking, Alex?" Hawk asked over the coms.

"You'd be looking much better if you weren't hovering that high off the ground," she said.

"I'll be down soon enough, but I need you to help me get to my target."

"Roger that," she said. "I'm tracking the location of the dirigible via GPS, so I just sent an app to your phone that will help you see the target's real-time location."

"Got it," Hawk said. "Thanks."

"Good luck, honey."

Hawk checked the coordinates and set a course for the dirigible. He hummed along for a few minutes until he crossed the Potomac River and entered the airspace above Washington, D.C. Pulling out his binoculars, he scanned the skyline for the target. A few long seconds passed before he finally identified it.

"I've got the target in sight," Hawk said over the coms.

"That's not all you've got in sight," Alex said.

"What do you mean?" he asked as he looked out both sides of the glider and then checked his six.

"Marine helicopters are heading straight toward you."

"What the—oh, just come on. This is ridiculous."

"Agreed," she said. "But you knew this was a very real possibility."

Hawk cursed as he figured that the helicopters would easily reach him before the dirigible, realizing he may not even get a chance to disable the dirigible.

"Alex, think you can help me out?" Hawk asked. "Maybe get me a direct line to the special agent in charge of this operation or a military commander who can get those birds turned in another direction before they make a horrible mistake."

"I'm on it," she said.

————

MORGAN MAY FIELDED a call from a number she was all too familiar with.

"Please hold for the President of the United States," a woman said.

Morgan drummed her fingers on her desk, ready to absorb the tongue-lashing from Norris. It was something her uncle had prepared her for if she was so intent on taking Hawk back. "He has that effect on people in power," Blunt had warned her at the time. And now she was getting to deal with the fallout for the first time.

"Morgan, I thought my office was clear about how we were going to handle the threat," Norris said.

"Yes, very clear, Mr. President."

"Then why am I hearing reports about someone in a hang glider heading on a collision course with the dirigible?"

"Because it's Brady Hawk, sir. And I authorized him to do so."

"Damnit, Morgan. I'm the President of the United States. You don't pull this shit with me."

"With all due respect, sir, your team didn't have a plan, if you don't consider a wait-and-see approach a plan. If so, it's one that could have disastrous consequences."

"We're going to shoot him down," Norris said.

"That's not a good idea, sir. If we don't get that bomb on the ground and in the hands of someone who knows how to disarm it, that bomb might still detonate."

"Right now, the dirigible is flying relatively unnoticed over the city. But if some nut in a hang glider gets near it, then who knows what kind of questions it will unleash."

"Stop worrying about your precious re-election and do the right thing in this situation," Morgan said.

"I am," Norris said. "I have my reasons for why I'm doing what I'm doing. Now, I'm not going to ask you again. Order Agent Hawk back to wherever the hell he took off from before he gets shot out of the sky."

"Shooting a lost hang glider out of the sky is definitely going to get you a lot of questions, maybe even some of the kind you don't like to be asked," Morgan said.

"He's got one minute to turn around or else we will engage," Norris said before hanging up.

Morgan sucked in a long breath through her teeth. "Alex, do you think you can talk Hawk into coming back?"

Alex winced and shook her head. "No. Why?"

Morgan sighed. "If he doesn't return to the airfield immediately, Norris is going to have him shot down."

CHAPTER
FORTY

HAWK STEADIED the glider as he closed in on the dirigible. He glanced at the ground around a thousand feet below. Before he took off, Maxwell had warned him not to go much higher than that, but the target was just above him at a height of about twelve hundred feet. Hawk determined to remain at Maxwell's maximum recommended height until he moved within a hundred feet of the dirigible. By his calculations, that was about two minutes away. And the Marine helicopters were certain to reach him before then.

"Alex," Hawk said, shouting on the coms, "you made any progress yet on getting these choppers off my tail?"

"Still working on it," she said.

"I've got a parachute and can abandon this thing if they fire."

"It'd be wise to be ready to jump out ASAP. If we can't get the White House to see things our way, you won't have any other options."

Hawk unbuckled his lap belt as he continued to check his six. Then he glanced over the edge. The dirigible's trajectory placed it directly over the Potomac River, but it had straightened out and was heading directly toward the Pentagon located along the west bank.

He couldn't hear the beat of the heavy rotors behind him, but he could feel it in his chest. The helicopters were getting closer and he was running out of time.

"Alex, any news?" he asked.

"Still talking with the White House, but no indication yet of which way they're going to go."

Hawk placed his hand on the throttle and tried to push it farther forward. But it was already opened up all the way.

"Come on, girl," Hawk said aloud as he patted the control bar. "Give me a little extra right now."

But Hawk felt a strong gust, making the aircraft dip about fifty feet as it slowed down.

"Come on, Alex. I need to know something."

———

MORGAN MAY SCREAMED at Norris's chief of staff Emma Washburn as she fielded the call intended for the president.

"There's no time for your bureaucratic bullshit, Emma," Morgan said. "I need to speak to the president right now."

"He's in a meeting right now with several of his security advisers," Emma said. "I can have him call you right back when he's done."

"I don't care if he's meeting with the Pope right now, you drag him into the hallway and hand him the damn phone."

"Morgan, I understand you—"

"You don't understand anything, much less have a clue what he's doing. He's threatening to shoot down one of our country's best black ops agents, who coincidentally is trying to save the lives of possibly thousands of innocent Americans. Get him right now."

A half-minute later, Norris was on the phone.

"This better be good," Norris said with a growl.

"Yeah, I want to find out why you haven't called off those helicopters yet. They're about to shoot down Brady Hawk, who's risking his life to help others. And you're literally condoning this."

"Sorry, Morgan, I already made up my mind. You were warned not to go after the dirigible."

"So, you have a plan to get it down?"

"That's what we're working on right now," Norris said.

"Well, that's what we're *actually doing* right now," Morgan said. "Tell those Marine choppers to back off."

"Can't do it, Morgan. Now, if you'll excuse me."

"No, I won't excuse you. In fact, I'm going to make your life a living hell if you don't stop those helicopters."

"Morgan," Norris snapped, "have you forgotten who you're talking to?"

"If you don't tell those helicopters to stand down, I'm going to release that footage to the media myself."

For once, Norris was silent.

———

HAWK LOOKED BEHIND him at the choppers which were almost on him. The headwinds had slowed him, but it had also slowed the dirigible. But they'd had no effect on the helicopters.

Hawk climbed higher, straining the hang glider's motors as it went upward. He narrowed in on his target. Maybe thirty more seconds and he'd be close enough to attempt to get Dr. Z's jamming device into the basket.

Hawk's mouth went dry as adrenaline coursed through his body. If he jumped out, he wouldn't have more than a couple of seconds to pull the ripcord on his chute. But there was no guarantee he'd be far enough clear of the hang glider to avoid getting hit with the blast. And if it stunned him for even a couple of seconds, that would be all it would take to kill him.

He thought about John Daniel and Alex. He knew she'd be okay, but John Daniel needed him. For a moment, he pondered abandoning the mission. But then he thought about all the other dads on the ground who might die from a blast contained in the dirigible as well. That was potentially hundreds of little John Daniels who'd grow up without fathers.

Hawk set his jaw and stared at the target. Despite the struggle, he'd managed to get the glider at the same elevation as the dirigible and was closing in. Meanwhile the choppers just sat behind him, almost as if they were waiting for something.

Then it dawned on Hawk—they were waiting for the orders to fire.

"Alex," Hawk said, "please tell me these choppers haven't fired on me yet because you've helped Norris come to his senses?"

There was a long pause.

"Alex?"

"Yeah, I'm here," she said. "Norris isn't backing down."

Hawk glanced over his shoulder again at the two helicopters. They were both preparing to fire.

CHAPTER
FORTY-ONE

KIRA GUSEV PEERED SKYWARD from the backseat of a white SUV at the dirigible floating overhead. She controlled it with the device in her hand, guiding it closer and closer to its final destination. Within the next five minutes, she'd drop a payload on The Pentagon and make her father proud. But she'd also be proud, too.

This is for you, Andrei.

Her cousin Andrei had been a soldier under Gusev in the Russian Army, seeing action in Kosovo during the Kosovo War. One night, he was part of an offensive that was ambushed by U.S. and other NATO peacekeeping forces. Gusev and several of his troops were captured. According to her father, each prisoner was interrogated briefly. She remembered him telling her that the interrogations were weak and obviously didn't result in any actionable intelligence. However, General Purcell grew increasingly agitated by all the Russians' rehearsed answers. That's when he turned in front of all the men and shot Andrei in the head. The way her father retold the events of that night, General Purcell didn't seem bothered by what he'd done, though he'd witnessed firsthand how war had ravaged so many good men and spoke solemnly about it often. "War will make you do things you wish you'd never done," he repeatedly told her, though his epiphany was never applied to enemy forces. The things the enemy did were always evil, and retribution was justifiable in every situation. Kira understood how intellectually dishonest her father's thinking was, but she agreed with his guiding principle—someone needed to pay the price for Andrei's murder. And exposing General Purcell as a killer when he'd reached the pinnacle of his career seemed to satisfy Kira and her father's thirst for vengeance.

As Kira maneuvered the dirigible with the massive explosive device inside closer to the final target, she wondered if her father was aware of what she was doing. The phone call he'd made signaled that it was time to initiate the plan. She'd trained for the past ten years for this moment, rehearsing everything over and over in her mind from how to evade capture from law enforcement by misdirecting them to how to quickly find the supplies necessary to build a bomb. But this dirigible she was controlling wasn't something she had cobbled together on the fly. It had been sitting in a Washington storage unit for the past five years waiting to be employed. Kira had been amazed at how smoothly the process had gone.

Papa was right about everything.

Her confidence grew with each passing moment. She continued to guide the dirigible toward The Pentagon unabated.

"Just a few more minutes, Nikolay."

The driver nodded. Gusev had arranged for Nikolay, a long-time member of the Russian embassy in Washington, to drive Kira when the moment called for it. With his extensive knowledge of the city's layout, there wasn't anyone better to handle the task. And Nikolay had readily accepted, affirming his position as a devoted patriot.

Even while Kira watched the dirigible hovering overhead, she noticed Nikolay continually checking his rearview mirror.

"Is something wrong?" Kira asked.

He shrugged. "I'm not sure, but I thought for a moment we

were being followed."

Kira turned around and looked out of the rear window. The traffic looked benign to her. "I don't see any U.S. government vehicles."

"There's one SUV that's been following us for a few blocks now."

"Aren't we on a main street?"

"Yes."

"Then stop being so paranoid. This town is full SUVs and it's entirely normal for one to travel several blocks with you."

"I don't know," Nikolay said. "This one seemed different somehow."

"It's only because you're worried you're going to get caught," Kira said. "My Papa told me that your record was spotless, which was why he chose you. It's why you'd be the last person the Americans would suspect would be involved in something like this."

"What if they were able to track *you*?"

Nikolay turned west onto the Arlington Memorial Bridge, and she ignored his question. "We're so close, Nikolay. I can almost see The Pentagon from here."

"Just a few more turns," he said.

She fiddled with the controller as the dirigible refused to move when she directed it to. "You need to slow down. We're getting too far away and it's making it difficult to control."

Nikolay eased onto the brake and slowed their speed. He glanced in the rearview mirror again.

"Just relax," she said. "There's nobody back there."

"If there's one thing I've learned after living here for so long, it's that you should never underestimate your enemy. Sometimes all it takes is a surprise to take you down. It's how every politician has their career ended in disgrace. Americans are very forgiving, but they will not forgive a corrupt politician who has been exposed until years have passed. If you can surprise someone, you can beat them here."

"What does that have to do with you thinking we're being followed?"

"If they surprise us, they might catch us."

Kira smiled and laughed before patting Nikolay on the back. "You give the Americans far too much credit. I'm not sure they even know we're here."

Nikolay leaned forward in his seat and looked up. "Then, what's that thing approaching the dirigible?"

"Probably just someone enjoying their hobby."

"I've lived here a long time, and I've never seen anyone hang gliding over the city," he said. "I'm quite certain that activity is outlawed."

"This is a nation of outlaws and exhibitionists, all trying to become famous. Why wouldn't you think the person is simply enjoying a recreational activity?"

Nikolay glanced in the rearview mirror again, this time holding his gaze. "We need to move. We're definitely being followed."

As soon as they pulled off the bridge, he turned south onto Washington Blvd. As soon as he found the first turnoff, he jerked the steering wheel to the right, sending them careening out of the congested area.

"Well, you surprised me there," she said. "Though you need to slow down so this low-frequency radio signal is close enough for us to transmit. I seem to be losing some of my capabilities because we're on the edge of the range."

"If we get caught, it won't matter."

He stomped on the accelerator as the car lurched forward.

Kira sighed and then looked out the rear window again. She spotted the SUV and immediately understood Nikolay's concerns.

They were being followed. And that wasn't all.

Overhead, the glider had edged dangerously closer to her dirigible—and no matter what she tried, it wouldn't go any faster.

CHAPTER
FORTY-TWO

HAWK SWALLOWED HARD as he looked back at the helicopters on his tail. The glider's engine whined as it struggled to stay at the higher altitude. With each passing second, he wondered if he had time to do what he needed to do. To better assess the threat, he wanted to get a look inside the dirigible's basket and see exactly what kind of explosives were contained in it. But there wasn't time for that.

He decided to ask if anyone on the team had made any headway with Norris in calling off the attack choppers.

"Alex, I'm out of time," he said. "Any indication they're going to back off?"

"Not from what I understand," Alex said. "Norris is being stubborn."

"Roger that," Hawk said.

He looked back at the helicopters one more time and made eye contact with one of the pilots, who gestured for him to take his glider down. Hawk situated himself so he was sitting sideways and had his right arm on the control bar, freeing up his left hand. After he dug into his jacket pocket, he produced the device that Dr. Z had given him. Flicking the switch to activate it, Hawk soared higher, this time a few meters above the dirigible. He took a deep breath and counted to three.

When he reached one, he let go of the control bar and leaped out of the glider. He had only one shot with no room for error.

As he dropped from the sky, he focused on the dirigible and was able to get just inches away from it before dropping the signal jammer into the basket.

"I hit the target," Hawk said over the coms.

A second later, he yanked on his ripcord, unfurling his chute as he drifted over the Potomac.

With Hawk's descent slowing, he was almost certain the helicopters would fire a missile to destroy the glider. But instead, one of the crews hooked the glider with a grappling hook that dangled from a rope. Initially, the glider bucked. But the canvas quickly ripped, rendering the glider inoperable.

Hawk looked up at the other chopper and gave them a friendly wave, which was met with an obscene gesture.

"Nice going, Hawk," Morgan said over the coms.

"Yeah, honey, that wasn't half bad," Alex said. "But you're not done yet.

"Now what?" Hawk asked.

"I need you to land on the west bank," Alex said. "There's been a development and you might be needed for backup."

"Kira?"

"Yeah, the FBI is tailing someone they believe to be Kira Gusev near your position."

"She was trying to stay off the radar by using such a low-frequency," Hawk said. "It also made her easier to find."

"Get down there and help out," Alex said. "We need to make sure the threat really is over."

"Roger that."

Hawk exhaled with relief as he guided his chute toward the west side of the Potomac. The Pentagon sat ominously a few blocks away, but it seemed out of danger for the moment. With the dirigible now under the Magnum Group's control and rising higher, the less likely an explosion could harm innocent people on the ground. And Hawk was proud that he could make that happen, as well as grateful that the chopper pilots exercised some restraint.

But all those good feelings vanished when he heard an explosion a few blocks from where he aimed to land.

CHAPTER
FORTY-THREE

KIRA WRESTLED the controls back and forth as she watched the befuddling activity occurring overhead. The man in the hang glider got close to her dirigible but bailed out when two military helicopters showed up behind him. A few moments later, the choppers snagged the glider and dragged it away. However, Kira was less concerned about that and more concerned with why the dirigible wasn't responding to her directions any more.

"Come on," she said, rattling the small joystick back and forth. "You're supposed to go up."

She looked at the read out on the screen designed to relay every piece of piece of information available about the dirigible's status. But all the digits turned to dashes, meaning that the device was out of range.

"Go faster," she told Nicolay. "I'm too far away and can't control it. We need to get closer."

Nicolay groaned. "I'm trying, Kira. But we've got some other problems right now. The SUV isn't pretending to be following us anymore. They might as well be broadcasting that they are pursuing us."

"Not my problem. And there's nothing I can do about it anyway."

"Maybe you could start shooting at them so they'll back off."

Kira laughed nervously. "Only if you want to die getting gunned down in the streets. I have faith in you to guide us out of here."

"That makes one of us," he said with a growl.

Nikolay whipped the wheel to the right, turning onto a less trafficked side street.

"What are you doing?" Kira said. "You're pulling me farther away from my balloon. If I lose my connection permanently, this entire mission will be lost."

"It might be too late for that. Even your father understood when it was time to retreat and regroup. This is one of those times because if we get caught, we'll spend the rest of our lives in a U.S. prison somewhere with a bunch of terrorists."

Kira took a deep breath and wrapped her fingers around the door handle. "Then I'll unburden you."

As Nikolay made a wide turn at the next corner, she slung the door open and tucked herself into a fetal position. Then she rolled out and onto the street, coming to a hard stop as she slammed against the side of a Toyota Camry parked against the sidewalk. While she wanted to lay there and complain about how hard that stunt hurt, she had the wherewithal to scramble to her feet and take cover.

Seconds later, a black SUV rolled around the corner, lights on the dashboard flickering.

"Good luck, Nikolay," she said under her breath.

She looked up and tried to establish a connection with her dirigible, but it wasn't happening fast enough for her. Then she glanced down the street in time to see a grenade flying through the air from Nikolay's car toward the FBI agents' vehicle. A boom shortly followed that echoed off the surrounding buildings and reverberated through her chest. The FBI vehicle caught fire before swerving off the road and careening into a long line of parallel-parked cars before tipping onto its side.

Nice work.

The Russian diplomat sped off, leaving behind the fallout of his slick maneuver. Curious onlookers emerged from the nearby buildings and crowded around the vehicle. A few people tried to help, but the car caught ablaze again, forcing them farther back to avoid another potential explosion.

Kira ducked down an alleyway and headed east, hoping to emerge closer to the river so she could see her dirigible and re-establish a connection with it. After determining she was safe to run, she hustled closer to the river's edge and then rang along-side it. She glanced up at the dirigible and then down at her machine. The readouts remained nothing but dashes, signifying the device was still disconnected.

She cursed in Russian before picking up her pace. But no matter how fast she ran, her dirigible appeared to increase its speed until it finally landed in a nearby green space. She pushed the button that was supposed to activate a detonation. However, nothing happened again.

Instead of giving up, she rushed along the pathway until she noticed two military guards running to the device. She tapped the button repeatedly.

Still nothing.

She shoved the device into her pocket and kept her head down as she walked by, furiously tapping the button to get it to detonate. But nothing happened.

As more guards raced toward the dirigible to form a perimeter, Kira took the first opportunity to turn around as discreetly as possible and head back toward the maze of surface streets. Running toward the nearest Metro station, she tried not to think about what had happened over the past week and the life she'd left behind at USC. Even if her reason for being there was all a facade, she'd grown to like the people she'd met. They were her friends, all likely to be telling journal-ists that they never saw this coming, that "Kira was so sweet." And she was.

But her loyalty to her father ran deep, as did her thirst for revenge. Someone still had to make General Purcell pay for what he did to Andrei. The world still needed to know.

And she was the only one left who could make it happen.

Kira glanced over her shoulder one final time before galloping down the steps, two at a time, to the train platform. She had one more stop to make, one more chance to make it all right and make her father proud.

The next train was scheduled to arrive in three minutes—and she was almost certain she'd seen someone following her.

CHAPTER
FORTY-FOUR

WHEN HAWK'S FEET hit the ground, he rolled to lessen the blow. While he'd jumped from lower heights before, the short jumps always had the more jarring landings. And this one was no exception, though he'd managed to master mitigation techniques. He bounced to his feet and collected his chute. After stuffing it into a nearby trashcan, he contacted Alex on the coms.

"I'm on the ground, Alex," Hawk said as he turned on his coms. "What's Kira's status?"

"She's still on the loose, I'm afraid," Alex said. "The vehicle she was traveling in sped away from the scene of an accident that resulted in an overturned black SUV."

"Had to be the feds trailing her," Hawk said.

"No doubt. And she did it all without exchanging gunfire." She paused. "But you have to find her at all cost."

"Of course."

"No, you don't understand. There's been a development since I last spoke with you."

"Give me the skinny."

"Mia's been combing through all of Kira's documents online and on her laptop. There's an encrypted document that is entitled 'Last Resort'."

"And?"

"Not only is it encrypted, but it's also written in some type of code," Alex said. "Mia is working on it and has a team of underworld types she's convinced to help us. But they're saying the best-case scenario is days, maybe even weeks, before they figure out what's hidden in there. You'll need to bring her in alive to interrogate her. Mia thinks there's another bomb out there, rigged to blow."

"Clever," Hawk said. "As long as she's valuable to the feds and has something she can hold over their heads, she's pretty much assured that she won't get shot. But don't worry—I'll find her."

"It won't be easy because she's already got quite a head start on you."

"But no weapon, right?"

"I can't confirm what she does or doesn't have, but I can tell you that she no longer has control of that bomb in the dirigible, all thanks to you."

"Team effort, honey. You, Morgan, Mia, Big Earv—speaking of which, where is that big lug? It sure would be nice to have him around right about this time."

"He's headed to your position, but I don't have an ETA on his arrival."

"I'll manage until then," Hawk said.

"Shouldn't be too much longer," Alex said. "He left a half-hour ago. But you have plenty to do until he finds you."

"Where exactly is she?"

"Thaaat's the one thing I wasn't excited about telling you," Alex said. "We lost her a few minutes ago, right before the car sped off. I spotted her on a satellite feed crouching behind a row of cars, all parked parallel along the street. But somehow, she disappeared a few minutes ago. She was about three blocks west of your position heading west on 12th Street in Virginia Highlands."

"Okay," Hawk said as he ran in the direction of Kira's last

known position. "If I was in her situation and needing to disappear, there would be two clear choices—the mall at Pentagon City or the Metro."

"Is the clearest choice always the right choice?" Alex asked.

"In this case, I'd say it would be. Even if we think we know where she's going, finding her would be a nightmare."

"Which would be more of a challenge? That's the only real question left to answer."

"I'd lean toward the Metro."

"Bingo," Hawk said. "I wouldn't even hesitate to head there."

"I'll start my search there now."

"Instead of doing that, can you do something else for me?" Hawk asked.

"Whatever you need."

"Can you stop all the trains going in or out of the station for say five minutes? Lock down the screens so the estimated time of arrival for new trains doesn't change."

"Why not ten or fifteen minutes?"

"We might spook her," Hawk said. "And that's the last thing we want. But I need to be on that train with her."

"I'll see what I can do on such short notice, but no promises."

Hawk put his head down and hustled toward 12th Street. Once he reached the intersection, he turned west and dashed down the sidewalk, weaving in and out of the other pedestrians. After a couple of minutes, Alex interrupted the scheming in Hawk's mind.

"Hawk, I could only convince Metro to delay the next arrival three minutes," Alex said. "And one more thing—you're going to have company."

"What kind of company?"

"The FBI has dispatched three agents to the area as well as a SWAT team in case a hostage situation occurs. You have to be ready for anything."

"You think something crazy is going to go down at the

Metro? Because as far as I can tell, Kira would've rather had her first plan succeed. I'm not sure she would've anticipated trying to get away here and planted something in advance. Besides, that Metro station is heavily surveilled since it's a stone's throw away from The Pentagon."

"I hope you're right," Alex said. "Every extra minute we can get will help us apprehend her."

"Let's just hope I get to her first instead of the feds."

"Roger that."

"One last thing," Hawk said. "What was she wearing?"

"I'll text you the best screen shot we have of her. Good luck."

When Hawk reached the station, the normal hive of activity had ground to a halt. Instead of the hustling and bustling among passengers transferring, the lines resembled more like a line of people waiting in a checkout line at the grocery store: people standing packed together but hardly saying a word, the frustration almost palpable. The near silence was eerie.

Hawk ran up the steps that led to the platform. He tried to put himself in Kira's shoes, thinking about what *she* might do, not necessarily what was the best *thing* to do. He would want to go in the most opposite direction possible to throw anyone trailing him off course. But Kira also had a job to do, one she obviously felt very passionate about as she was willing to give up her life at USC for it. This wasn't just a cause—this was a commitment, one that felt so rigid that it seemed like it was written in blood. She wouldn't be headed away from the city. No, she'd be going back to it to finish whatever it was she came here to do.

Hawk found an empty spot on a bench and stepped up onto it so he could survey the crowd better. He searched for the red baseball cap she'd been wearing. In some places, it would've made her stand out, but not in Washington. She'd obviously done her homework and was well aware of the popularity of the city's baseball team. The Nationals were still playing in October, entrenched in a playoff run, and caps with the team's colors were everywhere.

In the picture Alex had texted Hawk, Kira was wearing a dark coat, something else that didn't help distinguish her in the crowd. But Hawk had a clothing combination to work with. While scanning the crowd, he hoped she wouldn't be near the front of the platform.

As each few seconds passed, he felt a growing sense of angst.

Is Kira even here? What if I was wrong?

The fear of being wrong gripped Hawk. She could've hailed a taxi to get to her final destination. Or maybe she was just going to wait it out and hide out in shops for an hour or two at the mall. The second-guessing gripped Hawk.

"Find her yet?" Alex asked over the coms.

"Not yet."

"Okay, but I thought I'd warn you that the train service will resume in one minute," she said. "That's all you wanted me to hold them for."

"I know. I know. Thank you."

Hawk maintained his focus, going through each cloistered group of people and searching for the red hat-dark coat combination. He found a handful, most of them men. The one woman he spied with that same attire was rather portly. He'd almost searched the entire crowd and seen nothing of the sort.

Then Hawk considered one more thought: *What if she ditched her hat?*

He looked for a blonde with a dark coat but with the same result—nothing.

The train hissed, its brakes echoing as it chugged into the station. An audible sigh went up from the crowd as people anticipated the doors to open. Hawk made one last sweep before he noticed a woman with a red hat and dark coat exiting the restroom. She fought her way through the throngs of people before Hawk watched her take a quick glance around.

It was Kira.

"Found her," Hawk announced over the coms as he hopped down from his perch on the bench.

"Did she see you?" Alex asked.

"I don't think so."

He wove his way through the crowd, dodging and twisting his way to get to the front. The doors had opened, creating a colliding mass of humanity devoid of politeness. Some people intent on leaving the station as quickly as possible fought against those determined to get on that train.

Hawk embraced the station's collective focused hustle, pushing his way past strangers without a second thought. He could still see Kira's red hat bobbing up and down as she struggled to make it to the train. But she had a head start and was almost there.

A bell followed by a short announcement signaled that the doors were about to close. Hawk was still about ten meters from the train with a mass of humanity still in front of him and precious little space available inside. He spied Kira as she squeezed just inside the doors to Hawk's right, before turning his attention to the doors in front of him. He rushed past several people, hurdling one woman's umbrella stroller to claim the last piece of real estate inside the train. While he could feel the nasty looks judging him for his wanton lack of decorum, he didn't care. The commuters still stuck on the platform glared at him as the doors slid shut.

Hawk didn't care what they thought.

He was on the same train as Kira.

CHAPTER
FORTY-FIVE

AT EACH NEW STOP, Hawk edged closer to Kira. He kept his head down, mindlessly staring at his phone like everyone else aboard and texting updates to Alex. Kira seemed surprisingly cool, not like someone who was in the middle of an operation with its success hanging in the balance. Her blank facial expression and polite smiles to new passengers boarding the train belied her sinister motives.

At McPherson Square, she stepped off briefly. Hawk stood his ground, wondering if she suspected him and was testing to see if he'd follow.

As the seconds ticked past, he cast furtive glances in her direction. For someone who was in a hurry earlier, she didn't seem like she was going anywhere with urgency. She took a couple of steps toward the stairs before darting back aboard, squeezing inside as the doors were closing.

Hawk's eyes met hers and he gave her a friendly smile. "Got to be careful with those things. They'll try to bite you."

Kira nodded as she offered a thin smile, but remained quiet.

Hawk was almost certain that she was going to get off at Metro Center, but instead she remained aboard. The crowd had thinned out considerably, going from shoulder-to-shoulder to about fifty percent capacity.

A handful of tourists hand climbed aboard as had a high school on an apparent field trip of sorts. Several teachers acted as chaperones tried to herd the students, the girls clad in white blouses and plaid print skirts while the boys sported dark slacks and white oxford shirts with ties. They joked and laughed with each other as some of the class filled in the empty space between Hawk and Kira.

Two stops later, the train came to a halt in the Smithsonian station, prompting a mass exodus. Hawk gestured for the students to go first, all while checking on Kira out of the corner of his eye to see what she was going to do. Before they finished exiting, she wedged her way into the group and left with them.

Hawk remained calm as he watched the class empty out of the train. Then he followed them, scanning the area for Kira.

She remained with them as she kept her head down. After a few seconds, she glanced back over her shoulder at Hawk and the two made eye contact. In that moment, she didn't hesitate and started sprinting through the class.

Some of the kids shouted in response to the rude treatment and one girl was knocked to the ground. Hawk couldn't afford to wait, breaking into a full sprint to try and catch her. The encounter had created quite a scene with people moving out of the way and staring in awe.

"Please help me!" Kira cried. "That man assaulted me. Please help!"

A couple of men scowled as they heard the news before deciding to intervene on her behalf. One gentleman with a goatee and a skintight workout shirt stepped in front of Hawk.

"Please, sir," Hawk said.

"I'm not going to let you hurt that young woman," he said with a growl. "You'll have to go through me first."

Hawk shrugged. "If that's how you want it."

He kicked the man in the knee, sending him clutching for it.

As he did, Hawk delivered an uppercut to the man's head, knocking him out. The crowd that had formed groaned as they watched the would-be hero tumble unconscious to the concrete floor.

Hawk looked up and noticed Kira hadn't stopped, but she hadn't gotten very far. He resumed his pursuit, closing in on her rapidly. However, as she reached the stairs to exit to the street level, she doubled back with an incoming group of foreign tourists. They formed another barrier between her and Hawk, slowing him down and allowing her another chance to escape.

Undaunted by the move, Hawk darted through the group. As the people noticed how fast he was moving, they parted to make room for him.

"Help! Help!" Kira shouted.

Another man tried to be a hero, who was far less formidable than Hawk's last opponent. Hawk hit the man with a forearm while in full stride, knocking him to the ground. The move barely cost Hawk a step. He drew his weapon as he ran, leading to screams from commuters exiting the station.

Kira rushed back into the group of field trip students before using her arm to hook one of the girls around the neck and drag her against the wall. By the time Hawk was close enough to carry on a conversation with Kira, she already had her gun out and had it jammed into the girl's head.

"Come any closer and I'll kill her," Kira said. "And it'll be your fault."

Hawk lowered his weapon and held his free hand out in a calming gesture. "You don't need to do this, Kira. Please, let the girl go."

Kira set her jaw, her lips quivering as she considered how to respond. "No, I won't do it. You just leave me alone, okay?"

"We need to talk. Just me and you. Let that girl go. She didn't do anything to you."

"She's the only reason I'm still alive right now," Kira hissed.

Hawk shook his head. "That's not true, Kira. I need to have a conversation with you. I don't want to hurt you."

"I know how this ends," Kira said. "You're going to murder me just like you did my father—just like you murdered my cousin."

Hawk squinted as he looked at the Russian woman, struggling to know what to do in the moment. All the training in the world couldn't prepare her for having to make such heavy decisions under pressure. Her cool demeanor had vanished amidst the stress of the moment.

"I know about Andrei," Hawk said. "What happened to him was a tragedy."

"It wasn't a tragedy—it was murder," she screamed. "And because of your government, he's gone forever now. Such a sweet friend, lost because of the monsters created by your military."

"We could discuss the psychological effects of war some other time and how we can get justice for your cousin," Hawk said. "But right now there are more pressing issues, aren't there? Like first of all how to get that girl to safety and then how to make sure thousands more innocent people don't die."

Kira tightened her grip around the girl's neck as tears streamed down her face. She mouthed something to her friends. Unsure of what she'd communicated, Hawk glanced at them and shook his head.

"I knew you were following me," Kira said. "I just knew it."

"Your father trained you to be an operative, but he didn't train you for this. We're never truly ready for the crossroads we face in life. We have to pick a direction and hope it's the right one. And when it isn't—because that happens a lot—we try to make the best of our situation. You chose poorly, but all is not lost. What you do next is going to define what kind of life and legacy you'll have. Are thousands of people going to die because of what you've done?"

Kira glared at Hawk but said nothing.

"You came back here because you wanted to see the chaos you put into motion, didn't you? You wanted to do it for your father, who spent the rest of his life stuck in that moment when Andrei died. All your father wanted was revenge, and he was willing to sacrifice your childhood and the rest of your life to get it, even if he wasn't alive to see it. He killed himself, maybe to protect you or maybe it was because he was confident you could get the job done. Either way, it was a poor parenting decision, one he's not even alive to regret anymore."

Kira narrowed her eyes. "How dare you invoke my father's name like that? He did whatever he could to avenge Andrei's death. And I'm not about to let him down either."

"Where's the bomb, Kira?"

She smiled wryly and shook her head. "You're going to watch the fruits of his years of meticulous planning ... and weep."

After pushing the girl aside, Kira started to draw the gun up to her head. But Hawk recognized what was happening and reacted quickly. He took aim at her hands and fired.

The bullet ripped through her hands, forcing her to drop her gun. But the bullet deflected to her right, avoiding hitting her in the center mass. She stared at her chest, her mouth agape. There was no other wound to be found.

As she studied her hands, a pair of gunshots rang through the metro station. This time when Kira looked down, she found two spots of blood pooling around where a bullet had ripped through her jacket.

Hawk looked over his shoulder and glared at the FBI agent, reporting that he'd taken the suspect down.

Without a second to waste, Hawk rushed over to Kira and knelt beside her.

"It wasn't supposed to happen like this," he said.

"What—what is this?" she asked.

"Someone else shot you," Hawk said. "And I'll deal with them later."

Then Hawk spoke into his coms. "Alex, can you get paramedics to the Metro station at the Smithsonian stop? We have a suspect down who needs immediate medical attention."

The students in the area screamed at the scene that had unfolded as chaperones worked to usher them to safety. The FBI agent who'd fired the shot holstered his weapon as he strode toward Hawk.

"Back away," Hawk said. "I'll deal with you in a minute."

Then he turned back toward the Russian woman lying on the ground, trying to apply pressure to the wound. "Kira, I will get justice for Andrei—I promise. And I'll get justice for you too. But I need to know where the bomb is."

She sneered at him. "Why should I help you?"

"Your whole life has been about getting justice. And none of it will happen if you kill thousands of innocent people today. We know there's another bomb, but you need to tell me where it is."

"I'm going to die," she said. "What difference does it make anyway?"

"You're still writing the story of your life," Hawk said. "Wouldn't you rather it end in redemption than tragedy?"

Kira didn't say a word before she started to convulse with tears. "I never wanted to do this, but he made me."

"The General?"

She nodded. "I just wanted to be normal. I wanted to be a kid. And look where it's gotten me."

"The paramedics are on their way, Kira. Hang in there. You're going to make it and we're going to change your story. But I know that bomb is close to going off, isn't it?"

Kira nodded between sobs.

"Please, tell me where it is?"

Kira started coughing, spitting up blood. She tried to say something, but he couldn't make out what she said.

"What was that?" he said before putting his ear right next to her mouth.

She whispered something, which this time Hawk heard.

He squeezed her hand. "Someone will be here shortly. Please, hang in there."

Then Hawk jumped to his feet and started sprinting toward the exit.

"I know where the bomb is," Hawk said over the coms.

"Where is it?"

"Have a bomb squad meet me at the Lincoln Memorial—and get someone to clear the area."

"That's not going to be easy," she said. "The military is holding an event there right now. And guess who's speaking? General Purcell."

Hawk cursed under his breath as he shot a bike lock in half to borrow a bike chained to a rack. "Just get them out of there. And hurry."

CHAPTER
FORTY-SIX

WHEN HAWK ARRIVED at the Lincoln Memorial, a large crowd dispersed, completely devoid of any order. Men and women in their service dress uniforms sprinted away in every direction from the cluster of seats. Several golf carts driven by MPs wheeled away the top military brass. The rest of the crowd was yelling and screaming, holding hands with friends and loved ones as they darted down the sides of the reflection pool.

Hawk raced headlong into the crowd, juking his way past the onslaught of terrified attendees.

"What exactly did you tell these people?" Hawk asked over the coms.

"I reported a bomb scare under the Lincoln Memorial, just like you told me," Alex said. "Should I have phrased it another way?"

"Nope, you're fine. I'm just a little stunned at the reaction of soldiers to a threat."

By the time Hawk reached the stairwell leading to the basement beneath the memorial, everyone had vacated the premises. He scanned the area, searching for any explosive devices. After a few seconds, he concluded that there weren't any in plain sight.

"How long was that shindig supposed to go on?" Hawk asked.

"It had just started, but according to the itinerary I found, it was supposed to go at least an hour and a half," Alex said. "They were honoring General Purcell for his years of service as part of a ceremony introducing a new military initiative to help stop child slavery in impoverished countries."

"And Kira knew all about it, apparently," Hawk said. "What time was he supposed to speak?"

"According to this schedule, General Purcell was supposed to speak in about fifteen minutes."

"Was that itinerary public?"

"Uh, huh," Alex said. "Found it with a simple search on the Internet. It's been in the works for months now."

"Then I suspect we have about fifteen minutes to find that bomb."

"There's an FBI bomb squad on the way," she said. "But I don't know if they'll be able to get there."

"Well, first we have to find the bomb."

Hawk searched thoroughly over the next five minutes but couldn't find any signs of a bomb.

"I don't know what to do, Alex. I've looked everywhere and there isn't a thing here."

"Think she was lying to you?" she asked.

"Doubt it. General Purcell was here, remember? That's who most of her ire was directed toward."

"But what if that was a smokescreen?"

Hawk hadn't considered that as a sick feeling fell across him. He had to reckon with the fact that there was no bomb. The chaos over the bomb was exactly what she wanted. Kira never intended to kill all those people. Her hatred was directed at one person. Gusev's master plan was to embarrass General Purcell before killing him. It was the ultimate disgrace, a man's legacy destroyed just moments before he ushered into an early grave.

"Damnit," Hawk said, slamming his fist against the wall. "She played us."

"How so?" Alex asked. "She's gone."

"Maybe there were more agents," Hawk suggested.

"If there were, we didn't see any evidence of them. We can account for everyone on Kira's list from her computer."

"Have you decoded the 'Last Resort' file yet?"

"I just got the first part of it on my desk from Mia, but it's not complete," Alex said. "I'm not sure there's much here yet. Even without the decoded document, there are still initials representing people and places."

Hawk walked up the steps, all alone with the massive chiseled Lincoln monument. "Let's think. There has to be something that can help us tie what the Last Resort plan was to what's happening now."

He listened as he heard the rapid turning of pages.

"Finding anything?" he asked.

"Aha," she said. "The plan was to create a bomb scare at the Lincoln Memorial, never an actual bomb."

"Okay. And?"

"Let's see. It says here that a character named NA will be taking General Purcell captive by picking him up on the street corner."

"What the hell? How would he expect to do that? And who's NA? Can you cross-reference those initials with any of the sleeper cell agents, real names or pseudonyms?"

After a brief moment of silence, Alex answered. "Nothing. No matches."

"Well, where else would she get help? There's got to be some place."

"What about the embassy?" Alex suggested. "You know there are plenty of FSB agents there who might want to participate in an op like this."

"Then look at the list there and see what you can find."

After about a minute, Alex groaned.

"What is it now?" he asked.

"I wish it was cut and dry, but we've got a Nikki Anatov and a Nikolay Aslanov."

Hawk chuckled. "Sounds like almost the same person."

"According to the Russian embassy website, it's not. One is a striking blonde while the other is a former military officer."

"My money's on the officer," Hawk said. "Any ideas where he might be?"

Hawk heard Alex's fingers flying furiously across the keyboard. And then—nothing.

"He's clean, as far as I can tell," she said.

"Bullshit," Hawk said. "He's dirty and working with her. I just know it."

"You sure you don't want to look into the blonde?"

"No, whatever agent they hired would need to be able to overpower General Purcell."

Hawk walked up to the street and found the bodies of two MPs lying on the ground, one in the road, the other on the sidewalk.

"Have you got satellite footage of the chaos here from a few minutes ago?" he asked.

"Let me dig it up."

After a couple of minutes, she finally spoke. "Got it. I'm watching it now."

"I want you to focus on the street right near the monument where all the cars were delivering the military brass. I just found a couple of bodies of MPs on the ground."

"Roger that," she said. "I'm going back to look at the footage from a few minutes ago."

Hawk scanned the street for any other clues. As he did, the FBI's bomb squad rolled up.

"You Agent Hawk?" one of the men asked.

Hawk nodded. "I did a sweep of the basement, but I think this was a false alarm. It looks like this was a diversion to kidnap one of the generals."

"We'll check it out just in case," one of the men said before whistling for his team to follow him.

Hawk knelt and checked the pulses of the two MPs along the side of the road. They were both dead, a shot to the head and then chest.

Classic FSB.

Hawk studied the scene, trying to recreate what had happened in his mind.

Nikolay must've seized upon the chaos and took out the two officers before they knew what hit them.

The fact that a Russian college-aged student outsmarted him irked Hawk. But the danger wasn't over—and neither was the mission. General Purcell was a hostage. And while Hawk would've preferred to just let him twist in the wind like he deserved, letting him be ravaged by terrorists—Russian or otherwise—wasn't the right message to send to the world.

"Find anything yet?" Hawk asked.

"No," Alex said, "but Homeland Security just received a phone call from a man claiming to have General Purcell hostage."

"And?"

"He's been left at the base of the Washington Monument," Alex said. "And he needs to be delivered to the White House."

"Or else?"

"Or else there will be dire consequences for American citizens, according to this document."

"That sounds ominous," Hawk said with a shrug.

"Big Earv headed out to your position ten minutes ago. I'll have him pick you up and then you can collect the general."

"Roger that."

Hawk checked in with the special agent in charge of the bomb squad, who confirmed that everything was clear. A few minutes later, Big Earv rolled up to the sidewalk in an SUV and rolled the window down.

"You ready to ride, chief?" he asked.

Hawk hustled over to the vehicle and climbed inside, nodding as he did. "Never a dull a moment."

Big Earv flipped a small black device about the size of a ring box to Hawk. "Dr. Z said you'd know what to do with that."

Hawk smiled and pocketed the item. "Let's ride."

CHAPTER
FORTY-SEVEN

TEN MINUTES LATER, Hawk and Big Earv parked along the road running right by the Washington Monument. The towering obelisk cast a long shadow across the grounds on the autumn afternoon. General Purcell leaned against the base of the monument, ignoring the visitors who waited patiently to ride to the top and get an epic view of the city.

As Hawk approached General Purcell, he gave a friendly nod to them.

"You looking for me?" Purcell asked.

Hawk offered a polite smile. "It would seem so, General. I hear we need to deliver you to the White House."

"That's the plan," Purcell said as he rose to his feet.

No one spoke until they returned to the vehicle and were all safely inside. Hawk turned around and studied Purcell.

"What's really going on here?" Hawk asked.

"What's it look like?" Purcell asked. "I need a ride to the White House."

Big Earv reached down and pulled Purcell to his feet. "He couldn't be bothered to give you a ride all the way there? Seems rude."

"You don't know the half of it," Purcell said.

Hawk untied Purcell and escorted him to their van. They drove to the White House in silence. Hawk wasn't sure if that was due to all the trauma Purcell had just experienced or if he wasn't a talkative person. It was Hawk's first encounter with the man—and nothing was overly impressive about him.

When they reached the gate to the White House, Big Earv flashed his credentials.

"Nuh, uh, uh," the guard said. "Let me see that again."

Big Earv forked over his clearance card. "I was under the impression that you knew I was coming."

"Not exactly," the man said. "The lines of communication move slowly around here."

The guard house phone rang and the man picked it up and had a brief conversation before hanging up.

"So, apparently, that was the phone call I should've received a few minutes ago. You're clear to enter."

The guard waved them inside before Big Earv pulled the SUV to a stop and led them up the steps.

"Big Earv," one of the Secret Service agents said, "you finally made it back."

"And in one piece, Darren," Big Earv said, "which, as you know, is a small miracle."

"Good to see you," Darren said before the two men embraced quickly. "So, what brings you here today?"

"We have a special delivery for the president," Hawk said.

"A special delivery? Sounds interesting. Where do you want to put it?"

Hawk glared at Purcell. "It's not an it—it's him."

"General—"

"Purcell. General Peter Purcell, humbly requesting a meeting with the president."

Hawk activated the device and then handed it to Big Earv. "Don't let him out of your sight and don't touch a single button on this machine."

"But—"

"I'll explain later," Hawk said as he hustled away.

He went outside and contacted Alex over the coms. "Do you know what's going on here?"

"I'm in the dark more than you are," she said.

"Something doesn't seem right," Hawk said. "Purcell is acting strange."

"And?"

"His chest also looks somewhat bloated and abnormal."

Alex sighed. "You think he's wired to blow, don't you?"

"There's no doubt in my mind."

"What do you want me to do?"

Hawk explained his plan before enlisting her help. After she agreed to help, Hawk walked past the guard house.

"Agent Hawk, what are you doing?" the guard called after him.

Hawk waved dismissively at him. "I've got some business to take care of."

———

HAWK HUSTLED DOWN the street, searching for any suspicious vehicles parked nearby. The barricades along Pennsylvania Avenue made it almost impossible to be close by, not to mention the lack of parking across the city in general. The public transportation system in the nation's capital was more than adequate, but Hawk realized in this instance that proximity was important.

"You see anything?" Alex asked.

"Not yet."

"And you're sure he's wired?"

"As sure as I'm standing here."

"Why did you take him to the president then?"

Hawk sighed. "It's the only way to end this once and for all. Gusev's plan was to take out anybody who refused to listen to his protest about Purcell's war crime. Yet no one did. So, he was determined to get his own justice, even if it had to come from the grave."

"Why not just rig the explosives with a timer?"

Hawk continued scanning along the street. "There's no way to guarantee that Purcell would be in the room at the optimum moment with President Norris. But if Nikolay is listening, he can detonate the bomb whenever they're together."

"But why would Purcell do that?" she asked. "Why would he willingly walk in to meet the president while wired to blow up? That makes no sense to me."

"I understand," Hawk said. "Think about it for a moment. What would make you abandon almost every principle you ever had?"

"Nothing."

"Okay," Hawk said, "you're an anomaly. Now, imagine you're like everyone else and would be willing to abandon all your principles under the right circumstances. What would that be?"

She was quiet for a moment. "Maybe if someone was going to do something to John Daniel."

"Bingo," Hawk said.

"What makes you think that's the answer?"

"I looked it up on my phone as I was walking out to the street," Hawk said. "Purcell's son attends Georgetown University. And it just so happens his roommate hasn't seen him in two days."

"You're looking for a van, aren't you?" she asked.

"Yep," Hawk said. "And one big enough for both Nikolay and Pete Jr."

Hawk hustled along H Street behind the White House. He turned onto 16th Street and headed north. And just outside St. John's Episcopal Church along the street, he spotted five white vans all lined up. Each one had different business names on the side, all sounding legitimate. And all of them had the proper license plates, based in Virginia and Washington.

Hawk hustled across the street and searched for each one on the Internet. The first two checked out, but Pete's Plumbing failed to register anything. He did a quick search on the Virginia Secretary of State business page to confirm that the business wasn't real.

"Found them," Hawk announced.

"Hawk, this is Morgan. Do not engage. I repeat. Do not engage. I'm sending a team over to your location."

"With all due respect, Director, there won't be time if I wait," he said. "Once Nikolay realizes that Purcell has been compromised, he's going to kill his son."

"Just wait, Hawk, okay?"

Hawk ignored Morgan's pleas and approached the van. He knocked on the window, but no one answered. Then Hawk went around to the back and pounded on the door. A few seconds later, it opened followed by a gun barrel.

But Hawk was ready.

He had already slid to the side and grabbed the barrel with both hands, yanking it outside. Nikolay came outside along with it before the weapon was wrestled from his hands.

Realizing that his advantage had been stolen, Nikolay swept his foot under Hawk's leg, sending him tumbling to the ground. The gun skidded across the sidewalk as a few nearby pedestrians scattered.

Hawk eyed his foe as the two men were hunched over in a position ready to pounce. Nikolay grew tired of the dance and lunged first. As soon as he did, Hawk slid to the side and kicked the Russian in the head. However, Nikolay rolled away and reached for the weapon. Then Hawk dove for it, pushing it out of Nikolay's reach along the sidewalk.

The two men then engaged in hand-to-hand combat, delivering blow after blow. After a couple of minutes, Nikolay managed to pin Hawk down on the ground before Nikolay whipped a knife out of a sheath wrapped around his lower right leg.

Hawk stared up at the blade, hovering over him in Nikolay's hands. As the two men continued their struggle, Hawk used his hands to hold up Nikolay's, preventing a fatal strike. But Hawk weakened as Nikolay held the stronger position, edging the tip of the knife closer and closer to Hawk's throat.

Desperate to turn the tables on Nikolay, Hawk reached for his breast pocket and fished out the pen that Dr. Z had given him. It was designed to capture audio and video footage, but Hawk needed it for something else.

With just one hand to hold off Nikolay, the blade edged dangerously close to his throat. However, he grabbed the pen with his left hand and growled as he mustered up enough strength to jam the point into Nikolay's neck. Instinctively, he grabbed for the object now lodged in his neck, while Hawk squirmed free and picked up the knife. Hawk drew back and kicked Nikolay in the face, knocking him out and ending the threat.

Hawk hustled over to the van and found a young man, who looked about twenty years old, bound and gagged lying on the floorboard in the back. After Hawk untied him, the young man introduced himself as Pete Purcell Jr.

"Please tell my father to stop," Peter said. "He doesn't have to do whatever they're trying to make him do."

Hawk notified Alex over the coms. "The target is down and Purcell's son is secure. Let Big Earv know so they can get out of there."

"Roger that."

Hawk sighed as he looked down at the Russian bleeding out on the ground. His natural reaction was to help him, but Hawk was tired. And he didn't see any redemption possible by saving the spy. Nikolay had tried to murder the president. Hawk shrugged, and figured the Russian got what he deserved and it'd save Norris a big diplomatic headache.

"You all right?" Alex asked after a few minutes.

Hawk exhaled as he sat down on the curb. "I just want to hug John Daniel's neck and read him a bedtime story."

"Which one?" she asked.

"The one about that stupid teddy bear who gets lost in the department store."

She chuckled. "Me too."

CHAPTER
FORTY-EIGHT

THREE DAYS LATER, Besserman hosted the Magnum Group team for celebratory drinks. They sat on his deck, enjoying the view of the Potomac River and the foliage of the trees lining the banks. He lifted up the lid to his grill as the aroma of his center cut steaks wafted into the air.

"You'll never taste a juicier piece of meat," Besserman bragged while clutching a pair of tongs. "That much I can guarantee."

Hawk swirled the scotch around the glass in his hand. "Can you guarantee what's going to happen to General Purcell?"

Besserman shook his head as he closed the grill. "Unfortunately, not without being able to order the court martial panel how to rule. But I do think he's likely to receive a dishonorable discharge for what he did, even if he's not sentenced to prison."

"And his pension?" Alex asked.

"Gone. He'll never see a dime of it."

"Good," she said. "He doesn't deserve it after what he did."

Morgan sauntered over to the wet bar and poured herself another drink. "This is the kind of celebration my uncle would've appreciated."

"Except he would've complained that there wasn't any bourbon here," Hawk said.

Besserman chuckled. "I would've had some on hand if he'd been invited."

Morgan took a swig of her scotch. "Well, what I want to know, Mr. CIA Director, is the story about President Norris and General Chow."

Besserman's eyes widened. "I heard about what you did."

"What are you talking about?" she asked.

"Threatening to use that footage of Norris and Chow talking at a bar in Maldives? How did you even know about it?"

Mia raised her hand. "I can answer that one. Mallory asked for my help to see if I could enhance the audio. I couldn't, but I have a deaf hacker friend from China who could read lips. I edited a clip that only showed Chow's lips and sent it to her. She was able to read and then translate what he was saying."

"So you knew what their conversation was about?" Besserman asked.

Morgan nodded. "We only found out hours before Kira's attack on The Pentagon, which made it curious to me as to why he wouldn't want that story out there."

Besserman sighed as he stared at the bottom of his empty tumbler. "He wanted to control the narrative about his meeting with Chow and was afraid if the story got out there without him explaining the context first, no one would believe him. He later told me that he needed to gather all the proof before he released the footage."

"I started to wonder if there really was something he was trying to hide because of the way he backed off when I mentioned releasing it," Morgan said.

"As it turns out, that footage just endeared him to the nation," Besserman said. "General Chow's mother needed a rare surgery that no surgeon in China had ever performed, and Norris agreed to help her get the care she needed with a top U.S. surgeon. Then the president invested millions of dollars into a

Chinese investment firm that was funding cancer research there, another detail that could be easily twisted."

"You have to admit that without the audio, the whole meeting seemed sketchy," Morgan said. "Nothing good happens in Maldives. It's like the last outlaw refuge in the world."

"Fortunately, the doctor who performed the surgery on Chow's mom still had copies of her medical records to verify Norris's story," Besserman said.

"Hard to blame the president for thinking that story might get him in a bunch of hot water with the way the media could turn that into a fiasco for him," Alex said. "The way they operate today, they'd fill in the blanks themselves and create their own story."

Besserman got up and grabbed a beer from the cooler. "There was one brave journalist who tried to do things the right way named Glenn Feller, God rest his soul."

"I heard about him," Hawk said. "He was that political blogger who committed suicide, right?"

"Yeah," Besserman said. "And I was there, too. He was trying to get me to tell him more about the story by threatening to release it all. Then the Secret Service showed up to escort me to the White House. And Feller was already paranoid, but that sent him over the edge. It was sad because I wanted to help him, just not in the exact way he wanted at that moment."

Besserman checked on his steaks before flipping them.

Hawk drew in a deep breath, inhaling the smell of the sizzling meat. "I'm famished and sitting out here isn't doing me any favors."

"Soon enough," Besserman said with a wink.

Morgan stood and faced the group while leaning against the deck's railing. "There's one more piece of business we need to discuss."

The team turned their attention to Morgan as she took a long pull on her glass.

"We're listening," Big Earv said.

Morgan nodded subtly. "We've had a lot of good news today, but there's something that happened in the midst of all this that I wasn't ready for. As you all know, I was close with Capt. Hal Dellinger, the pilot who was killed at Leavenworth in our sting to out the mole in our midst. And while we were able to figure out who the mole was, our plans to use him to learn more about who's running The Alliance are useless now."

"Useless?" Alex asked. "How?"

"Nick Slavitt is dead," she said. "LAPD found his car at the bottom of a ravine at the Inglewood oil fields. The car had been set on fire but he was shot in the head first, which the coroner said was the cause of death."

"So, where does that leave us with The Alliance?" Hawk asked.

"Still not sure," Morgan said. "But they obviously knew that we knew about him, no matter how discreet we were. Maybe I shouldn't have promoted him, I don't know. Either way, it's back to the drawing board to figure out what's going on."

"I'm sure you'll figure it out soon enough," Besserman said, "but in the meantime, I propose a toast to my favorite black ops team. You saved the president's life and the lives of hundreds maybe even thousands more. Here, here."

The team raised their glasses to the toast.

Besserman smiled. "J.D. would be proud of all of you."

"Maybe," Morgan said. "But he hated loose threads. And The Alliance is one that's still dangling. And I feel the same way as he did."

"So, what are you going to do about it?" Besserman asked.

Morgan grinned wryly. "We're going to find them and snuff them out."

The End

THE PHOENIX CHRONICLES

The Shadow Hunter
The Reaper
Covert Invasion
The Cobbler
The Widowmaker
A Bridge Too Far
The Deadly Alchemist

ABOUT THE AUTHOR

R.J. PATTERSON is an award-winning writer living in southeastern Idaho. He first began his illustrious writing career as a sports journalist, recording his exploits on the soccer fields in England as a young boy. Then when his father told him that people would pay him to watch sports if he would write about what he saw, he went all in. He landed his first writing job at age 15 as a sports writer for a daily newspaper in Orangeburg, S.C. He later attended earned a degree in newspaper journalism from the University of Georgia, where he took a job covering high school sports for the award-winning *Athens Banner-Herald* and *Daily News*.

He later became the sports editor of *The Valdosta Daily Times* before working in the magazine world as an editor and freelance journalist. He has won numerous writing awards, including a national award for his investigative reporting on a sordid tale surrounding an NCAA investigation over the University of Georgia football program.

R.J. enjoys the great outdoors of the Northwest while living there with his wife and four children. He still follows sports closely.

He also loves connecting with readers and would love to hear from you. To stay updated about future projects, connect with him over Facebook or on the interwebs at www.RJPbooks.com.

Made in the USA
Monee, IL
19 October 2022

16224007R00177